The Ark of the Marindor

The Ark of the Marrindor

Larry Targan

MacMurray & Beck
Denver

Printed and bound in the United States of America

1 2 3 4 5 6 7 8 9 10

Library of Congress Cataloging-in-Publication Data
Targan, Barry, 1932–
The ark of the Marindor : a novel / by Barry Targan.
p. cm.
ISBN 1-878448-80-3
I. Title.
PS3570.A59A89   1998
813'.54—dc21   97-49973
                                           CIP

MacMurray & Beck Fiction: General Editor, Greg Michalson
The Ark *of the* Marindor cover design by Laurie Dolphin,
interior design by Stacia Schaefer.
The text was set in Granjon by Chris Davis, Mulberry Tree Enterprises.

THE *ARK* OF THE *MARINDOR*

Midway life's journey I was made aware
That I had strayed into a dark forest
And the right path appeared not anywhere.
                              —Dante

For Alexandra Hart Targan

prologue

In Cuthbert's Yard the giant blue-black machine moved slowly toward the water with the *Marindor* swaying slightly in the slings beneath it. The machine hunched over the boat like a great insect bearing prey. At about one foot a minute, the machine and the boat eased out on the steel beam ramps over the scummy water into which the boat would be lowered and set free. It was an odd union, the overpowering twenty-ton machine steaming with noise and exhaust and the acrid odor of hot grease as it held a boat designed to survive not by brute power but by abiding the terrific forces of wind and water it might encounter. She watched the boat as it swayed toward its liberty.

Once, in a yard like this a boat would have been hauled up to be worked on and then relaunched on a wooden cradle set on carriages of railroad wheels. The boat and cradle would have been pulled together up the inclined rails out of the water into a dry dock by a roaring engine attached to a taut wire cable three inches thick that wound around a large screeching drum; it was all resistance, then and still. The dry dock and the carriage lingered, rusting eventually into dust, but now it was done differently, this way, the old way gone.

Over the water the machine began to lower the boat, forty-five feet long, gleaming white topside, darkest green below the maroon waterline. The boat was a very old design, still in wood, stately. Nothing like it was

1

built any longer; nothing like it had been built for fifty years or more. And this boat was well known along the Atlantic coast to those who knew boats, their histories and heritages. None would have been better known than the *Marindor,* this daughter of Joshua Slocum's immortal *Spray,* this princess. Once this boat had also been called the *Spray* after its namesake, but the current owner had renamed it. The *Marindor.*

"Here we go, Captain," Cuthbert said to her. "Down we go." He signaled to the man at the controls high up on the machine.

With the boat halfway down to the water, the machine shuddered and stopped. The heavy engine whined and popped and was silent.

"Lost something," the man high up at the controls shouted down. He tried to start the engine, but it would not come alive. "What it is, I think it's the glow plug's gone. Got to replace it. Got to start with that at least." He scrambled down the steel ladder.

"Now don't you worry, Captain," Cuthbert said to her. "Fifteen minutes and you'll be afloat. Nothing to worry about."

But there was.

All sailors are to some degree superstitious. It is not that they believe they can control fate, only that fate gives them something to appease. Katherine Dennison did not entirely think that way; like all sailors she thought every voyage must presuppose the only success that mattered: a safe conclusion, an arrival. Omens reminded you of the danger. But it was not death that blue water sailors feared most: death was an abstraction. What sailors feared was failure—like the failure of a piece of equipment. But mainly of yourself. Things could always go wrong. The boat hanging helpless ten feet above the water required apprehension. And it is that, the doubt high above some steeplechase we dare, that cracks us, and we fall.

Her father had told her tales, once about a crew that discovered in a coil of line a gull that had hatched without a head. The men were reluctant to sail on such a ship, and when they finally did sail, it was with a muttering bitterness within the crew that did not disperse even after a thousand miles when the ship came to a safe port. Sea lore was heavy with such forebodings, as if sailors needed an excuse for what might happen, the satisfaction of being right even in catastrophe. Of having paid attention.

Just four days ago she had come into Noank with expectation. For the first time in three years, she had allowed herself once again to consider possibilities. And now this had happened. A signal had occurred. It was her job to be concerned, to accept doubt. She must not ignore it, but she must contain it. Portent itself could destroy. And Cuthbert, who had himself sailed far for many years, understood that.

"Nothing to worry about, Captain. Nothing at all."

But there was much to worry about, much. This had only reminded her. She was the captain, both in figure and fact. She was, more accurately, a master, legally certified by the Coast Guard to command a ship up to two hundred feet. But she was bound by a deeper commission, deeper than that to the people, the two young ones who would go with her, or to the intriguing Mr. Agare, who would be waiting for them in Charleston.

Four days ago she had allowed herself to believe the nearly incredible story that Agare had told her; its very implausibility had convinced her. She had accepted the seductive oddity of his story because sometimes the improbable makes more sense than not. He had made her curious. Perhaps that in itself was also a sign, like a dove returning with a twig indicating land after all this time at sea, that the rains will stop, the waters recede.

But now the boat had gotten hung up. This had happened to remind her that things break, go astray, that accident was her theme. And it was not that she had accepted once again a future, even if only a two-week future. That is not what disturbed her. It was the idea that maybe after all she had locked up in the past, especially herself, she had forgotten what that past had warned her of: that her past was prologue.

1

There was no wind inside the steep, rock-walled cove, and outside it, only two or three knots from the southwest, a light and variable wind. What clouds there were hung in the sky and did not move at all. The boat swung gently in random arcs against the fulcrum of the anchor line. Tethered like an animal grazing in a meadow, the boat moved freely in one direction until it was snubbed and then moved back against the pressure of its own momentum until it was snubbed again. Back and forth in easy oscillations, the thick pine mainmast ticked against the blue September sky like a metronome at its slowest setting, an effortless largo. Secured to the larger boat was a smaller boat, fourteen feet, broad shouldered and deep for its size, a lap-straked sailing craft, cedar on oak, with a long run of keel. It also looked as if it could take care of itself in heavy weather. The *Ark* was the name she had given to the fourteen-footer, which hung on davits over the transom. It was a lot of boat to be hung so, but not too big for a boat like the *Marindor* to handle. She had worked out the problems of keeping it tight to the larger boat even in the highest seas. But she could launch it easily. It was a sturdy boat, strong and powerful like the *Marindor* itself.

The tide was at its lowest ebb, at perfect slack just before it would begin to turn.

And then there was no wind and no movement at all, or nearly so. The boat was as motionless as a boat can ever be, but a boat can never be perfectly still. No matter how slight, there is always some tremor of movement in it, a thrum of energy. Like the sea itself. Like life itself, she thought, except perhaps her own.

She lay in the pilot's berth in the starboard quarter with her eyes closed and remembered sailing into this cove on the last of the small wind. She thought about the deftness with which she had twisted the large boat around the hook at the northeast arm of the spit that formed the cove, how she had let the boat shoot to the precise point where she could swing the helm to starboard and follow the thin seam of deeper water between the rocks into the pool in which the boat now rested. It was a difficult maneuver for a large, full-keeled boat drawing seven feet of water, and a dangerous one, and even more dangerous on an ebb tide. There was no margin at all. The seam through the rocky shelf was only maybe twenty feet wide. You either went through it exactly or else you hit the rocks and bounced off them with possible damage to your hull, or maybe worse. But she would not use the diesel engine until after her boat had come to a stop. Then she would drop the anchor and run the engine in reverse to set it. This was the sort of thing that had become important to her, this reduction to small, precise executions in which she need depend upon nothing but her own exact skills. "If I stay within the knowable limits, I can go on," she had written him, but Joseph Mackenzie had compared such a life, her life now, to living in a coffin. He said she was burying herself at sea. After that she had not written to him for two months, for how did she defend herself against the blunt truth?

She knew this cove perfectly, as she knew most of the coast. She had spent much of her life exploring it, or at least the better part of that life. The best part of it, she thought now. And she knew this boat, the *Marindor*. Her mastery of it. All that was left in her life, the last of ownership—the *Marindor* and the fourteen-footer tied off at the stern. This little residue of excellence, all that was left of what she could trust. Her skill, but not ever herself. Only her skill. And the *Marindor*. And Joseph.

Now that she was alone, she would often do this, review an action. But this retelling was an old habit. She thought that maybe the point of doing anything, but certainly the point of much sailing, was that after the anchor was safely down, there was something to think about. Or better, in the shorebound winter, there were memories to count and stack up and play with like golden coins.

She looked up out of the pilot's berth. On the overhead she had epoxied the two medals with which she had bought so much of her life. Next to them the framed citation: to Katherine Dennison, the artist of the most distinguished picture book for children, 1971. To Katherine Dennison, the author of the most distinguished book for children, 1971. The book was *The Marindor*.

And in 1971 she had married Tom Lecourt. She did not take his name because already she had become Katherine Dennison to the world. It would have been cumbersome and, her agent and her publisher had pointed out, disadvantageous to be two people, the old Katherine Dennison and the new Katherine Lecourt, to have two identities. She might have answered that there were already other Katherine Dennisons, more than a few of them, in fact, and famous Katherine Dennisons at that. Or she might have answered, at least later she might have answered, that after she married Tom Lecourt, she did not have even one identity. Still, when they did divorce, it had made the settling of things just a little easier, at least for the lawyers and accountants and the other managers of her life.

And in 1971 she had bought with her first great flush of fortune this boat, the *Marindor*. She was thirty-one years old then, but she could remember exactly the pleasure as she walked about and through the boat and marveled at the craft in it, the perfectly laid teak deck, the scarfs so precisely cut that you could not tell where one plank began or another ended. Even now she could reconstruct her thrill in the details of tulip wood and holly trim, the ash stringers, or how the sole in the two cabins had been set tight against the white oak framing that the builder had brought straight up out of the bilges and into which he had ingeniously inlaid a grate where one could sweep dirt. The drop-leaf table in the main salon in widths of mahogany that would even then have been difficult to obtain. Every through-hull fitting doubled and sometimes even tripled. The lovely long curve of the sheer line, the upturned tuck of the hull into the broad stern that would accept and shoulder aside the largest following seas. All, all a testament of intelligence and care. A kind of honor. She had kept it all as good as she had found it, kept at least this honor bright.

Now, twenty-four years later, she had money in banks she hardly bothered with. But this was what she had left that mattered to her. The *Marindor.* Her medals. Her competence at sea. Her memories. Her daughter, Sally. And under her berth, in a battered small leather-covered case, a thick file of the letters she had received from Joseph, as early as September of 1962, when she had gone away to college. And the beginning of a newer kind of correspondence: July 17, 1966, when she was in Vietnam.

She had flown into Donyang with a company detached from the 103rd Reconnaissance Battalion, an engineering unit attached to the Second Corps of the Eighth Army. The 103rd was sent into the Donyang valley to determine the precise elevations necessary for the planning of a major spring offensive. The company from the 103rd was ordered to get into Donyang and out in forty-eight hours, but almost immediately after the unit had landed and deplaned, the airfield came under intense bombardment from the artillery the Vietcong had struggled to haul up into the mountains that completely enclosed Donyang. It was the first and only use by the Vietcong of a fixed position against the Americans. Not since Dien Bien Phu, where they had caught the French in a similar cauldron and destroyed them, had the Vietcong dug in.

The attack continued for ten relentless days. All the American air strikes could not dislodge the Vietcong. On the sixth day, the recon company was ordered out of the valley. It had managed to get the information it had been sent for, and Command needed it sooner than it had planned, because now the 103rd was ordered to steal its way out through whatever crack in the mountains it could find.

She could stay behind in the bunkers of the regiment and wait out the bombardment, or she could move out with the 103rd and take her

7

chances. If she got out, if she got her film to Blue Star in Saigon, they would have to take her in, get her out of the serfdom of freelance and take her into the illustrious Blue Star stable, turn her official, get her real press credentials. Then eating for her would not depend upon the next photograph she sold, the photograph that she had to take because the others, the official photographers, could afford not to.

After three days she had run out of film, but by then there was nothing more to see. And nothing at all of what she had come to find: some intensity of hope, the naive élan of courage. For three more days she had hunched over in the terrible cold and waited for the artillery shells to stop falling, but they never stopped. In the dark and the cold of the bunker, all of them driven down into the small safety of their most private selves, which were located elsewhere—the Kansas prairie, the southern California beaches, the clatter of Philadelphia, New Orleans, Providence—no one could tell or bothered to care even if they knew that she was a woman. Their kind of misery all looked the same.

When the unit made its move on the sixth day at 1800 hours, she decided to go with it because this was the chance for which she had taken all the other chances. If she had not wanted to be here, then she would not have lied and cheated and fucked her way to Korea in the first place, to San Francisco, to Tokyo, to Saigon, to a hundred different units and patrols through seven months, and at last to a company of the 103rd Recon Battalion about to crawl out of the Donyang disaster either to freedom or an ugly death, because if the Vietcong artillery found them out in the open by first light, they would all surely die, and death by artillery is the ugliest of deaths. That is what she had written to Joseph three months earlier after she had visited Poyuk fifty kilometers to the west to observe what American artillery had done to the small city of Pohang-dong.

"You accuse me of doing an emotional stunting, like those little airplanes that corkscrew straight up into the sky and then dive straight down in spinning loops, pulling out just one hundred feet above the ground. But the thrills are not so cheap, are maybe costing me more than I can afford. If I were a man, you would call it machismo. You think this is all only an outrageous search for excitement on my part, 'an act without principle' I remember you called it when I told you what I was going to do. But so

8

what? Why is bravado a less worthy emotion than any other? The point is not what emotion or idea we explore but that we explore it vigorously. So maybe I am here to find what it is I want to explore vigorously, not the least being myself. God knows I spent what seems like the last four years in college staying up half the night talking to my girlfriends about the 'search for identity' and 'finding oneself.' I think all that talking was a kind of pose. Innocent enough, but ineffective nonetheless, although maybe that is partly what college was for, shallow babble, the trying out of the taste in our mouths of serious ideas. So what have I discovered here? More than I can imagine how to say. What I've learned maybe is that you don't learn anything until later. First you have to survive. But I've learned at least two things. Increasingly, I want to paint. As you know I always have wanted to paint, have painted. But now it seems as if my life depends upon that desire, that if I do not get killed here it will be so that I can make a life painting. Can you believe that even now, in the midst of all this, I draw, sketch? I don't have decent paper, not even good pencils. And no color. I use chunks of charcoal I gather out of old fires. Still, it focuses me. Maybe it is that I draw in the aftermath of the terror and the horror and the cold, and that the drawing makes me think I'm safe, unlike photographs. The second thing I've learned is that I do not want to be a photographer. I certainly wasn't a photographer when I got here, and I am not now, though that is what I do. But for me at least photography is a kind of curse. It is too powerful. I am not strong enough for it. I need a distance that photography cannot afford. The blunt immediacy is too overwhelming. I am not cool and tough. I watch the professionals at work and admire the detachment of someone who is doing what he is supposed to be doing, who knows why he is here. (Some paradox!) I don't think I am that kind of person. Painting allows me to be, more than anything else, alive in a moment that does not exist. I think I always knew this. I can hear your response. Why did I have to come to Vietnam, to the edge of death, to discover what I always knew? I don't know the answer to that. And I also realize that I don't want to be a writer, about this or anything. The poems I've sent to you are a kind of painting too. Let me weather this chaos and mayhem and maybe sit with you again on Macken Island in a September and try to figure it all out. At least I'll have some material to work with."

This was the letter to which he had finally responded. He had been so opposed to her Vietnam adventure that he had refused to maintain their old correspondence that had gone on ever since she had started college. His letter had reached her just before she flew into the Donyang valley. In the flickering of small light she had read it over and over.

She thought it was marvelous that his letter had found her, had followed her through the fantastic space-time of war, from one very temporary office to another and then to another. It was one of the small but countless anomalies of war that the priority of mail should be so high and effective, that there was the dogged belief that a "letter from home" would make life under unendurable conditions somehow endurable. But perhaps it was true after all, not that the men were cheered or reassured by the cheerful and chatty—Dear Frank, Mary Ellen got a job doing short-order at the Crossroads Diner. Can you imagine her frying eggs! Dear Bob, Well, your brother has really gone and done it this time. Dear Bill, Dear Mike, Dear Sonny—but rather by the belief itself, by the believing, like a magic, in the power of the mail from home. And maybe it was true, maybe men at war were sustained by their superiors' belief in the mail simply because it was the only belief available in circumstances where any belief at all was obscene beyond description.

"There are no atheists in foxholes? What crap," she had written to Joseph. "In foxholes no one believes in God, but there are plenty of men trying to make pacts with the devil, willing to sell what is left of their souls for another day of life, another hour, for anything that could be guaranteed at all." The next meal. A cigarette. If only you could count on it. Why was it that men sought their salvation in a believable devil but not an abstract God? But she knew the answer to that: God had already forsaken the battle zones of Vietnam, had lifted the dainty skirts of His goodness and had left the men to work out their deals with the evil that had stayed.

No wind and no tide in the equation of the September afternoon. Not even the gulls moved about in patrol. They must wait for the freshening breezes and the thermal updrafts that would come with the new wind to hold their bodies up, the thickened air that they could bear against and be lifted by in spirals high enough to see the bait fish fleeing from the slashing mackerel that would begin to feed on them in the changing tide.

In the silence Katherine could sense more than hear the slap and flutter of the approaching boat. She sat up and looked out the bronzed port above her head. About two hundred feet off, nearly the entire width of the cove, a small boat labored in. It was a shambles of a boat, about twenty feet, the kind of boat built roughly in a backyard out of cheap plywood, lumberyard spruce, polyester resins, and romantic assumptions. There was a small cabin, hardly sitting room in it. Even without wind, she would have seen that the sails were completely blown out, and ripped and patched as well. But now the sails flogged uselessly. The helmsman pumped the rudder, barely sculling the boat forward. It was a young woman, her hair long and free. She had no idea where she was heading, what she was heading into. Katherine should warn her. She had probably sailed over from Cob Island and lost what little wind there had been and now could not get home. Katherine doubted the girl had a chart, or if she did surely she had not read it, or could not. There was barely enough deep water in this cove for one boat, the water the *Marindor* was already in. But before she could move, the little boat grounded with a shudder and a grating; the exhausted wooden mast, badly fitted and slackly stayed, whipped sharply forward and then jumped up and fell back into the mast step heavily, a hard and nasty sound to hear in an old and nearly broken boat. Katherine watched the girl go to the centerboard and slowly haul it up. And then she saw the tiller stiffen and leap upward as the rudder jammed itself into an underwater crevice.

The girl did not seem surprised or alarmed. As the boat was clenched and settled into the grip of the rocks, she stood up and looked around the way one does after setting down the anchor for the night, as if now there was a chance to appraise and enjoy the surroundings. Katherine reached for her binoculars and focused in on the girl.

Her beauty startled her. But why should that be? She thought it might be the effect of the binoculars, exquisite Zeiss 7×50s that brought the girl to within ten feet of her and, in the limited field of view, focused her features with an unnatural sharpness. But it was also that, hidden, below decks, through the binoculars, through the port, she was a kind of voyeur. To look at the girl this way, sharpened the senses. Made her a peeping Katherine. She smiled at the aptness of the image, but not happily. It was too much like a kind of truth about her life, and truth is not what she had sailed to find or deliver; it was, in fact, whatever truth was or might be that she had sailed away from. Looking at the girl now, in this way, made Katherine think of Sally, her own daughter, probably the same age as the young woman on the broken boat. There was no young woman she looked at who did not make her think of Sally. And thinking about Sally made her think about all the rest. Certainly about her son, Steven.

Then the girl began to undress. In a few seconds she was out of her shorts and shirt. She stretched her arms upward as if flagging, sending a message in the language of semaphore, the arms upward in a V, the hands moving, ironically the semaphore signal for *attention*. But there were no actual flags, and Katherine knew that the girl would have no idea what to do with them if there had been. But surely the girl must know that someone was aboard the larger boat. Where else could they be? Or maybe the girl simply did not care. She was going for a swim. She swung over the side of her boat and into the water. For ten minutes she swam around her rock-bound boat, dove under it, stood upon the cradle the rocks had become.

Katherine came up on deck. She walked about pulling at gear, trying to make the point that she was not looking at the girl. Then the girl hauled herself into her boat and took a towel out of the cabin and dried herself off, flinging her long, thick golden hair over her head and rubbing it emphatically, and then thoroughly working the towel over the rest of her body, working carefully into all the numerous places on a body where dampness could be held. Then she saronged the towel around herself and finally turned and waved to Katherine. What else could Katherine do? She waved back.

2

Although she kept a traditional ship's log, a fundamental habit, she also kept a personal log, but not in the form of a journal. She wrote letters to Joseph on his island just on the north edge of Penobscot Bay, about fifteen miles south-southeast of Belfast. Macken Island.

Mackenzie Island it had been, but somehow it had gotten shortened. In a spare and economical existence, who needed more when less would do the job? Macken it had become, and when the chart makers had come to make the coast permanent, that is what was entered on the charts. But the island had been there, and theirs, the Mackenzies', for as long as the Cabots had commanded Cabots Cove off Pulpit Harbor on the west side of Northhaven Island. In fact, William Mackenzie had sailed with John Cabot in 1497, had been John Cabot's first officer. So there had been a Mackenzie and a Mackenzie Island for as long as there had been a North America inhabited by Europeans.

Maybe that was why Katherine had written to Joseph all these years. He was, for her, the island he lived on and gave life and continuity to her life, the one still point in the swirl and tumult of her life, the lode to which her compass turned, measured its deviations from, computed her compensations and adjustments. Without him, without the island and his being there, she did not know what would have become of her.

A year ago, anchored in a cove much farther south, she had written to him: "I am like the Flying Dutchman. How I envy you your island, 'a fixed form in the massive fluxion,'" she had quoted a poet. And he had answered, "You don't have to be a Flying Dutchman (Dutchwoman?). You've got options. And unlike the Dutchman, you have no argument with the sea. You are not laboring under a curse, even though you prefer to think otherwise. If you want to come ashore, then do so. Come to Macken Island. Even the Dutchman can be redeemed by a faithful love." And he had ended, with his characteristic flick at her, "And don't be so melodramatic."

He was, of course, the man she should have married. But she had not, and now he was at 64 degrees, 8 minutes west longitude, 44 degrees, 14 minutes north latitude, and she was wherever she might be. At that moment four hundred sea miles southeast of him, but where would she be tomorrow? For if she were not the Flying Dutchman, then surely now she was a Wilson's plover, one of those birds that live their entire lives aloft, endlessly at sea, only coming to land once to breed. That was her exactly, a pelagic wanderer. Now, a year later, she was not much closer to him on his island. To a landing. And what breeding she would ever do, she had done.

The afternoon drifted away. A slight but steady offshore wind developed. The tide came in. The girl in the boat gave no indication that she would leave. Even in the small cove, the boat was not close enough to be intrusive. Katherine had anchored in countless other situations where boats were much closer. Unless there was loud music or a giddy party, she hardly noticed. But in this cove—her cove—the small boat felt like an intruder. At other times small, shallow-draft fishing boats had come in to poke at the ledges for tautog or black bass in season, but at night they always left.

What was this about? Katherine wondered. What was the girl to do? Had she brought food with her for her day sail? Clothing or a sleeping bag against the September chill? Would others be looking for her, worrying? But at that age what could the girl worry about except herself?

What had Katherine at that age—twenty? twenty-one?—worried about? What even now did Sally worry about? Not others. Not discomfort. Not even disaster.

The night fell upon them, the two silent boats disappearing into the darkness. Katherine thought that perhaps she should row over in the inflatable and tell the girl what she had gotten herself into. Offer advice or, better, help.

She shook herself out of her thoughts, put on a heavy woolen sweater she had owned for twenty years, leaned back in the cockpit to read until the light was no good. Then she went below and prepared her supper. It was her routine, this taking of the day into the night. After supper she might come up on deck again and watch the stars, and then, after a final check of the boat, and particularly the set of the anchor, she would go below and sleep. She would arise before first light and go up when the air and the sea were undifferentiated in a perfectly seamless sublimation and all was poised in the apprehension of dawn. There she would attend, nearly holding her breath, as the miraculous occurred once again—the division of the sea and the sky, the emergence of the apparitional land, the first slap of the waves as the water began to move again, the creak of the boat, the muffled cries of the stirring gulls. This is what it must have been like after the Deluge, she thought. This is what Noah saw when he opened the hatch for the first time, full of awe and wonder and uncertainty.

But with the other boat, or rather the girl alone in the boat, which remained unlit, Katherine felt ill at ease. The boat was in trouble, and therefore the girl, but she had given no indication of concern, had not called for help. If anything, her indifference seemed to forestall Katherine's help as though this were something the girl was purposefully doing, something she understood even if Katherine did not. At last she pulled herself into her bunk and down into sleep.

At about 0200 hours Katherine did hear her, heard first a scratching and a thumping on the hull of the *Marindor,* then the girl's voice.

"Hey," she called. "Help. Get me aboard. Come on. Come on. Help, help, help," she shouted, but without panic or even much alarm.

Katherine came out of sleep quickly. It was the practice of a captain; you always slept with a piece of yourself listening for the wind to increase or to a new pattern of waves, feeling the boat turning into the new wind and maybe pulling the anchor free and dragging down onto the rocks.

She slept in a sweatsuit, ready to go. In moments she had pushed into a slicker and was on deck. There was enough ambient light for her to find the girl bobbing about midship on the starboard side.

"Swim back to the transom," Katherine said. "Can you move? Are you stiffening up?"

"What's a transom?" the girl said. "I'm OK. I mean, I'm not drowning yet."

"The stern," Katherine said, and pointed. "The back of the boat. Can you make it?"

"Sure. I'm all right." She pushed away from the boat and swam to the transom, where already Katherine had flipped out the thick handhold/steps that were built into the massive rudder. The girl came around the boat.

"Here. Can you see these steps? There's one more right at the water-line that you'll have to pull out yourself. Can you feel it?"

"Got it," the girl said. "Here I come." She pulled herself out of the water and up the rudder easily. All she was wearing was the t-shirt and shorts from the afternoon. "I sank," she said. "My boat sank. Sank nothing," she said. "It disintegrated." She gestured out over the water into the darkness. "Can you imagine?"

Katherine could imagine. What must have happened was that as the tide rose, the boat did not; it was wedged too tightly into the rocks. The rising tide had splintered the rotted boat like a fragile toy.

"I was sleeping, and suddenly I was getting wet," the girl said. "Evelyn Kinski." She put out her hand.

"Katherine Dennison." The girl took Katherine's hand briefly and then headed for the hatch of the forward cabin. "I know you," she said. "I know who you are. Jesus, I'm cold. It's worse out of the water. Can I borrow some clothes?" She started down the steps. "Whoa," she shouted suddenly, holding back. "How do you do this?"

"Backwards," Katherine said. "You go down backwards."

The girl turned and scurried down. Katherine followed. She lit the oil lamps, gave the girl a towel, and then pulled out another set of sweats for her.

"What do you mean you know me? How do you know me?"

Quickly the girl was dry and dressed. She looked around the cabin. "Wow," she said. She walked to one end of the main cabin and back. "This is just so great. Do you have coffee? What a place. What a fantastic place." And without a pause, "Everybody knows you, don't they? Katherine Dennison? I've known you all my life. You made *Cat's Bundle* and *Lovely Snakes*. And *Sea Time*. *Once upon an Island* is nearly my favorite. I know them all, at least those you wrote up to when I stopped with kids' books, you know? And *The Marindor*. That's my all-time favorite. But I guess that's everybody's all-time favorite. Isn't it? And isn't this something, here I am on your fabulous boat actually talking to Katherine Dennison, to *the* Katherine Dennison."

Katherine started water for coffee. And she thought that Evelyn Kinski had not happened into this cove or even into her boat by happenstance. That the boat sank was an accident, but nothing else.

"What's going on, Evelyn?" she said even as she pointed for the girl to sit down. "Instant coffee OK?"

"Instant's fine," Evelyn said. "Going on? What do you mean?"

"You're not a sailor; you end up in the smallest cove on the Atlantic seacoast, nearly an impossible cove to find unless you know what to look for. It doesn't even have a name. Now you're in my boat, and it sounds as if you knew who would be on this boat. Me."

"You think I sank my own boat?" she said, her mouth already full of biscuit. Katherine watched her. In the soft amber of the oil lamps, the girl's enormous health, the healthiness of her youth, had already overwhelmed the shriveling cold. Already she was as brightly burnished and glowing as the mahogany that trimmed the cabinetwork of the boat, lustrous and smooth. And the girl was beautiful, far more so than Sally Lecourt.

"Of course not. I don't think you sank your own boat. But I also don't think you got here accidentally. It feels as though you were looking for me."

"The *Marindor.* The boat's the *Marindor.* It's got its name on the ... the ..."

"Transom," Katherine said.

"Transom. Yeah. The water's ready," Evelyn said. "It's a famous book. It's a famous boat. You're a famous person."

"Not so famous," she said. "Come on, Evelyn." She poured the water into the mug and pushed the sugar jar toward her. "What's up?"

"Tomorrow," Evelyn said. "Mr. Agare. He'll explain everything. It's nothing to worry about. He'll explain it all. And much better than I could, that's for sure. I'd just get it all confused. I don't even have it all straight myself. Tomorrow. Mr. Agare wants to meet you. He has something he wants to ask you. Mr. Agare knows everything about you. We didn't know half the stuff. You've done everything. We only knew about the books. We didn't know about Vietnam," she said. "Neither of us."

"Us?" Katherine said.

"Me and Alan. Alan's my boyfriend. You'll meet him tomorrow too."

As the girl finished her coffee, Katherine went to a locker and took out a bottle of Old Bushmill's Irish whiskey and poured herself a couple of inches. Evelyn looked up at her.

"Do you have any vodka?" she said.

"I do," Katherine said.

"Can I have some? I can't drink whiskey. I mean, I don't like to if I can help it."

"Can't you help it?"

"Oh, sure. Sure. I don't drink much. Beer, vodka when I do. And I don't do drugs. Maybe a little MJ once in a while, but that doesn't count. Nothing hard, no mean stuff, you know?" Her eyes had opened wide and serious. "And Alan too. He's very clean. It's because he's a diver. He's got to keep himself straight. In top condition."

"Is that what Alan says?"

"Right."

"There's some vodka in that locker; help yourself."

When the girl was settled, Katherine said to her, "And you? A little while ago, you could have died. And that boat? How could you have sailed over here in that? Did you come from Cob Island?"

"From Bald," she said. "Bald Island."

"In that boat? And you can hardly sail, can you?"

"I can sail enough. As long as there isn't too much wind. But we don't sail it hardly at all. Alan uses it to dive from. Actually, we've been living on the boat for the past month. Very crowded. You couldn't even sit up all the way. But business hasn't been so good. There's not much business for scuba up here anyway. In the summer Alan gives lessons. And he does a little repair work at the boatyards. But it's been slow. I was waiting tables in Mystic in the summer, but after Labor Day, forget it. I work a little on weekends now, but that'll end soon. But it's good now. Mr. Agare has made it very good. We're going to get a really good boat, a motorboat, and go south in it, all the way to the Keys. Alan's got it all worked out."

Katherine could see there was no way she would be able to get the girl to respond directly. She would, indeed, have to wait for this Mr. Agare. Perhaps it was simply better that she did. If she wanted to know precisely what was happening, what was about to happen to her, or might happen, she would have to wait. This did not frighten her. Katherine was not a person easily frightened, and the circumstances were too bizarre to be ominous. Fate always caught you by surprise. That is what she meant by fate, not predetermination but surprise itself. Still, she could not help but press the girl. It all seemed so preposterous that it bred curiosity.

"But why didn't you wait for Mr. Agare? And Alan? Why did they send you if they're coming themselves?"

"Oh, they didn't send me. They'll probably be pissed when they find out. But they were going away all day to get the equipment, and I just thought, well, it was such an easy-looking day, why not? What else did I have to do? I never have much to do. Thought I'd sail over and scope you out and sail back. Who'd know? They're not coming back until this morning."

"And you'll be gone. What will they think?"

"They'll probably figure it out. Alan will. He's always saying how he knows just what I'm thinking." She sipped at her vodka.

They sat for another half hour and finished their drinks. They hardly spoke. Katherine wandered to the brink of tomorrow. To Alan. To Mr. Agare. But then she drew back.

"Well," she said, "I guess we had better turn in. Get what's left of a good night's sleep. Got to be fresh for Mr. Agare. And Alan."

"Right," Evelyn said. "Right."

Katherine pointed to the entrance to the forecastle. "There's a bunk in there. A sleeping bag. I'll show you the head and how it works."

But Katherine could not sleep. She could not resist thinking about what was about to happen and how she would describe it all in her letter to Joseph.

She had first met Joseph in 1949, when she was nine, he five years older. She remembered that day vividly because he had saved her life.

She, her father, and her mother had sailed the *Far Horizon,* a fifty-foot full brigantine into Camden Harbor in Maine in middle June. This was what her father did, deliver boats. In the fall, after the good, constant southwesterlies had begun to fail, her father, Michael Dennison, would get a job sailing one of the great boats south. In the spring he would sail it or some other wealthy man's boat north, to somewhere in Maine or to Newport or Marblehead or into Oyster Bay or Larchmont. It was not the business that it would become decades later when people could own a boat and keep it anywhere and fly to it in three hours. But even in the 1940s, or even earlier in the grinding maw of the Depression, there were families with enough money to put their boats wherever they wanted them: the Bahamas, the Keys, anywhere in Florida, in the Gulf of Mexico. Enough for Michael Dennison to make part of a living moving them about. Or during a season he would lease a boat and run charters. Even through the war, with all the restrictions and warnings, moving sailing craft along the coast did not altogether stop.

More of Michael Dennison's life, however, was to stay with a single boat and run it year round, sailing it for the owner during the sailing weather of whatever season, whether in Maine or in the south. If the boat stayed north in the winter, as more often it would, he would oversee its maintenance, which was a considerable job. The boats were all wood, the rigging nearly all rope or galvanized wire. The boat would be hauled at Camden or East Boothbay or Rockport or Brooklin and be scraped and caulked if necessary and painted; the sails mended, grommets and reefing points replaced, sheaves and winches disassembled and meticulously cleaned, the brightwork varnished. He did much of the work himself and saw to it that what the workmen did, they did properly.

Katherine was actually born aboard such a boat, in July 1940, the *Carlyle,* which had sailed out of Galilee in Rhode Island a month earlier. A thirty-eight-foot double-ended Colin Archer schooner, and her father's own boat. It was the only boat of size he would ever possess. He had gotten it out of default proceedings and in two years lost it back to the bank. But this is where Katherine was born, in a hard blow (force 8, her father would remind her) in eighty fathoms of water about sixty nautical miles off the end of Cape May, New Jersey. He delivered her himself, which is why he alone was a true delivery captain, he would always say, and after securing her and her mother—his word, *securing*—he ran the *Carlyle* up the Delaware Bay and into the Maurice River, where he anchored and then went ashore to find a doctor and to register his daughter's fabulous birth.

Officially the certificate said she was born in Bivalve, New Jersey, Cape May County, but in fact she had been born at sea, out of one amniotic fluid into another.

After they lost the *Carlyle,* Katherine would still see it over the next twelve years and come to comprehend what it was as she grew older and could understand. And though she never longed for a land life, for a stable platform of a life, for formal schools and a consistent society, she longed for the *Carlyle,* even though she could not remember actually living on it; longed to return to it much as someone might long to return to the family farm, as if, in the hard blows in the years to come, if she could get back there, she could get back to where all her strength had come from and maybe start over. In one place or another, up and down the Atlantic coast in those more intimate years of sailing craft and their fellowship, they would cross the *Carlyle* at Watch Hill or Mystic or somewhere in the Chesapeake, and she would ask to go aboard, and her father would show her the exact berth where she had been born and where she had played.

In 1951 the *Carlyle* went down off the shoals of Sable Island, and she had wept at the report.

It had been a remarkable, exceptional, and often astonishing life every day. No wind was ever the same, no tide. Channels shifted. She was taught to read and write and count and to identify the countries of the world, all that she would have been taught in a schoolhouse, but she also learned to be alert and rigorous. By age eight she could take the helm in any reasonable weather, by nine she could tie in reefs and trim sail, by twelve she could pilot and navigate by the stars, take sun shots with the sextant, compute the moon. From her father she learned to read the weather by the feel of it in hand, the scent and taste of it—the sound of it—the way a north wind chopped sharply like a slap, high and sibilant, but southerly winds sloughed like a quiet sighing. Dreaded easterlies whistled in the rigging shrilly and at a particular pitch, a shriek that set the teeth on edge. It was only at twelve, when she finally came ashore, that she felt lost.

In 1953 her father was called into the service, the Coast Guard. At fifty-one, married with a child, he was exempt, but the government wanted him to train the men who would be handling the landing craft in the Korean conflict, someone who understood the problems of riptides and breaking seas and shallowness, the running of bars. He accepted a commission and went off to Korea and never returned. At the landing on Inchon, which he had partly designed, he went in with one of the craft, a landing ship tank. He had figured it right. The landing was a success. But his LST took a direct hit. It was all spelled out in the letter her mother received from Rear Admiral Kershner.

Once, before that day, she had fallen overboard into Camden Harbor, where the water was under fifty degrees. She would have only about three minutes to struggle to the bulkheads, which were too far away, or to the mooring rafts anchored in the harbor. She was nine years old and her parents had left her at her chores, mostly splicing some new lines together. She had tied a bowline in one end of the line and gone to work, and as the coil grew she was careless and tripped on it and fell into the harbor.

Joseph Mackenzie was in his peapod pushing out toward his uncle's lobster pots, which even at fourteen he could manage to haul. He saw her fall and got to her before she locked up altogether and hauled her in much as he would a lobster pot.

"You better get warm quick, or else you'll die," he said. "Are your folks aboard?"

"No. Ashore," she said, her lips already hard to move. She could feel the cold squeezing her chest, her throat. But it was not the threat of death, rather the humiliation, she remembered years later. To fall overboard! To be so careless! You got only one chance, her father had explained to her, and that one chance was to stay in the ship. You had one chance to stay aboard, that was all.

Joseph got them to the boarding ladder, which they could reach from the platform of the peapod. He was strong, big for fourteen. He managed to get her up. And in the cabin he undressed her and rubbed her down until she could move herself. He poked the stove to life. In thirty minutes she was Katherine Dennison again. With no more chances left and a whole life to be gotten through.

After that she saw him often enough over the next four years as they sailed up and through Penobscot Bay, and they became friendly. When her father went off to the war, she and her mother settled in a small house on the lip of tiny Ducktrap Harbor, a little north of Lincolnville Beach and the ferry to Isleboro. And after her father's death, that is what became home for her and her mother. She and Joseph became deep friends.

Like her father, many of the men of the region had gone off to the war. There was much left for the young to do, and Joe, by the time he was fifteen, had taken over the lobstering from his uncle and two others and had a good piece of work in the Gamage shipyard taking boats apart and putting them back together again, comprehending the huge, rough diesels of the fishing boats, welding the broken and rotted steel of the fishing-boat cranes. In any slack time, he could always pick up work in the limekilns over at Rockport. Sometimes he would even ship out for a few days to work on the trawlers, dragging for bottom fish.

And she hung around with him. Her mother worked in the sardine cannery, and Katherine went to school. But Joe did not. She marveled that he could openly walk past school without being hauled in and set down. But it was a time for other needs. Just as in the north of Maine, in Aroostook County, the schools were shut down each fall for two weeks while the children worked in the potato harvest, and now, with so many of the men gone, there was even more that the younger people had to do.

When she was not in school, as increasingly she was not, she trailed Joe and helped. Soon enough they became a kind of team, she working beside him, splicing rope, reweaving the netting of the lobster pots, hammering the new slats, painting the floats, scraping paint, raking clams, handing him wrenches as he hung nearly upside down wrestling with the stuffing box around a worn propeller shaft or as he took apart a transmission to replace a busted gear. She learned all that from him.

She taught him about reading. In the years she had spent with her parents, where time was measured by the fixed speed of a displacement hull through water, where ten constant knots an hour was a fine but absolute pace, she read. Her mother stocked up. She was herself a reader, and her daughter followed her. Katherine spent hours, days, reading, below in foul weather or on fine days sitting forward resting back against a mast as the ship bore into the sea. From Nancy Drew to *The Last of the Mohicans* to *Ivanhoe*.

As Joe worked, she read to him. He didn't live on Macken Island then; only occasionally would he go to it to see that the house was still soundly sealed up, that nothing much had gone amiss. She asked him if he missed it, the island. "Every day," he said, "I miss it a little in some way."

"Will you go back there? To live? After the war?"

"Oh yes," he said. "No doubt."

"Why?"

He said he didn't know the answer to that altogether, only that he felt he had no choice. And he wanted no other choice. It was where he felt he belonged.

She went to the University of Maine in Orono, up the Penobscot River, where she majored in literature and art. Without her understanding why, the letters she wrote to Joseph Mackenzie, at least once a week or often two and even three times a week, became more and more the axis of her time, what everything else she was doing and learning turned around. She told him everything, sent him copies of her reports and term papers, the stories she was starting to write, sketches, poems, all her news.

She rehearsed for him her angers and arguments, wrote to him about the boys who were increasingly interested in her, her dates, their fumbling attempts upon her. And she created a certainty in him that nothing had happened. Nothing. She sent him lists of books he should read and even the books themselves.

He wrote back about the menhaden schools, the quality of the lobstering, the births to and deaths of people they knew, the houses that burned down, those that were built, what was happening in the shipyards. In his letters all of her own sea life came back to her. Each envelope she opened revealed the smell of low-tide sea wrack, released plumes of fog.

In the summer she would return to Ducktrap Harbor and work with her mother in the cannery. On weekends Joe would come for her and take her to Macken Island. But not until the summer between her junior and senior year did they make love couched in the low juniper and cedar pruned by the salt spray, then held on to each other in a cusp of rock overlooking Eagle Cove, a favored place where they had been children together.

Katherine awoke as always before the dawn, at the end of the midwatch, the dogwatch, twelve to 0400, and started the coffee. Quietly. That was a difference. Not in three years had someone been aboard the *Marindor* to stay, to sleep aboard. Not since Steven, not since Sally. She took her coffee and settled in with a novel once again, and waited. After the sun came up enough to cut some of the chill, she would go for her morning swim.

Three hours later, Evelyn awoke the way the young often do, as if she were born the very moment she opened her eyes. She stumbled out of the forecastle, puffed and stretching, yawning, not at all certain in that instant where she was or why. Katherine watched as the girl's systems gathered into a person. So often she had watched the process in her own daughter. Had she herself ever been like these young women? She remembered only being poised to jump—or pounce—upon her life. In the main salon Evelyn stretched as Katherine changed out of her wet bathing suit.

"Sorry," she said, and started to turn away.

"It's OK," Katherine said. "Not a problem." She finished toweling herself off and reached for her sweats.

"What's that?" Evelyn said pointing to a two-inch blue, puckered scar across Katherine's right breast.

"This?" Katherine said, putting her finger to it. "I caught one. In Vietnam."

"You were wounded in Vietnam? Wow. That's a story," Evelyn said.

In the battling around Koto-ri Katherine had fallen in with an ordnance unit bringing ammunition to a questionable perimeter when the Vietcong surprised them. The skirmish was brief. She got some excellent pictures. And she got wounded. The explosion of the grenade knocked her out. She awoke in a medical evacuation tent getting first attention before being lifted out to the rear. She was not in much pain, and she remembered with delight the doctor's reaction after he scissored through her clothing and discovered her breasts. "Holy Christ," he said. He looked down and saw that she was awake. "Who the hell are you?"

"Katherine Dennison, Blue Star," she said. "Are you going to fix me up, or are you just going to look at my chest?"

It was a good story, but too good a story. She became the story: the intrepid Katherine Dennison, the Margaret Bourke-White of Vietnam. The wound. The doctor's surprise. Other reporters used her when there was nothing else to file. But two months later High Command reached out and plucked her out of the action. Too dangerous for a woman, they decided, more than a year after her year of danger.

"I was thinking that maybe you're worried," Evelyn said. "Me showing up, Mr. Agare, Alan. There is nothing to worry about here, Katherine. It's just a business proposition. Is there something to eat? I'm starved."

3

About ten o'clock she heard the high snarl of a large outboard motor coming straight at her, slow and heavy. It would be they. She had been sitting in the cockpit reading leisurely. Sometimes she would put down her book and look around to see where the girl had gotten to. Evelyn had taken the inflatable and was rowing all around the cove, splashing and poking with the delight of a six-year-old, or rather with the abandon of someone who could take immediate and total pleasure in the angle of a rock, the flowering of seaweed, barnacles and limpets, all that was new, that was always new to the Evelyns of this world.

Or sometimes Katherine would look up from her book and consider what course to set herself, whether to stay north through September until after hurricane season or to start down the coast now. To where? Should she stay outside, keep to the blue water off soundings and go around Hatteras and head for the Keys, or go inside, down the Chesapeake and into the Intracoastal? But how could she decide that? Possibilities meant a future, a purpose. She had nothing of this, only the small clamp of the comfort of her boat, the sweet society of her gear and tackle, the capacious sea, "annihilating all that's made/to a green thought in a green shade." She had taken it to be her emblem.

The motorboat swung around the edge of the island and throttled back, gliding on its momentum. It drew little water, even as low and squat in the water as it rode now. There were two men in the boat.

"Alan," the girl shouted and began to row quickly. "Alan, Alan, it's me. I'm OK."

The boat came up. "*Marindor* ahoy," the older man shouted. Mr. Agare, she assumed. "Can we come aside?"

Katherine stood up. "Yes," she said. She noticed that the motorboat had already placed fenders down. "Give me a line," she said. He threw a line toward her, but he handled it badly, the line bunched and not coiled. He was no sailor.

"Alan," the girl was squealing, "the boat sank. Wait till you hear."

"This is Alan. Alan Sonderson." Mr. Agare indicated the tall young man, well made, sea- and sun-bleached blond, youth and strength streaming from him. He smiled at Katherine and waved as if he knew her, just as Evelyn had assumed her easiness with Katherine. Katherine enjoyed him, them. Just the fact of them.

"I'm George Agare. Evelyn has preceded us, I see. We were worried but guessed she would be here. Has she told you much? I had hoped to explain it all myself."

He was in his midfifties, about her own age, dressed like a working seaman, or at least that was what he tried to look like. His clothes seemed like a costume, a rough sheath of sea-bleached jeans, a stained Caphartt work jacket, a faded cotton shirt, everything properly tattered and torn. He even wore a navy watch cap far back on his head. He wore half boots as if he were ready to stand for hours in fish guts while he filleted the catch. But it was not really his style, inappropriate to his softer core. He did not look burned or wrinkled, salt cured. And the way he stood in the boat marked him. He did not move with it at all, seemed ready to grab on to a handhold even in the gentle swell. But he was not concerned, not nervous or uncomfortable, almost at ease, not at sea or in a boat, but at ease in the masquerade itself.

"May we come aboard? I'd like to have a little talk."

The boat was about twenty feet and fairly flat, a plumb stem and not much of an entry. It was basically a fisherman's boat, a modification of a lobster-boat hull but without any superstructure. A nice boat. Old and firm and used. She looked down into it. There were air tanks and other scuba diving gear. A generator and air compressor. Crates of provisions. Baskets of food. What looked like some cartons of wine. Two gleaming aluminum suitcases. Two heavy-duty twelve-volt batteries. Two large seabags that probably held clothes.

"I imagine you're curious. Let me come aboard and assuage your curiosity. At the very least, I've come to feed you. If nothing else, we'll have a gam, I think it's called."

"That was in the nineteenth century, a gam," she said.

"An excellent century," he said, and clapped his hands, clasped them.

He was a gleaming man. As curious as anything else was the tension between how he was dressed and why, when he was so clearly not in his own clothes.

"Here," he said, laughing. He took one of the aluminum cases and held it up to her. "Go on. Take it. Open it up. I'll wait here."

By now Evelyn had reached them. She scrambled into the motorboat and lunged at Alan.

Alan said nothing. He smiled at her and continued to hold the stern of the motorboat against the larger boat. Then he said, "You're something else, sweetie. You surely are."

Katherine took the case and opened it. It was stacked neatly with packages of twenty-dollar bills. It was full. It looked exactly like what she had seen in movies and on TV, like the way big, illegal payoffs were made.

"A hundred thousand dollars," Mr. Agare said. "Yours. Aren't you amazed? Certainly you must be curious enough to want to know why, what? Yes?

"Not drugs," Mr. Agare said, anticipating her. "Nothing at all to do with drugs. And nothing illegal at all. Nothing unethical. Nothing like that. Oh, you must be dying to know about this. Invite us aboard. Or would you feel better if only I came aboard?"

"Come aboard. All of you," she said.

Soon enough Mr. Agare was in the cockpit, but before he settled into his explanation, he offered her food. "Let me feed you some exquisite things. Alan, there. That basket. Oh, please," he said to her, "refuse my business, but not your own pleasure. I've gone to such trouble, to soften you, of course. But you'd have guessed that. But then, why not? What's the point of not using the occasion to delight ourselves? And look, it's close enough to noon to start an early picnic." Even as he spoke, Alan dropped back into the motorboat and swung up out of it with a lidded basket, beautiful yellowed willow strips woven into a totemic design, and in the basket a cornucopia of fishes and eggs and jellies and sauces and pâtés and meats. Four baguettes broken in halves so that they would fit. A bundle of platters and knives and forks. Two bottles of champagne. Small compotes of fruits. Tins of English mints, toffees.

"A fete," Mr. Agare said. "What's the counterpart for a fete at sea?"

"No fetes at sea, Mr. Agare. Hardtack and salt pork and rum." She thought he would ask her to call him George, not Mr. Agare, but he did not.

"But yes, but of course. Still, let us depart from tradition. May we? I presume upon you, but obviously I'm trying to woo you."

"Seduce, you mean?" she said.

"Convince," he said.

"Mr. Agare," Evelyn said across the deck, "can we have the marmalade? That is so good." She and Alan were forward, giving them room. Distance.

"Yes, yes, my dear. Whatever you want." But he looked at Katherine. "Permission?"

It was a European gesture; much of him was. Continental in an old sense, a movie-mode sense. He spoke with no discernible accent, but he did not seem American either, and was certainly not a man who worked with his body. There was a constant but soft, sumptuous movement to him, an elegant lethargy. As he spoke, or looked up into the rigging of the boat or directly at her, or gestured to the young people, he seemed comfortable and unhurried. But with purpose too.

Evelyn began to open things and hand them about. Out of every container she took a small taste.

"This is great," Alan said. "Superb." He was digging into a fairly large tin of caviar that must have come from the Caspian Sea.

"Superb," Evelyn mimicked him.

"Superb, my dear," he said.

"Superb indeed, Alan dear."

"Salty," he said. "But superb."

"Superbly salty, yes," she said, and giggled.

The case of money still lay open. A small piece of smoked mako shark had fallen on it. Mr. Agare made up a plate for Katherine and handed it to her.

"Open the champagne, Alan, please."

"Oh, look," Evelyn said. "Look!" She pointed across the cove to where the inflatable bumped against the cliff.

"Later," Mr. Agare said. "We'll retrieve it. Do you know what this is?" he said to Katherine and pointed to something on her plate she could not identify. "These are eggplants. A puree made from Greek eggplants. Baby eggplants. The preparation is Greek. You cannot buy these easily, even from the best of provisioners in this country. What do you think? Go on, try."

She took a small taste. It was sharp, a surprise, the softness of the puree and the sting of the food, but it was the afterglow that he must have meant for her to enjoy.

"Isn't that delightful? It's nothing like what you expect. Maybe life is that way, eh? The delight is in the unexpected?"

"That's not been my experience. For me, the opposite."

"But of course it depends upon having expectations. Accidents don't count. It's important that you have an expectation, the more specific the better. Do you see what I mean? The savor depends not on not knowing but on expecting to taste something only to taste something else."

And he spoke of other things. The air, the coast, the marvelous boat, the joy of appetite. He seemed happily involved in nothing more than being here, all his business incidental. He noticed her book. He admitted to not reading as much as he would like, or thought he would like. But he was so busy. He lived his life like a projectile. He had almost no control over it.

She enjoyed him—his gleaming, his lilting spirit. A fete indeed! A fete gallant! This graceful man in his costume, Alan and Evelyn rooting around in the basket like bear cubs smeared with honey, the spangled

31

day. And the seduction. Oh, certainly he was playing her, certainly he was conscious of his amiability and the tightening of the string. At one point he lifted the lid of the aluminum case with his toe and closed it, dismissing the mundane. There was time; there would be time for that tiresome element.

He had drawn her into talking, if only out of politeness. Her voice at first sounded strange to her, but she understood that: long-distance sailors, solitaires in general, but singlehanded sailors particularly, would go days or weeks without speaking. The sound of their voices became disconnected, their voices and yet not their voices. It took an interval to bring the two together again.

She was explaining to him the virtues of a wooden ship in this age of fiberglass and exotic plastics, the way wood kept you warmer or cooler. A good boat to live in. And you could fix a lot of things yourself if you were working with wood. She explained the good sense of gaff rigging and a yawl mizzenmast and topsails and double-headed foresails. The advantages for a singlehanded sailor. "All too arcane for me," Mr. Agare said, "though interesting still." He drew her on. She explained the system of tanks for water and fuel and how they served equally as ballast. At one point she even took him aft and lifted a hatch cover to show him the very large lazaret. "They don't make boats today with that kind of space," she explained. In it were the supplies of paint and solvents, tools, a bin for firewood, and a larger bin for coal. Later, she said, she would take him through her boat for a proper tour.

"But how do you sail it alone?" he asked.

"Do you mean how does a woman sail it alone?"

"Perhaps."

"It's not a matter of great strength. You use blocks and winches. Even a very strong man can't deal with heavy wind. You can't haul these anchors by hand. A windlass, a comealong. A small engine; a donkey engine, it's called." She pointed it out to him. "Let me tell you, what is maybe more important than handling the boat is dealing with chafe, replacing fittings in time, anticipating problems. That's where boats are lost. Under stress, something gives way. Something you counted on. Must count on. Do you understand that?"

"Very much so," he said. "And you are confident? You could sail a boat anywhere?"

"This boat. Yes," she said. "I have altered it to my purposes. Anywhere, yes. Yes."

She started to explain the provenance of the ship, that it was built by the legendary R. D. Culler, who lived on it and sailed it for twenty years, that the boat was a close replica of the legendary *Spray,* Joshua Slocum's boat. Slocum, the greatest of all mariners, had sailed the prototype of this boat around the world alone with no electronics or motor or devices.

"Yes," he said. "I know."

"You know?"

"It's your story. It's been told. A wonderful story. I accessed it easily. I read about the *Marindor* and about you in *Cruising World* and *Sailing,* in at least half a dozen places. CompuServe can find anything. I found you when I made the decision."

"The decision?"

"Why I'm here." He touched the case with his foot. "What I want you to do for the money."

4

But he did not explain at once. He looked off eastward out of the cove into the open sea, at the light breaking across the slight chop into slivers and chips of silver and gold.

"Do you smoke?" he said.

"No."

"Do you mind?"

"No. Not above deck."

From inside his rough costume, he fiddled out a silver cigarette case and a matching silver lighter. He extracted a cigarette and tapped it, placed it in his mouth, and lit it. He exhaled extravagantly, his head thrown back in theatrical pleasure. She smiled.

"I haven't seen anyone smoke a cigarette like that since maybe Adolph Menjou did it in the movies forty years ago."

"It is an affectation," he smiled back. "But this tobacco is so wonderful, it forces you. Balkan Sobranee cigarettes. Lots of choice latakia from Bulgaria. Difficult to obtain, you might imagine. Very difficult. And that's a pleasure too, isn't it? The obtaining of what is difficult to obtain?"

"Like the eggplants," she said.

"Exactly."

Alan and Evelyn were now far forward, wondering at the boat on their own, the complication of gear and tackle and lines, laughing, snuggling, bumping their hips against each other like teenagers. Comic-book love, Katherine thought with envy. Like eating ice cream without getting fat. It was what youth was for.

"You have something in mind that involves me? Why are you dressed this way?" she said. "A drugstore sailor. What is this all about, Mr. Agare? This is like something out of a TV movie. What is this all about?"

"Do you watch much television?" he said.

"Hardly any. None now. With the children. When they were young. Ashore." It was as if she could not connect the words into a sentence. Only fragments. Shards. What remained of something badly smashed.

"I've watched a lot of television these past few years," he said. "On little portable sets. It's all that I have time for now. I used to read a lot, but now TV fits more neatly into my movement; it doesn't require continuity. And let me tell you, it reveals to us much about the human condition." He drew deeply, luxuriously, on his cigarette.

"You're kidding," she said.

"Not at all. Sex. Violence. Eh? Soap operas, talk shows?"

"There's sex and violence in *Anna Karenina* and *Madam Bovary* and *Hamlet*," she said with unaccustomed force.

"But there it is ennobled, the sex and violence made tragic. TV, on the other hand, holds, as it were, a mirror up to nature. The soap operas? The talk shows? The advertisements for soft toilet paper? The relentless vulgarity? No tragedy here. On TV there is always a happy ending. The bad guy always gets caught; the good girl always gets her man. The abusive husband always gets shot. The endings are always happy. Life's a situation comedy, a series of one-liners. TV, however, tells us what we want."

"So cynical?" she said.

"Alas," he shrugged. "But there we are."

"There *you* are," she corrected him, though her defense felt automatic. What, after all, was she defending? "But to the point, Mr. Agare. What do you want from me that is worth so much money?"

"Yes. To the business at hand." But even then he spurted away, or seemed to, lapsed back into a reflective mode as if he resisted leaving the

35

seemingly indolent pace of the morning, as if he would extend it, delay, draw back from what he had come to do. "The natural condition of humankind is to be evil," he said, the melodrama gone to drama. "We all live in constant anger at the humiliation, the embarrassment of death. Everything we do is an attempt to mitigate the chagrin. Sex, violence. Sexual violence, violent sex. Or good food. Tobacco. A marvelous boat." He swung his hand about him. "Them," he said, pointing to the children nuzzling forward in the bows. "Victims."

"What has that to do with why you are here?" she demanded.

"Perhaps nothing. Except that always at the very center, at the absolute nick and tickle of purpose, are assumptions, which is where we all start. Why am I here? I would like to stay here a long time and be laved by this marvelous day. But time takes survey, yes?" He looked at her. "I'm sometimes surprised how far behind I have left what I was or wanted. This. This is such a time on this boat, a moment. The essential stillness. Everything else is an intrusion." He looked off and then back at her.

"So. Well, this is the situation," at last breaking away, and now quickly all about his business. "It is very simple. I want you to take Alan to a point in the ocean and to bring him back. Two weeks. Not a day more. A small airplane resting in about ten meters of water there. In the airplane is a small box. Alan will dive to retrieve it. Here. Do you know what this is?" He handed her a piece of paper: 9960-Y-72130, 9960-X-26530, 9960-W-15410.

"These are LORAN coordinates," she said.

"About a third of the way between Bermuda and the eastern United States. South Carolina, yes? The Carolina Canyon? You have heard of it? You can find it? For a hundred thousand dollars?"

"I've heard of it. Yes. Of course. We've sailed over it. At least, years ago."

"It's still there," he said. "Let me thin out the mystery. Obviously there is something of unimaginable value in the small case. The plane carrying it failed. It is still there. I want it. The small box. A hundred thousand for your effort. A hundred thousand for the children." He nodded forward to indicate Alan and Evelyn. "In the other aluminum case. Do you want expenses for the boat? Ten thousand? Done. Will that suffice?"

"What I want is to know more. And why me? Why this way? With this kind of money you could charter a much faster boat, a full crew. Professional divers."

"And far too much attention. A motor-driven boat large enough to get there would be strongly noticed. The Carolina Canyon is not fishing water, not commercial and certainly not sport fishing. It's the middle of the ocean, maybe three hundred miles offshore. Any boat other than a sailing craft would be spotted by the Coast Guard at some point. It would have to be accounted for. An eighty-foot seagoing trawler, say. The Coast Guard would stop such a boat, search it expecting drugs. But a sailboat sailing toward Bermuda in September? What could be more natural?"

"But why me?"

"This boat. The *Marindor,*" he said as if the answer were too evident to need explication. "Whoever might notice it or report it or talk about it on the radio would not imagine an adventure, this adventure. Instead of suspicion, people would say with delight, 'We crossed the *Marindor.'* They would write it down in the log. Isn't that what sailors do? The Coast Guard would disregard you. On the registry they would check and see the *Marindor,* Katherine Dennison. Nothing. Out for a sail. In fact, you could be doing little else but being out for a sail, a jaunt to Bermuda most likely. Very plausible. Sailing to Bermuda in September. Nothing to draw attention. Indeed, your notoriety, the fame of the boat itself, would be a cloak."

"I had no specific plans," Agare said. "It was, indeed, a quandary. For a week I was casting about, trying desperately to imagine what to do, when I encountered your boat in Mystic. One look and I knew what I needed. And when I discovered you were the master, who you were, *what you were,* I knew I had the solution. Perfect.

"If the coordinates are right, Alan could dive and get the little case in an hour or so, I would guess. Or more? Half a day? You would sail to the closest port. Give me the box, what is in it. And then we would all be gone. You could go wherever. Why should you hesitate? Is it the money? Name a price, then. Two hundred thousand? Done," he said. "On your return I'll get you the rest of the money. Another aluminum case of money."

He pointed to the fishing boat tied off the side of the *Marindor* and at the equipment in it. "Alan can bring this aboard. You can sail out of here today." He had finished his cigarette. He flicked it into the water.

"With so much at stake, there must be danger. You are not telling me everything," Katherine said.

"Then I will tell you everything. What is in the precious case in the airplane? A 3.5-inch computer disk. A common disk. You could use it in any computer. What is on the disk? Numbers. Letters. But these are very special numbers and letters. They exist nowhere else in the world. You have heard of the seven gnomes of Zurich? It is not a children's book. Ha."

"Switzerland. The banks?" she said.

"There is the facetious legend that there are seven men in Switzerland who directly or indirectly control all the money in the world. Sooner or later, the myth is, they will have ultimate stewardship. It's not their money; it is the control of it that they have, the shifting of it, the making of it available. But above all, perhaps, there is the protection of it, the sequestering. The hiding."

"Numbered bank accounts?"

"Something like that, yes. In a manner of speaking. In simplest terms, yes. But the hiding of money is expensive. And difficult. In effect, what you pay for is what you get. The more secret, the more it costs. The larger the amount and the greater the secrecy ... well, so it goes. And it is not cheap. It is not a simple savings account, you understand. Well, the numbered account in Swiss banks that we all know about, that's not much secrecy, really. Right off there are minor clerks who know, who possibly could be bought. And the international banking community can tap into the information in some instances. Governments can often gain access. Oh, the fabled numbered Swiss account is not nearly as secret as you might suppose. It is used by gangsters, drug kingpins, dishonest politicos, American dentists, and so forth. Small potatoes is what you call it in America."

"Drug money, Mafia money? That's small potatoes?" she said.

"By comparison, yes. To what is on the disk."

He paused and withdrew another cigarette. "Not usual for me, two cigarettes so close together. But this is an occasion, almost a celebration.

Everything is out of the ordinary. This is all so different, I hope you understand. And so much is involved." He inhaled deeply. "Coffee?" he said to her. "I have a thermos of fresh coffee. Marvelous Kava. And the cakes! Ah, I have forgotten the cakes! Every day these cakes are flown to the United States from Paris. Every day. Imagine. From a patisserie in Paris. What are we, I ask you, who will fly cakes across an ocean; what kind of species are we?" He seemed suddenly angry, his question an indictment. "And I have forgotten them to you." He started to call forward, but she stopped him.

"No," she said. "No coffee, no cakes. Don't interrupt yourself. Go on. Now. Please."

"Yes, well, where was I?" he said as if the good coffee and the cakes from Paris were just as important as the disk on the ridge of the Carolina Canyon. "Ah, yes. There are varying degrees, ascending degrees of secrecy, at increasing cost. And it is a simple process and progression. All you do is have fewer and fewer people know who belongs to what accounts and what is in them."

"And at last you get to the seven gnomes?" she said.

"Three, not seven," he said. "Actually, there are only three."

"You are serious?"

"I am here, am I not? The money is real, yes? I assure you I am serious, this that I am telling you."

"But your explanation is not complete."

"Even three is not safe enough. They, or even one, could be suborned, as unlikely as that is."

"Or kidnapped," Katherine added for him. "Tortured. Racked until he told all. Bamboo slivers under the fingernails." She laughed.

"That has all been considered, I assure you. To prevent even such unlikely exposure, each of the three holds only a part of the critical information."

"But the three could get together and take control, or sell the information," she said. And again she laughed. It was not that she did not believe him. He was real enough. Intensely present. With a little reflection, she could easily imagine and accept that there must be some arcane mechanism of great secrecy about the moving of vast sums of money. It was that *she* was here and listening to him that amazed her and in some respect convinced her. I respond, therefore he is.

He disregarded her. "Everyone knows who the gnomes are. *They* are not the secrets that they guard. This has to do with more than money, the gaining of money. Oh, money is made or not made—great sums—but money is just the medium, a kind of lingua franca. This all goes far beyond the money itself. Perhaps the simple analogy is to a game. There is only one game. And it is played in Zurich. Consider, the players in this game are wealthy beyond imagination. They play because it is what they do, what they have always done. Why do rich men gamble? Or why do rich men go to work in the morning? It is for the pleasure of the action itself. Painters paint, novelists write. Moneymakers make deals. The money is nearly incidental. And there is something else, something wonderful to consider. Zurich is the only place on earth, in all of civilization, where there is something perfect. Trust. Perfect trust. In international finance no one lies or cheats about the money. If they did, even once, they'd be out of the action."

A slight wind was coming up, nothing strong but enough to stir the air and the sky, enough to push the water in the cove against the surrounding rocks. Katherine watched the inflatable butt against the rocks, hit and bounce and hit again.

"What is important is the information. So this is how it works. We have devised a simple system whereby the critical information, the numbers and letters, so to speak, are encoded into a computer in such a way that when the information is removed from the computer, it is, whatever could possibly be left in the computer, destroyed. The information can only exist in one form at any one time. The code is set up so that only when it is activated does the information exist. And once it is put on a disk, it ceases to exist in any other form. It can only be copied once. A simple system. Little more than an exercise used in computer training programs in college. But very effective.

"This is what happened. Resources in the Bank of Nassau were removed; the disk was to be flown to the U.S. and then taken to Switzerland. The Bank of Nassau was just a conduit, part of a mechanism for which it was well paid, but the resource never entered into its knowledge or control. In effect, all we did was rent its computer, so to speak. For a short period. An easy and safe way to dissemble. So there it is."

"But wouldn't there be a fail-safe plan, a backup?" she asked.

"If two plans, why not three?" he said. "Do you see what I mean? That is moving in the opposite direction from what is desired. It doubles the risk. Triples it. The fail-safe idea has been considered, and there are, of course, other factors, other details to this process, but they are not important now. What is important now is that the access to the resource is in a small, tightly sealed case in a small airplane resting in what we hope is only ten meters of water on the edge of the Carolina Canyon three hundred miles out from the mainland, maybe, what? six hundred miles from here. And I want you to sail there so Alan can retrieve it. There and to the closest mainland. In two weeks altogether. This will leave me time to get to Switzerland."

"In two weeks?"

"Yes. The time is critical. Absolutely critical. You see, after two weeks the information is worthless. Utterly worthless."

"Worthless? But you must be talking about millions and millions," she said.

"Billions and billions," he said. "Amounts that are not easy to imagine or describe. But it is not the money, it is what the money implies, the possibility of its use, the actions that can be based upon it. I can't tell you all the particulars; I am not even myself privy to them. I am just someone in the system, little more than a clerk, actually—though a fairly highly placed clerk." He smiled. "It works this way. If someone, some force, say, wants to create a special sort of weapon or fund a coup. Or if an international corporation wants to dam a watershed in, say, Zambia, or control a rain forest in Brazil or determine the flow of wheat or cotton between a large buyer nation and a large seller nation, it must negotiate. Or, say, if a country like Saudi Arabia is facing a severe fiscal problem and it needs to borrow a vast sum of money, it can't just borrow it openly. It can't go to the World Bank and arrange a loan, not under such circumstances. Its credit would evaporate; outside capital would flee. International markets would tumble. There are sometimes public negotiations, or what appear

to be public negotiations. Sometimes. But there are *always* private negotiations. Subterranean negotiations. Nothing you find in the newspapers.
Agreements are made, actions are taken, money is bought and sold in a
private market transaction, and in a year or two or ten, events transpire.
In a day or a week or a month, the Bourse or the City or Wall Street rises
or falls. Earth moving commences. Armies are formed. Prime ministers
tumble. Nations revolt.

"At this moment such a negotiation is going on. A very large one,
possibly one of the largest ever. It depends in great part upon Party A as-
suming that Party B has the financial weapon required. Now there is also
a party C, let's call it the Luxembourg consortium, that could be a part of
the negotiation as well, could replace B, but it can't move against B because B has the power. Or at least all the parties involved assume that B
has the power, but the power is actually in a small plane on the Carolina
Canyon in ten meters of water. What B needs is simply to know that it
has regained that power. In two weeks it must demonstrate it. If it
doesn't, the procedure stops. It is over."

"And C moves in?" she said.

"Oh no. The whole thing comes apart. Fails. A, B, C. The deck is
reshuffled; a new hand is dealt."

"And the resource? The money? What happens if it is never recovered? What happens if the plane slips off the ridge into a thousand
fathoms of water?"

"Well, for all intents and purposes, nothing," he said. "Only this
record of it is gone, or the means to reveal it. The money is still there,
somewhere. The books or something have to balance at the end of the
year, so to speak.

"But you see, you think of money as if it were something real. Like a
dollar bill or a piece of gold. But it isn't. Money's a concept, an idea. It's a
mechanism. It's a configuration. The dollar bill is just the sign, a symbol
of a small piece of power. But the power is actually the faith that the
power can be transferred. Faith. It's all a matter of faith."

But Katherine persisted. "It's money that belongs to someone, isn't
it? Someone, some entity will have less rather than more money, right?
They'll know that, won't they?"

"What do you imagine, Katherine Dennison?" he said. "That someone lugs thousands of bags of paper bills or hundreds of pounds of gold
bars or trunks of diamonds into the vaults of Nassau? It is only when you
pin it down and talk about the specific things that you can *do* with the
money, like buy a million metric tons of wheat, and who is going to pay
what price for it.

"There are consequences, of course, but for whom? At what level are
the consequences felt? Do the 115 families who own the land of Central
America care about money? Can they lose their land? Or their power?
Of course not! Without the information on the disk ,we create a new configuration, restructure the energy of the money. The *energy* of the money.
Do you understand? It is the way the electrons in salt or the electrons in
steel are the same, all electrons are the same. All the particles are the
same. It is how they are configured that makes them salt or steel."

Long ago Katherine had learned that the simulacrum of order we
assume we live by is only a scrim through which we see figures and
shapes acting in what we interpret as civilized attitudes. When we see behind the scrim, we see that all is chimerical, only a play of
phantasmagorical light and shadow upon which we put interpretations.
The play's the thing with which we'll catch, if not at conscience, then at
consciousness. Is that what she was thinking about? Except for love,
there is no magnitude or dimension to anything. Only in love or in the
loss of love do we know that we exist or not. Pain is indeed the fulcrum.

"But still, your own secrecy? What of that?"

"A small precaution. Look, I understand how this must all appear,
my sudden appearance, the abstruse concepts, the large payment. The
enigmatic me. But think about it. Does all that I'm representing to you
now *not* happen in this world? I think you understand better. The com-
plications of power and the mechanisms that create and direct it ... oh, in
fact I think little actually happens that does not happen this way. If there
had been more time, a more usual presentation, a lesser time constraint,
then this would all be a simple action. It's the mystery and the intriguing
aspect that creates suspicion, which feeds the incredulity. But it's only the
form here, not the fact. I want you to understand that I understand this.
But what I'm telling you and what I want from you are not so strange

after all. I mean, who could imagine what you observe on the talk shows? Who could have believed such people existed, or the millions of people who watch such people? Seventy percent of the population believes in angels. Or in a literal Satan. And how many believe in aliens? Or a risen Christ? Or in Nirvana? How many believe in whatever it is they want to believe in? Junk bonds? Star Wars systems? Reincarnation? And who could have believed the orderly designed mechanism of the Holocaust? The officious disappearing of people in Argentina and Chile? Come, come, Katherine Dennison. I represent something that is, at the end of the day, much more likely than most other things. In a global economy, global financial structures have evolved. That's all that this is part of. And the disk and what it represents are actually no different from the power that a letter of credit drawn on London had when presented to a spice merchant in nineteenth-century Bombay. And more than a few ships sank with their letters of credit in them. So financial structures in India, say, had to be changed. Please, please, don't confuse this stage acting with that reality. All the world—life—is a stage, after all." He paused, but only for a moment.

"Will you do this? It is a kind of lark, after all. As I promised, no drug stuff, nothing illegal. A lot of money. A cruise upon the September sea. The best time for a sail, I'm led to believe."

"The best time, yes. Or the worst. Hurricane season. Tropical depressions. It's either very good or very bad in September."

"Will you do this? Two hundred thousand?"

"It's a lot of money," she said.

"Yes. And you're Katherine Dennison. Adventure is what you're about. I told you before, I read all about you. You're perfect for this enterprise."

"But the point is," she said, "adventure is what I've given up."

Still, she began to think that the money could be a splendid gift to Sally for her marriage. Instead of an adventure, then, she could think of what Agare wanted as a job, a temporary employment not much different from a charter, not much different from what she had grown up doing with her father, not a change in what she had determined three years ago her life would henceforth be.

He looked about. The last of the cigarette was burning down. He seemed to understand that she had not truly decided. He would wait. There was nothing more he could do. Offer another hundred thousand dollars? But it was not the money. She would do it or not by counsels of her own. And she was demonstrating Agare's ideas to herself: it was not the money that would determine her; like the three gnomes, like A and B and C, something much larger was involved. Money was only the sign, like the wind; you could not see it, only the effect of it, the crests of the waves being blown away, the wind turning the spume into missiles that hurt you when they hit.

"It's like the oldest kind of story, isn't it, the hunt for buried treasure?" she said. "Instead of a map, LORAN coordinates. No X marking the spot on the pirate's map. Now it is the crossing of three electronic beams. And now we can even read our position from satellites in space."

"Yes, yes," he said. "Exactly the same. Exactly. What the Spanish wanted with the New World gold was the power to shape Europe, to determine all of empire. The jewelry, the plate, the trivial decoration? Nothing. That was nothing. It was Philip saying to the pope, 'I will regain England for God.' It was Drake saying to *himself,* 'Spain shall not.' Do you see what the true excitement of the game is? Do you see?"

She considered how Joseph would respond, what he would advise. He would tell her to do it, not for Agare's purposes or even because of the money but because he had been urging her to do something, anything. To once again be affective. Since Steven's death.

Steven, Bobby Lockridge, and Tom Lecourt had spread out the charts on the dining room table in her house in Cushing. They were all knowledgeable, but she especially, about the coast of Maine, the fifty miles of it from Owl's Head to Southwest Harbor on Mt. Desert Island, that the three men would travel along in the next week. They would island hop more or less depending on the conditions they encountered, but they would aim for Weir and Lamb and Little Sheep and Apple, to Hen just below Swan and thence behind Great Gott and up the Western Way into Soames Sound. Steven had drawn in the line, written out the compass headings along it, and had interpolated all the information about tides and tidal currents, time lags, and wind characteristics directly onto the charts. He had even shown where they should figure on heavier big-boat traffic. He did just as she had shown him to do, taught him all his life. And carefully, as she had also taught him, as her father had taught her, he drew in alternatives and contingencies, anticipations, "just in case" lines, redundant lines, fallback positions. Alternate islands, lee shores. But you could not draw them all in; you could not anticipate suf-ficiently. You could not divine.

They would travel in three sea kayaks, Bobby and Tom in new Easyriders and Steven in his beloved Nautriad that had come from France. Dinged and patched, torn and plastered, it was still in good condition.

It was an ambitious voyage, but not beyond them. Nothing of the voy-age was new to them. They were, the three of them, like a team, as expert as you could get, and they had poked into the islands from Casco Bay through the Penobscot even up east of Schoodic. From sixteen onward, and now at twenty-two, Steven nearly lived in his Nautriad. He had worn out a wet suit. He was first in, last out of the waters in spring and fall.

By the age of sixteen, he was a master mariner, like herself at his age, capable of taking a boat, even a large sailing craft, anywhere. Through anything. She had taken him and Sally onto the *Marindor* and raised them there as much as on the land. She had sailed with them as they grew older down the coast into the Caribbean and all around it. She and Steven and Sally and Tom. But with his discovery of sea kayaking, Steven had left the high decks of the *Marindor* and dropped down into the sea itself, settled into the molded curve between crests. Bobby Lockridge, his old-est friend, soon followed him. And then Tom Lecourt, his father, from whom, by then, she had been separated for a year.

"We put in here," Steven said with his finger on Owl's Head, "at Conklin's Wharf. No problem. I called. We can leave the vehicles. We put in at six o'clock and make for North Haven right away. We get a two-mile lift from the tide, see. Going our way." He continued to describe their journey with the deftness and assurance of an admiral. They had all, of course, gone over the charts and the plans a dozen times, had hatched them together, but it was Steven who led them, maybe because Steven himself could not be led by anyone.

They were leaving in the best of weather time, the last of August, the beginning of September. The great enemy, the notorious September fogs of Maine, was still a few weeks off. Still, you had to figure possibilities. He checked out the handheld VHF radio, the EPIRB transmitter that she had urged on him, the extra compass. She had taught him well.

"So what do you think, Mom?" He turned to her.

"It looks great. I can't think of anything you haven't thought of."

"Oh, this is good; this is going to be such a good one. Sometimes you can feel it, you know?" he said to all of them, straightening up from the table.

She did know. There were times when she had sailed with an inexplicable assurance that the wind and the tides and the weather would coalesce, that the ship would take a bite on the sea and hold tightly, rooted on a long, firm, unalterably perfect tack. As if all the probabilities had been for this time suspended, and this once certainty was possible.

He would not have the wind to sail, only his strong arms to propel him, his litheness, his energy and strength. Sea kayaking was tough business, but he had prepared himself, the regimen of diet, of running, of proper weights, the paddling contraption he had rigged up in his bedroom to keep in shape through the unbearable winter. At twenty-two he was tall and handsome, smart, indomitable. And full of a blessed passion.

She worried, because she was his mother, that he should have a future, that he should continue his education (he only went to college each spring semester in order to be free to kayak well into November somewhere along the Atlantic coast). She worried that he should meet a woman "right for him." She worried for him in all the oldest maternal patterns.

She worried about the dangerousness of his sea kayaking ventures, but only within the natural boundaries of such concern. There she had parameters to work within. So much of her own life had been lived at the edge of danger that she knew there were limits to such concern. People who did not know the limits always imagined them to be far larger than they were. People who did not know about sailing grew anxious when the boat heeled even a little. The terrific danger of large cities was always worse to those who did not live in them. Sickness, business failure, whatever was not perfectly predictable always had more of fear than was useful to fear. Katherine Dennison had sailed through more bad weather by the age of twelve than anyone other than professional fishermen ever sailed through. In the midst of war, she quickly came to understand that the disabling discomfort, the debility, was worse than the death. We do not fear death until it appears to be inevitable. *Appears* to be. She had read that men in actual combat will not panic until what appears to be 30 percent casualties. They do not count and conclude; they advance into battle and die and do not stop until this appearance of the inevitability of their own death destroys their will.

She worried about Steven and his ventures within the reasonable, but she worried more about his larger taking hold in life, getting on, finding a purpose and a way. She worried about him exactly as she had worried about herself at his age and beyond. Maybe always. Maybe still. And yet, concurrently, she did *not* worry about him in the same way she had *not* worried about herself at that same age, when we are swept away by the overwhelming beauty of being young, sailing as if without effort into the strong apparent wind.

"Do you know what would be better?" He looked at her. "Instead of leaving the truck at Conklin's Wharf and then spotting a car at Southwest Harbor, what would be better would be if you just drove us down to Owl's Head. Bring back the truck, and come and get us where we come ashore. I mean look, suppose we end up here instead of here?" He touched the terminus of the main course line. "Instead of one of us hitchhiking to the spotted car, you could just come and get us. One vehicle. What do you say, Mom? Come on."

"I don't know. Sally's coming out tomorrow. I'm going to pick her up at the airport at Bangor. I'll be driving all day. And what if I'm busy when you get ashore? What if I can't drop everything and come and get you?"

"Drop what?" her husband said.

"Don't start," Steven said to him quickly. And to her. "Don't start, or I'll have to send Bobby out of the room. Bobby, go out of the room. You don't want to hear this; you don't have to hear this shit."

"No. OK. I'll do it," she said. "Gladly. With goodwill. Honest." Her fight was with Tom Lecourt, not Steven. She could easily give him what he asked her for. And certainly now was not a time to take energy from them. Every voyage should start fresh with innocent promise. And omens were important to sailors. Obedience to omens implied that there were forces you could placate: if you could offend, then you could also appease. Before a voyage you poured a libation. Offered a sacrifice. It would be easy enough to put on the altar what little was left of her and Tom.

When after three days the telephone rang, she did not think the call would be from them. But it was Tom. He told her directly. There was no other way to say what he had to say. Steven was lost. Presumed drowned. He was silent.

"Go on," she said. She wanted to say, go on, you fool, tell me. Don't make me say anything or ask anything. Tell me. But it was not Tom at whom she was angry. Only angry.

"We were between Shelter Island and Cornerstone. Yesterday late. A little fog came in for about two hours. We kept pretty close. Shouted to each other. Blew whistles. We kept a course to Sumner Ledge. About five o'clock we picked up more than a little wind. I figure it set us off about five degrees to the northwest. Not a lot. Then the fog lifted. I was about a hundred yards from Bobby, but we couldn't see Steven. Nothing. We thought he had kept a better course and had gotten to Sumner Ledge before us. We corrected for it and got there about seven o'clock, but no Steven. We waited. What else could we do? We thought he had settled for another island, Trinity or Spruce, or any of a dozen. We tried to raise him on the VHF. The second day, yesterday, we waited at Sumner Ledge. We figured he would come here; it's the way we planned—stick to your rendezvous point. By noon he should have gotten there. We struck out straight for shore. Picked up a lobster boat in half an hour and radioed in to the Coast Guard. They've been searching ever since. This morning they found the kayak." He stopped.

"And?" she said. Hurry up. Get to the point, she wanted to say. But there was no point, no conclusion, only a recitation and a stop. Neither of them had any control over the shape or pace of this event. Tom Lecourt was silent.

"What should I do?" she said. "Is there anything I can do?"

"Nothing to do, Kate."

"What do you mean, nothing?"

"There's nothing anyone can do but continue the search. The Coast Guard is still looking. They've been checking out every island, every rock. But it's not a large area. There's not much ..."

Chance, she thought, blotting out whatever he was saying. Not much chance. No chance, they meant. She slammed down the phone.

"What?" her daughter said, but as if she already knew.

"Steven," she said. "He's gone. Lost."

Too stunned to weep, how does one take the next step? she wondered. Do you sit down to lunch, a cup of tea? How could you dare to continue with the quotidian and the mundane? But equally, how could you afford not to? And Sally, she was struck dumb, crushed into shock, clinical shock. She wished that Sally were not here. She resented her presence. She did not want to share her grief; she wanted it all for herself. She wanted to howl and scream and smash cups against the wall. She wanted to weep and curse, do something. Sally prevented that. Her being there.

Denial, anger, grief, acceptance—she did not go through the stages, she embraced them all in the same, mixed the sharp primary colors of them into a middle-gray value, a seamless blur of nothing.

Steven had died with the suddenness with which the young always seem to die, like a breaking, like the quick and sharp shattering of glass, nothing of the fading, the diminishment, the used-upness or the exhaustion of age. The young died with no chance to relinquish, to give up, to back off and away. To reconcile. They do not live long enough to acquire debts of guilt or doubt or sorrow that take a lifetime to indemnify. That is why it felt so wrong. No chance for the young to take to themselves what mystery they can. She remembered the deaths of the young men in Vietnam all those years ago, no older than herself and often younger, how death always seemed to come to them as a surprise, a mistake. It took her thirty years to understand that it was no mistake.

She took Sally in her arms and held her against the convulsive shaking that seemed as if it would snap and splinter her. She dosed her with Valium and put her into bed and got Mrs. Crandall from down the road to look after her for the two hours she would be gone. Then she drove over to Rockport, where she would pick up Tom. Bobby Lockridge had called friends to come get him. She found Tom at the town wharf with his kayak and gear. And Steven's kayak. They loaded both on top of the car, and she drove them back to Cushing, where he had left his truck.

What was there to say? The acrimony that had risen up to poison them over the past two years had drained away, the lancet of their son's death piercing the corruption. Maybe that was what they could talk about, maybe that had become their more recent theme, the feverish infection of outrage and resentment, but they had not been able to approach it: we remember the wounding long after it has healed; the scar itself, the memory, becomes the issue, and even that fades.

"We're not as bad as we've been to each other," she said.

"No," he said.

She drove hard, looking straight ahead, tight to the road. She sensed him looking at her.

"Why are you looking at me?"

"I'm looking for answers," he said. "Maybe something I'll see in you."

"Answers?" She didn't understand. "There are no answers."

"Not Steven," he said. "Us. How do good people go bad the way we did?"

"You had an affair. It made me angry. Anger begets anger, especially if you're the cause of the anger."

How easy it was to say that now! How she had screamed at him, wept and shrieked, pushed him away! Licked her injury. And now how little any of that mattered. She wondered if he was responding the same way.

"Is it easy now to talk this way, to be together? For you? It is for me," she said.

"Yes," he said. "It's as if what we did to each other—it all seems so trivial, so inconsequential compared ..." He did not finish the sentence.

"We want and we take if we can get away with it," she said. "But the truth is too terrible to accept, so we want to be otherwise, so we build magnificent structures of intellect, we teach and honor them. And so we should. But do you see, that's the problem, the friction. To do good, to do what makes us *better* than we are, we have to go against *what* we are. It's a marvelous idea. Very exciting."

She could tell that he felt it was the incident of Steven's death that was speaking, a specter using her body, haunting her. But it was not. It was an idea that in one murky form or another she had come to embrace, was coming to embrace anyway. What Steven's death had done was codify. Piloting a boat along the coast, to find where you were you took bearings. Lines of position, they were called. Where all the lines crossed, that was where you were. The more lines, the smaller the margin of error. Steven's death was the last bearing. Henceforth she would know where she was, even if not where to go. And that is why, driving to her house, she could be as she was—calm, level. Or maybe just inert. And would remain.

Back in Cushing, she helped him with his kayak.

"Take Steven's kayak too," she said. "Please."

"Kate ..." he began.

"No. Don't misunderstand. It's not that I'll enshrine it. Memento mori. But if it's around I'll keep thinking what to do with it, what should be done with it. I couldn't give it away or destroy it. It would just be always *there*. I don't want that. And there is another reason. I'm going to sail. I'm going to get on the *Marindor* and sail away. I'll probably even sell the house eventually."

He loaded Steven's kayak. Sally was deeply asleep. They agreed it was best not to wake her. She would call and tell him when she was leaving. Sally could be with him for a while until she could get back to her job in Baltimore. He agreed. He'd come get her. In two weeks, they agreed. Then she said, "Tom, let's finish with the divorce. Let's just do, settle. Let's just leave each other alone. I'll split the house, whatever else. And I'll give over my counterclaims. But not the *Marindor*. I can't share that. I can't sell it. But let's be done, OK?"

"Sure," he said. "OK."

She thought that if they were free of each other, totally free, then they would be to some extent free of the pain they both now bore. If they were to end the deliberations of worth and equity, if they were to share nothing, then maybe they would not share this. But what was the ratio? How could you ever establish such proportions? Still, the instinct was right. End! What was ended, end! She leaned up and kissed him lightly on the cheek.

"I never did *not* love you, you know," he said, as he sat in the truck, the motor idling.

"I know," she said. "I always knew that, even in the worst of it. Maybe that is what made it so hard. Maybe if there was no love at all, we could have been easier on each other. Take care, Tom. Take care of yourself." She stood back from the truck as it backed and turned and drove away.

In the house the telephone rang. She flinched and as quickly remembered that nothing more could happen. It was Joseph.

"I just heard," he said. "I'm on the island. I'm coming down. I'll get to the mainland in an hour and then I'll drive. I'll be down by midafternoon."

"No," she said. "No, not yet, Joe."

"You shouldn't be alone."

"Sally's here."

"She'll take more from you than she'll give. Let me come down."

"No," she said. "What I really want right now is to be alone. I'm OK. I mean, I'm not breaking down. I'm actually as hard and as cold as an ice cube. I'm shocked at my own balance. If I didn't have so exact an idea of what I've lost, I'd question my love for him. Joe, don't come now. Let me write to you."

"Come here, then. Let me get you and bring you here. Sally too, if you want."

"I should be alone, Joe. I can't come to you. Together we'd turn Steven into a ghost. I wouldn't want that. I couldn't stand that. I'll write to you. Immediately. This afternoon. It will be very good for me to write to you. It always has been."

"You've always written to me."

"And you to me. There's nothing I cherish more."

"There's more that you should cherish," he said.

"More than you?" she said.

"More than writing letters."

"We've done more than write letters. Anyway, I've made an important decision. I'd rather describe it in a letter. Writing it down may even help me better understand it. I'll write. Immediately. Good-bye, Joe."

She wrote to him that she had decided to leave, to get on the *Marindor* and sail away. For a long time. "I have this need to be profoundly alone," she wrote. "The sea has always been better to me than the land. I've lost a husband and a son and my confidence in life. My life's been governed by accident. Even when I was winning, I wasn't. Right now only the sea has meaning for me, or more exactly my mastery of the *Marindor*. My only regret is that I can't come to you, to Macken Island. Not now. Not yet."

When Sally awoke, Katherine told her what she had in mind.

"Leave? Just leave? How can you just leave?" her daughter said.

The Coast Guard searched for three more pro forma days and then gave it up.

In a month she had outfitted the *Marindor* sufficiently. In mid-October she weighed anchor, sailed down past Port Clyde, and never returned.

"I can't leave today," she said to Agare. "I'd need to top off the water and fuel tanks, provision us properly, make some maintenance checks. You don't just sail out so far without getting ready. I should really take a week, two weeks at least. Think about it," she said. "Think what you're asking. But you don't know what you're asking. You don't know anything about the sea, do you?"

"But two weeks is all we've got to work with," he said. "And get ready for what? You sail a mile and then you sail another mile and then you've sailed six hundred miles. Get ready for what?"

"That's what you don't know. That's what you get ready for. I'll need at least two days. I'll go into Mystic within the hour. I've got to prepare the boat, at least as much as I can. But I always keep the *Marindor* fit for any sea, so you're lucky there. And my crew?" she gestured forward and shook her head as if to reject even the possibility of the idea. "I'll have to train my crew. Imagine that," she said to him.

"But you'll do it? Excellent. Two days, then. Fine. Excellent." He clapped his hands. He stood up and called to Alan to transfer what was in the fishing boat to the *Marindor.* "What about the other boats?" he asked. "The sailboat? Can you pull something like that through the ocean? It seems a little large."

"I unship the mast. I carry the *Ark* on davits." She pointed out the sturdy cranelike arms extended over the stern of the boat and the special bracing she had designed to hold the boat from moving. "Just like a lifeboat. The inflatable I keep on the forward deck lashed down. If the weather gets too bad, I deflate it and store it below."

"It is probably best that we don't meet again," he said. "Not until after you return. When you give me the disk." He smiled. "But as soon as you have it, contact me on the radio. That I know you have retrieved it is vital. There is the radio equipment. As powerful as radio gets. Can you operate it? Single sideband? I hope so. I can't explain it to you. But I assume you are able. You are probably already well equipped. Ah, Katherine Dennison, I assume so much about you." He hugged her. He wrote out for her where he could be contacted, how the message should be phrased. Returning, she should sail to the nearest port, probably Charleston, and he would meet her there. "We'll fly out. I'll have a chartered plane ready. I'll take you to Zurich, yes? Would you like that? Would you like to see the gnomes? Meet them? But now I am off," he said, but he paused. "Why, Katherine Dennison? What made you agree?"

"Perhaps it's that I've never done anything for which there were consequences. Maybe this is such a chance. I have a good friend who would think so. He would advise me to do it."

"But surely, surely you have acted with consequence. Think of your life, of your achievements. Your books. Your poems."

"Consequences for *myself,* yes. But for others? I think not. I've never done anything that has turned lives. It has always been my life that has been turned. I haven't even sought out on my own a way to do that. I waited for something like you to drop down upon me. No. That's not true. I wasn't even waiting. I just happened to be in Mystic getting ice."

"But your books," he persisted. "Think of their impact upon others."

"My books? Those weren't books. Those were children's books. Entertainments at best. Impact? Evelyn Kinski, do you mean? Do you think I influenced her life?" she said.

"Ah, well," he said as if to shrug. "Well, yes. Yes. I suppose."

"I mean consequences you live with. That enter into the rest of your life."

"There was your son," he said, softly, gently.

"That's altogether different. That *happened* to me, that's all. An accident. Everything has always been an accident. The story of my life. The end of the story."

"No," he said. "You can start a story with an accident, but you can't end a story with an accident. Aristotle," he said. And then, "You are surprised?"

"No," she said. "You seem capable of Aristotle."

"Or at least of aphorism." He smiled and swung himself clumsily down into the motorboat.

"Can you handle that boat? Do you know anything about what you're doing?" she said. "Maybe Alan should take you in; I'll meet him."

"No, no, no, you keep Alan. I can manage. I'm resourceful. I'm very resourceful." He was alight now, his exuberance pulsing, shining through the motley that was already beginning to slip off him, shedding, returning to his own plumage.

In the boat, he started the motor. She saw that he would understand enough to manage, and the sea was calm enough to allow him. He would be safe into Mystic. She held the line, and before she cast off she said, "You assume my loyalty to you? I have your money. Alan has his. Suppose I don't do it? Suppose I just keep sailing on to Florida, or wherever? Then what?"

"Nothing. Nothing at all. I told you. None of this—the money—has anything to do with anything important to the players. It is not even their own money that they play with. It's all in the game itself, Katherine. The game itself. That's all there is. All our games. Imitations of order." He waved and pushed the boat into forward and slowly eased away. "But there is no order," he shouted to her over the motor. "Only the imitations." Then he turned the boat around and tentatively felt his way out of the cove and into the open sea beyond. Soon he was gone, and the sound of the boat was gone. Do I wake or dream? she thought.

The clanging of Alan on the deck of the *Marindor* moving the boxes and bags and scuba tanks that he had unloaded assured her. She turned to the task.

"The generator, Alan. We'll use the boom and the topping lift to haul it over to the port side. We'll lash it there to those ringbolts." But Alan hardly knew what a boom and topping lift were. She would explain, or better, she would show him. In an hour the equipment was in place, stored and mostly secured. They would finish on the two-hour run under power into Mystic. She sent Evelyn below to various tasks. In the cockpit she began to tutor Alan in the handling of a large vessel. He was adept, quick to learn. A pleasant young man. Nice kids, the two of them. A little daffy, but hopeful and earnest. This would work. This would be something a little like pleasure again. She set the boat on its course. It would be an hour before they picked up the first important marker. She went forward to write a letter to Macken Island that she would mail immediately from Mystic.

5

It took four days rather than two to make the *Marindor* as ready
as it could be made for what it was about to do. But Katherine was not
unduly concerned. As she had told Agare, she continuously kept the boat
in excellent condition, always sea fit and ready. The boat was hauled and
the bottom painted every year, even beyond necessity, the masts slathered
with grease, all the brightwork varnished, the decks honed. The boat was
fifty-five years old, but its carvel planking was as tight and firm as it had
ever been. No seams had opened to any important extent, and those that
did open had been quickly recaulked, and the boat had not lost any of its
shape. No ribs or frames had cracked, never any rot. As for the standing
and running rigging, she replaced immediately whatever looked even
slightly suspicious, any shackle or block or length of line.

In Mystic she stopped at the shop of the chandler with whom she had
dealt for years whenever she made this harbor, S. Clemenson & Son.
Simon Clemenson, though Simon had been dead for a century. But his
business went on, prospered. Even now Clemensons were still involved.
Maybe that was why she gave them her business, or her *custom,* as Simon
would have had it. And it pleased her that though she might not stop in
for months, or years, she would be remembered by the older clerks.

She left them a list of her requirements and asked that they put it all
aboard the *Marindor* where it was berthed in Cuthbert's Yard up toward

Noank. She also bought the additional charts she would need. She updated her Coast Pilot, the Light List, the Coast Guard's Notice to
Mariners. Most of this material she would not need once she was off
soundings. And the information about the shipping lanes she would be
sailing through had not significantly changed; she had that nearly by
heart. She also bought the most recent publication of the *Nautical
Almanac*. She had not navigated by the stars or taken sun shots consis-
tently for years, except for the novelty and entertainment of doing it. And
with LORAN and Radio Direction finders and radio fixes all about, and
with the appearance of global position satellites, the sextant had become
redundant many times over. But she was going well off soundings now,
and she would be prepared. Redundancy was a good thing. And celestial
navigation, once you knew it well, you never forgot.

Looking at the high-scale charts, she quickened. She had not sailed
into such blue water for a time now; in the last three years she had
coasted, poking around the Atlantic seaboard, as far north as Sable
Island, as far south as the Florida Keys. Coasting. She smiled at the aptness. Me and *Marindor* coasting along.

She and the *Marindor* had been born in the same year, a fact that had
always delighted her. The sister she had never had. Now they were just a
couple of old ladies coasting along. But now they would head out, the two
of them. The kids—Alan and Evelyn—didn't count; they were cargo.
But Katherine and *Marindor,* like old times when they were fit for each
other, boon companions. She ran her fingers over the chart. She even
identified the point on the Carolina Canyon where the Learjet should be,
where they would be in few enough days. It all seemed so easy, so magical, like astral projection. It felt almost as if she could simply transmit
herself along the LORAN coordinates directly and be there. But that, of
course, would hardly be the case. She knew better than anyone that under
the fantastical there throbbed the truer rough magic of the sea, where
even what was easy was hard.

To be truly at sea again. Yes! She could not have done it without this
small adventure to prod her. She exulted in her decision to do it, delighted herself in the provisions she bought. Agare had been right:
whatever else, why not eat well? Whatever Agare had packed for them,

whatever was left of yesterday's feasting, she would provide for herself. Delicacies, excellent wines, fresh fruit. It was a giddy indulgence. She considered a new pair of boat shoes, a sweater that she admired. Still, they could not sail on caviar and Belgian chocolate. She stocked up on pasta and rice and beans, cans of stew, ham, chicken. Sugar, coffee. Oil and spices and mounds of fresh vegetables and salad.

Alan and Evelyn had rather disappeared. She had made a list for them of the clothing they would need and whatever other personal effects. It was a long list, but then, they had nothing but what they were wearing. What was in the duffles they had brought aboard in the cove were more like play clothes, what they imagined they would use in Florida. They had no idea of what was at sea. And everything else had gone down on their little boat. It couldn't have been much. She told them they must get exactly everything on the list; it was all important. She told them that she would inspect. They listened with respectful seriousness. Ma'am, Alan had called her. "Yes, ma'am," he had said, all attention. She let that be for now. Let her be ma'am. Let them get the feeling of a captain, the necessity that they respond without question to her. Later she could become Katherine to him.

Alan and Evelyn did not sleep aboard. They would taxi back from Mystic with their packages and dump them and leave. They were staying with friends. They were "bon voyaging," Evelyn said. Katherine had laughed. It was a wonderful phrase. "Have a good time," she said, "but don't forget. The day after tomorrow, ten o'clock. An outgoing tide. Sharp now." They promised as solemnly as Boy and Girl Scouts. She did not know where they had put their case of money; she suspected it was on the boat, but she did not ask. She hoped, except for what they were spending, that they had deposited their money in a bank, safely waiting for them when they all returned so that they could purchase their future, whatever it was that their future looked like to them now at the beginning of their lives. It thrilled her to think of that, and she wanted them to be, just now, if not wise, then at least not unduly careless. She wanted to tell them what she would have told Sally and Steven, but she held herself back. She was not their mother, she was "ma'am." In two weeks or ten days or less, more than likely she would never see them again.

She had the water tanks pumped and filled with fresh water as well as the water casks that were permanently lashed far forward in the bow just behind the windlass for the anchors, which were lashed with heavy, old-fashioned manilla lines, three-quarter-inch to the cathead just abaft the twelve-by-twelve-inch stem where the bowsprit ran into the head of the boat. She arranged for some work to be done on the pintles of the rudder and for some adjustments to the diesel. And at the last moment she decided to change the turnbuckles on the port shrouds. And the more she checked around her boat, the more she found to tinker with. But changing the turn-buckles and the work on the pintles, that was important and could be done only in a yard. The boat would have to be hauled to do the work on the pin-tles. That is what cost the extra days. She had to plead and finally offer twice the work rate, but money was not a consideration. It was not her money. And what was the money anyway, after Agare's lecture? And was this not all a part of the fantasy she had entered into: in for a dime, in for a dollar? In for $200,000. Incredible. The ease with which he had thrown the money at them all. More than anything else, it was the trivializing gesture of the money that had convinced her he was telling the truth.

About him she wondered more and more. Was he in Mystic, now in a new disguise, hovering around, keeping an eye out, waiting for her to leave, basing a new strategy on other contingencies? Maybe what he did, working in a continuum not unlike the sea, adjusting to waves and wind, brought him closer to her than at first she might have imagined.

She called Sally to tell her what she was doing, but she would not go into great detail, would mention no names.

"Hi," she said. "It's me, Captain Katherine. I'm in Mystic. Connecticut."

"Hi. What's up?"

"I'm going for a sail," she said.

"You've been going on a sail for three years, Mother."

"Right. But this is different. This is a kind of adventure. I'm going to look for a sunken treasure. I've even got a diver aboard."

Sally leapfrogged over that, refusing to respond to the delight in her mother's voice. "But I'm getting married. You promised you'd be here. You promised. What's *wrong* with you?"

"No, no. Don't worry. I'll be back in less than two weeks. This is a very short-term adventure. Just a tiny piece of one, really. I'll fill in all the details later. I'll be there. It's not for a month, right? The wedding. How's Jack?"

"Jason," her daughter said. "Jason, not Jack. You should meet him sometime."

"Please, Sally. Don't be hard on me. Please."

"I'm sorry if I'm hard on you. Maybe you're hard on me. I have a life. I wanted you to be part of it. All you are is an occasional phone call. Letters."

"It's the kind of life I live. A lifestyle," she started to plead. "It's not something against you."

"No, it's not. It's not a lifestyle, it's a deathstyle. You've been mourning for three years. Well, it costs me. It costs *me*."

Not three years. Fifty-five. I'm mourning for fifty-five years, she wanted to say. And I don't know exactly why. But whatever answers I find, I'll find them at sea or nowhere. But she could not say that to Sally. Sally would explode. She had said something like that often enough since Steven to have rubbed her daughter raw.

"I'm sorry, honey. I really am." And then she was stuck. Sorry was taken for granted, but it wasn't enough. It wasn't what Sally wanted. What she wanted was her mother back. And especially now, a month before her wedding. The way it was supposed to be. It didn't matter that Katherine would be useless. Sally did not want her help. All she wanted was for Katherine to be there, to be more than a voice calling from a pay phone on the edge of a harbor somewhere.

"I'll be there, Sally. Please. Don't worry about that. Don't doubt that. I'll come early. We'll spend some time. Don't hate me, Sally. I love you."

"I don't hate you, Mom, but you make me angry. You make me very angry. I'm sorry. But you do." Katherine could hear the edge of her daughter's tears. "I've got to go now, Mom. Be careful. Call as soon as you get back. Good luck with your treasure hunt." And she clicked off before either of them could say anything more, even as Katherine started to tell her that she could call her from sea, that she could patch through to her.

But Sally was gone. I'll surprise her, then, Katherine thought. I'll call her from the Carolina Canyon.

The morning of the twelfth of September, 0700 hours. Katherine went ashore for breakfast. When she returned she found a dinghy tied up to the modified gangway she used when on a mooring to get in and out of the *Marindor*. *Filigree* was the name across the transom of the dinghy. Katherine had noticed earlier the boat that owned the dinghy, a sixty-foot Hinckley. The kids must have come back and could not reach her on the shore-to-ship phone at Cuthbert's to have her come get them in the in-flatable. She would have to set them right about borrowing someone else's dinghy. That was not to be done. But she couldn't find them in the boat. Perhaps the dinghy had gotten loose and a passing fishing boat on its way out had caught it and tied it to the first boat it passed so that it could be put ashore or returned. She tried to raise the *Filigree* on the VHF, but there was no response. Weekend sailors. She would tow the dinghy into Cuthbert's and ask them to take care of it.

When Alan and Evelyn called, heavy with more bundles, bright and chirpy, she retrieved them and dropped off the dinghy. And now the time had come, the leaving, always a special moment regardless of how often it occurs. The profound separation. She cast off from the mooring, and they powered away from the congestion of the inner harbor and through the outer harbor, and then she hoisted sail and left Mystic and Noank with a good southwesterly wind pushing the *Marindor* steadily and firmly. Katherine struck a line on the chart, almost exactly east-southeast, and brought the boat onto a nice, tight beam reach in wind that had mounted into nearly twenty knots, and the great boat took wing. From Mystic she would sail easterly across the end of Long Island, past Montauk, and then strike a course directly down to the Carolina Canyon. She would not go through Plumb Gut but would stay outside. From this moment she estimated four days to the Carolina Canyon, but quite pos-sibly less. Even within the last two hours, she had carefully monitored the weather. Nothing was happening in the next four days that should alarm her. What weather systems were stirring were still far off the coast of Africa or down and blocked by the Yucatán.

She taught the helm to Alan for about an hour and then to Evelyn, how to feel the surge of the boat, how to compensate and not oversteer. She showed them how to aim the boat along some fitting, how to look behind at the wake to see if they were twisting and yawing instead of staying straight. Above all, she showed them how to avoid an accidental jibe, how to prevent the wind from coming in back of the sails and swinging them violently across the deck. If you are ever in doubt, turn into the wind. Always know where the wind is. Both of them had a good feel for the helm. That was encouraging. Even with the self-steering mechanism that would mostly be used, it was important that they should be able to steer. The self-steering mechanism was relatively crude because she had wanted to keep it that way. It was less technical and more reliable than the usual semi-hi-tech mechanisms. She had run various other important lines back through a series of blocks into the cockpit, the halyards and sheets, the vangs and preventers. She would hardly ever need to go forward, and when she did the boat could manage itself.

She didn't need Alan and Evelyn to sail the ship, even if the weather should become mean, but they could be useful. She would let them handle the halyards and trim the sheets, and it would be easier on any voyage to be able to have them take a trick at the helm, especially if she ran into any kind of disturbance or while the *Marindor* was in the shipping lanes. But she did not need them. She could sail this boat anywhere alone.

"Wow," Evelyn said. "Oh, this is fun. I just love this. Isn't this terrific, Alan?" she crooned as the *Marindor* rose on a sea and surfed on it for at least a hundred yards before it fell softly down off the back of the wave as the wave sped out from under.

"Yeah," Alan said. "Terrific. Just terrific."

They were sailing at a good and constant eight knots, about as fast as the *Marindor* was willing to go without being pushed. "We'll keep on this heading for another three hours if we can." Katherine had explained to them how to respond to the compass, how to stay on a course. "Then we'll come up about fifteen degrees and head off the wind a little. Slow down a little. Still, it's a good brisk start. A fair offing."

Even in the golden bright day, the heavy sun, the wind, and the swift movement of the boat made for a chill. It is always colder at sea if a boat is moving. Evelyn and Alan had dressed themselves in their fashionable clothing. Bright and stiff with newness, they looked like a couple on the cover of *Cruising World* or *Sail*. A handsome couple. Alan, wide eyed and sandy haired, with boyishness lingering in him, peeking out through the mask of his ascending manhood. And Evelyn was a beauty. From the first, when her boat grounded in the cove, she had expressed an easy certainty of it, the un-self-consciousness of those people who from the core out are beautiful to look at. Now, more naturally than the highest fashion models, she projected what the designers of such upscale sailing clothes and gear wanted. Against them, Katherine, in her brine-cured clothes, felt tattered.

She saw too that they had bought the most expensive gear available—Patagonia windbreakers, Harkens shoes. The heavy-weather stuff, the slickers, were Henri Lloyd, close to $800 for jacket and bib. She had made more modest suggestions, but a salesperson must have led them otherwise. It was the money in their pockets, Katherine knew; that is what had really led them. What were a few hundred dollars more or less when you had a case of money under your bunk in the forecastle?

"We'll get there in no time," Evelyn said. "Oh, I could get to like this. Alan, maybe we should get a boat like this. Maybe this is the boat for us. Could we get a boat like this for a hundred thousand, Katherine?"

"It's not always like this, Evelyn," she said. "Sometimes it's very cold and wet and scary."

"Not this trip," Evelyn said. "Not this trip. I can feel it. It's going to be smooth sailing all the way. Wooooooow," she shouted as they surfed on another wave. The meter read nine knots for another hundred yards.

Katherine turned the boat over to them. "I'm going below now. I've got some things to do. Lunch to start thinking about. You're in charge now. She's a forgiving boat. Give her half a chance and she'll keep you out of trouble. She'll take care of you. Just stay alert. Call me immediately if anything changes."

"Wooooooooow," Evelyn said.

And maybe it would be smooth sailing, downhill all the way. She had checked weather reports as far forward as possible and there was nothing coming their way. Once clear of Montauk and sailing closer to the wind, the *Marindor* would drop back to five knots. The problem would not be getting to the Carolina Canyon even if they needed more time, even if there was a shift in the wind and the weather. The *Marindor* could go pretty much where it pleased and when, and the season favored them. Four days to get there plus the four already spent in Mystic still gave them the margin of a full week. If they could contact Agare once they had the disk, they would have done most of what was necessary. Even without the actual disk in his hand, as long as he knew it was safe, he could go ahead. From the Carolina Canyon to, say, Charleston, the nearest land, even on a dead beat windward, they could easily make it back in three days. What would matter most was how quickly they could find the plane and how quickly Alan could retrieve the disk. And for him to dive, they would need calm weather. But it all looked good. Very possible. A race. A game, just as Agare had said. And a game that she could not lose. He could lose it. A or B or C in Zurich could lose it, but she could not. And even their loss, according to Agare, would not be such a loss. But if she could not lose, if she had already won, *what* had she won?

She turned to the electronic equipment. She needed to tune it, make adjustments, check it out, test. Align. Be certain of her compasses. Even with the easy availability of time checks, she kept her father's sublime chronometer accurate. She arranged the radio that Agare had brought. It duplicated her own, but it was far more powerful and all digital. State of the art. She glanced at the literature. She would study it later, but she saw at once that it would be easy to operate. She knew enough. She paid special attention to the LORAN. And to the fathometer. In the depth of her concentration, at first she did not hear Evelyn call down to her, and when she did hear her, she could not understand what she was saying, could not make sense of what the girl meant.

"Katherine," Evelyn said, "you'd better come up here. We have guests."

"Guests?" she said. "The Coast Guard?"

"No," Evelyn said. "Men. Two men. Here."

"Hello," one of the men said, appearing over Evelyn's shoulder. He pointed a gun down at Katherine. "Come up and join us. Please. But hurry. I don't feel so good."

Katherine climbed up the companionway into the spacious cockpit between the two cabins. Alan was still at the helm, his eyes bent to the horizon, flicking down to the compass in its binnacle and up to the horizon again just as she had taught him. The ship still moved solidly, taking the beam seas easily. The day had brightened even further, but everything was the same, except everything had changed.

"I am ... me," the smaller man with the gun said. "And this is ... him." He pointed to a second man. "But excuse me, I'm going to be sick." He looked around as if figuring out what to do.

"That way," Katherine said, pointing to the lee rail that was canted down toward the sea. "Don't get sick to windward."

"Gotcha," the man said. "Like pissing into the wind. Thanks." He slid down to the rail, bent over the life lines, and vomited.

Katherine turned to the other man. He did not hold a gun in his hand, but she was sure he would also have one, probably in his belt. He was large, thick across the chest, and his arms looked to Katherine to be heavy with muscle, but like the other, smaller man bent over the lee rail, he was also dressed in a more or less touristy style, fairly light fabric, colorful, open. Both of the men wore shoes that were all wrong for a boat, she thought, or even for strolling around Mystic. Expensive, hard, and leathery, they would be slippery in wet weather. The large man was over six feet, she guessed, but big boned, hard. His hair was dark, dense but receding. She could not understand his skin. It was granulated, not scarred from adolescent acne and not the sun-cured skin of sailors or farmers, only striated all over, finely etched. A mezzotint surface, she thought. It was a highly distinctive feature, the first thing you noticed. Unfinished, the way a piece of furniture is before it is finally smoothed and filled and varnished with a tight skin. His eyes were flat blue. Cerulean blue, she thought, brilliantly colored but opaque, impenetrable. Gouache eyes, not watercolor eyes.

And immediately she thought of Agare. He and this man would be about the same age, her age. Midfifties. But how different! Even in the instant she'd had to look at him, she could sense the stolidity in him, the wrench-tightened hold of the man. He looked at her without expression. She looked back.

"Ah. Better," the small man said. "But not good. I don't feel so good at all."

"Where did you come from? What is this all about? This must be some crazy mistake," she said.

"There," he said, pointing to the lazaret. "We hid in there. The hiding was easy. Over two hours. It wasn't so bad at first, but after a while …" He shrugged at the obvious.

"But how did you get aboard?"

"It was easy. We watched. You were all gone a lot. Coming, going. We saw our chance this morning and took it. There are little rowboats all over the place. We took one. We were going to do what we had to do quick and get out, but you came back before we could leave. So we hid. And here we are. Only I don't feel so good," he said.

So Agare's plan had foundered. C had found him out after all. Then for whom was she working now? Or was this Agare's idea? Despite his disclaimers, had he sent his own representatives to ensure the work be done? Yes, she concluded, but too quickly.

"Are you agents? Did Agare send you?" she said. "Is that what this is about?"

"Agents?" He laughed. He seemed as volatile as the larger man seemed not. "Federals? Narcos, you are thinking? That *is* a laugh. Na, na. We're robbers, that's all. We're here to rob you. It's very simple. There's nothing complicated. Agents?" He laughed again. "Hey, how about that, Barstow? Agents. Is that a hoot?" He motioned to Katherine and Evelyn. "OK. Let's get on with it. You two go over to him." He pointed at Alan. They did so. "Now, where's the money?" He waved his gun at them.

"Come on. Quick. I want to get back to land before I'm sick again. Already I'm feeling sick again." He fired his gun just above their heads. Evelyn shrieked.

"What money?" Alan said. The man fired again.

"The money you have been spending all over town. *That* money. You're spending that kind of money, some big money, we figure you've got more, a lot more," he said and fired again. "Get it before we have to start looking for it. Come on, come on. This is all taking longer than it should. Don't make it take no longer." Evelyn began to sob. The large man named Barstow came and stood beside the other.

"Tell Louis where the goddamn money is," he said. "We get the money, you take us back to land. It's easy. Or it can be hard." Katherine had no doubts. This was only a simple robbery, and it had nothing to do with Zurich and gnomes. Simply, she had come back too soon. Which left her with only one conclusion: do what they say. Get rid of them.

"The money is in an aluminum case under my berth," Katherine said. "Take it."

"Where?" the large man said. "Take me."

She led him to the companionway down to the stern cabin. She even cautioned him down. She could see he was, like Agare, unfamiliar with a boat, with the sea's motion, but he was lithe, athletic. Tensile as Agare was not. She pointed.

"Get it," he said. "And don't do anything stupid." He had not yet shown her a gun, but she knew what he meant. "Or I'll have to kill you. There's no need for that. Is that clear?"

"Of course," she said.

She took the case out slowly and put it on the berth.

"Open it," he said. She did.

He looked at the money as she looked at him. He was not suddenly possessed by it, a big score. The excitement of having what you want. He was studying the money, thinking something through.

In that moment he became very interesting to her.

"There's more," he said. "There's some more money somewhere. Are you going to tell me, or am I going to have to find it? I can be very rough on your boat if I have to find it myself."

The VHF began to chatter, the scruffy sound of voices crackling out of nowhere, a sound that was always more strange at sea than on land.

"What's that?" he said, quickly alert.

"It's the radio. It's a law that you have to monitor channel 16, the emergency channel. In case you hear something, you can relay the call, or you can use the channel to make contact with another ship and then go to another channel to talk. Not an emergency." But he wasn't listening to explanations. Radio. Contact. He was making another calculation.

"Out," he said. "Take the money up." She closed the case and did as he said. He did not follow her at once. They waited on deck. He appeared shortly and threw out another case, an old-fashioned briefcase, as old as her college days. The case she kept all of Joseph Mackenzie's letters in. He had looked under the berth and come up with this.

"What's in there?" he said to his partner, and ducked back down into the cabin.

First Louis opened the aluminum case. "Jesus fucking Christ. Oh my God. How much is that?" he said to her. "Come on, take a guess."

"I don't have to guess. A hundred thousand dollars. All twenties."

"Oh my God. A hundred thousand dollars. Jesus fucking Christ. This is not what we were expecting, let me tell you. Jesus fucking Christ. And in there?" he pointed at the briefcase with his gun.

"Nothing. There's nothing in there. Only letters."

"Open it."

"I'm telling you, there are only letters in there."

"Open it, Mrs. Dennison. Don't make a fuss."

"How did you know my name?"

"Barstow," he shouted toward the companionway, "hurry up. I'm getting sick again. Jesus," he said to her, "I feel rotten. Do you ever get seasick? I just want to get off this goddamn boat. Jesus. Barstow! I got to puke again! Jesus, just look at me. I'm sweating terrible. This is awful. Barstow! You," he said to her. "You steer the boat. You," he motioned at Alan. "You and the girl go back there, as far as you can go. Go on. Quick." They did it. "Anyone moves," he said, "bang bang. Oh, shit." He ran for the rail and threw up again, heaved up at nothing. After each contraction, he looked up quickly at them. Then down again. Four times. Ludicrous. A comedy routine. Then he came back. He took the briefcase and opened it and reached in and withdrew a handful of letters and threw them into the wind.

"No," Katherine shouted at him. "Stop that." But he did not. Handfuls of letters. Years. All gone. He turned the briefcase upside down and shook it to be sure, then he threw even that over the side of the speeding boat. Fury shook through her, but emptiness as well. It was like living in a sine wave, swinging in rapid oscillations between negative and positive poles. Nothing so far had so sharply driven what was happening into her. She felt herself splitting apart. She could have charged at the man, but the letters were gone. She must clutch herself together. She must remember what to do in a storm.

Barstow appeared halfway up the companionway and threw the VHF radio out into the cockpit. He disappeared for a moment and then reappeared and threw out the LORAN, the radio direction finder, the radar, the single sideband, everything that looked electronic to him. Then he came on deck.

"Why?" was all she could say to him.

He took the equipment and threw it over the side.

"Nobody can call you. You can't call anybody. And whatever else was in that, you don't need it to get us back. You can see where we were. It's only over there." He pointed to the purple flush of land that was still easily visible. Even some smudge of buildings on the hills could be distinguished. "And you've got a compass. You can use that." Then he said to the small man, "Listen, Santucci, there's more money somewhere."

"I'm sick, Barstow. I really feel terrible. Like I'm going to die."

"You just feel like you *want* to die," Barstow said. "It's not the same thing. We'll get the money, you'll see how much better you'll feel."

"And I'm cold. Jeeesus, it was so nice in Mystic. Warm. Now I'm cold."

"You," Barstow said to Alan. "Give him the windbreaker."

"Are we going back soon, Barstow? We got a hundred thousand. She told me. A hundred thousand. Good, huh? Unbelievable."

"There's more," he said.

"How do you know there's more? How do you know that?"

"I looked at the money in the case. It's all there. None of it has been spent. Not one package of the twenties is gone. Not one."

"So?" Louis said. He was greenish white now, a classic seasick. To Katherine it was like watching a play, outdoor theater.

"What's going to happen?" Evelyn said, but to whom? The wind wound through the rigging.

"I don't know," Katherine said to her. She wanted to say not to worry, but that would not mean anything, not even to Evelyn. Alan had taken off his windbreaker and brought it forward. Louis put it on.

"How do I look?" he said.

"The kid has been spending money for three days," Barstow said to him. "But not this money. So what money?" He came to Katherine and even motioned Alan and Evelyn toward him, as if he owed them an explanation.

"So how do I look?" Louis asked again. "Do I look like a sailor? I don't feel like a sailor." But no one was listening.

"You're Alan," Barstow said. "So what's your name?"

"Evelyn Kinski," Evelyn said.

"Well, Alan and Evelyn and Kate. Is that all right?" he said to her. "Kate? Katherine?"

"Kate is fine," she said, surprised at his punctilio.

"Well, Alan and Evelyn have been spending a lot of money. And Alan has also been paying back some debts. Fairly big debts and all at once for a guy who had nothing. With nice, neat packages of brand-new bills. The wrappers still on them. People notice this. Especially some people. Especially people who lend money to other people. So word gets around. Sometimes it gets to people like Louis and me. And we figure, what's going on? So we see him and Evelyn hanging out now and then on this swell boat with this famous lady, as it turns out. Famous lady, swell boat, sudden money. You follow me?" he said to them, but mostly to Katherine.

"I follow you, but it doesn't mean there has to be more money. He could have gotten it out of a bank or ..."

"Please," he said, "spare me. No bank. Alans don't have bank accounts. *This* Alan has a bank called a shylock, you understand? He owed a lot; he owed for a long time. They were getting nervous. End of the season, you know? People go away. Alan, he figures, I got the money, so why not pay off? Get out of here clean. And with no arm or leg broken."

"He could have sailed off like now. Gotten away."

"To Florida? To Key West? To wherever? That is not getting away. He ... they were telling everyone they had come into some money. Who knows why or how? Good fortune had come to them. A ship had come in. A ship was going out. So he splashed around a little money, paid off some serious debts ... what, five thousand, is what I hear. So anyway, no one cares. No one is interested. Except people like Louis and me. So I'm figuring that he didn't spend this money in this case, so where is the money he is spending? I'm guessing it is on this boat. So why not? If it's not, it's not. If it is, it is. For us, for Louis and me, it's a win-win situation. For you folks it's a lose-lose situation. So don't make it a lose-lose-*lose* situation. Where's the fucking money, or do I start looking for myself? You don't want that to happen."

She looked at Alan to see that Barstow's scenario was true.

"It would be a shame to throw up on this nice jacket," Louis Santucci said as if somehow that had been the point of what Barstow had been explaining. "Hey, Barstow. I can't think. You know me, I'm not a thinker. That's what I've got you for." He smiled at them all. "I'm not a thinker, I'm a *doer*." Even beneath the shrunken skull that his head had become, his happiness rayed out. A great score. Probably the biggest score of his life, by far the biggest score. "What brains I got, I think I upchucked them. Come on, let's turn around."

"We've got plenty of time, Louis. Time enough to find the money, or if there is money. You want to lie down somewhere? I think that would be all right. These nice people aren't going to do anything to you. In two, three hours, we'll be out of their lives."

She saw the two men look into each other. Barstow was far more complex than she had first seen, or had not seen. He was, little as he had done to demonstrate it, a clever man. Deliberate. But she could not see into him what his partner could, they into each other. In themselves they could read their shared history. These were not the first people they had robbed, odd as the circumstances were. She could admire their professionalism, even feel secure because of it, safer, at least, than if she were at the mercy of amateurs. But she was clever too, so she had to wonder what they would do about detection. Surely they knew that they—the robbery—would be reported. And their names came too easily to their tongues to be aliases. They would be easy to describe. How did they imagine they could escape eventual detection with such witnesses? Destroy the witnesses occurred to her, but she dismissed that. It seemed too out of scale. Too unprofessional. It was the nervous, doped-up eighteen-year-old robbing the 7-11 who shot people for the $38 that he grabbed out of the till. It was the gang of youths who wanted money for the movies who killed for the price of admission, maybe a couple of beers after. But for $100,000 you did not kill. It was too clumsy. There was too much boat to contend with, too close to land. Still, what? How would they escape? Who had caught whom? Perhaps she could forge an advantage.

She decided it would be better to give them the money, force them to return to Mystic, force them to act out their plan. Somehow she would seize the initiative. She would get rid of them. Maybe even get them caught, even retrieve the money. Agare would understand. Would not even care. Perhaps there would even still be enough time to try again. And certainly Barstow would have a plan of escape. She must make it possible for him. Expeditiously. It was easy. Give them the money.

Barstow did not have a plan, but he did have an operational mode. She found herself admiring the flexibility he allowed himself, the tactical stretch. "You have got to be thinking," he said to them, "how do you get out of this? You think you'll promise not to tell the cops, but you will. So what protects you? Why don't we kill you? Don't you even think that way."

"Right," Louis Santucci said. "Don't even think that way. It makes you think all wrong; you start to maybe do wrong things. Listen to Barstow."

"We go back. We go ashore in the boat you're carrying back there or even in the rubber raft." He pointed to both. "Either way, we take both boats. Now you don't have a radio. So you shout and wave something.

But we have a head start, even just a little one. We have our car waiting. We get to shore and go. The point is this. Maybe eventually we do get picked up. But when? A week? A month? Whatever, not quickly, I assure you. It's easy to not get picked up quickly if you're not stupid."

"Easy," Santucci said.

"What? You think all you've got to do is make an accusation? So? You say this, we say that. So? You've got witnesses?"

"You've got no witnesses," Santucci said. "What witnesses? We're out here in the middle of the Atlantic Ocean. With banks you have witnesses. Cameras. Here you've got nothing. Seagulls."

"We've got alibis. We will *have* alibis," Barstow continued. "So this can be neat and clean. We get the rest of the money. You take us back. In the darkness we get to shore. You catch us, you can't make a case. We have tough laws about this, I know."

"Is this a great country or what?" Louis Santucci said.

"The rest of the money is forward," Katherine said. "Alan will show you."

"Katherine," Evelyn shouted, "how could you? How could you? Now we'll never get our boat," she wailed. "We'll never get to Key West. Oh, Katherine, you really disappoint me."

At which they all laughed. Even Alan, out of his grimness. Even he could see what must happen.

It was suddenly as if a decent business deal had been made. The release from negotiations that allowed the flowing of goodwill. Laughing and smiling, Santucci motioned Alan forward with his gun.

"O brave new world," Katherine hollered up into the sails, at Evelyn, at the paper-thin level of her understanding of anything. Everything. "O brave new world," she shouted again.

"That has such people in it," Barstow said.

And now more than at anything that had happened in this bright and zephyrous day, she was surprised. People like this working on the blunt edges.

"I'm a robber, but don't think that's all I do," he said, perceiving her surprise. Expecting it. Goading it.

"Well, you are apparently not who you are," she said.

"I am *what* I am," he said, and for the first time opened a little, the veil of blue in his eyes seeming to rise. "First Corinthians 15, 10. Paul. 'But by the grace of God I am what I am.'"

"Popeye," Katherine said.

"What?" Barstow said.

"Popeye. 'I am what I am.'" She looked up into the rigging, a sailor's glancing, then back at him. "That's what Popeye used to say."

"I hadn't thought of that," he said.

"I'm surprised too," she said. "Robbers quoting the Bible. The devil quoting scripture."

"My mother was very religious," he said. "Her favorite verse. All my life I heard that. It was her excuse for the life we had. It became my excuse as a kid."

"And now?" Katherine said. "What is your excuse now that you're all grown up?"

"Now I don't need an excuse. All I need is a gun. Now I understand Paul. Paul's right. The truth."

"Got it," Louis shouted as he emerged from the cabin. On the deck he braced the other aluminum container and opened it. It was nearly as full as the other. But not as full. A noticeable even if small difference. Barstow had figured correctly.

"This is absurd. An absurdity," Katherine said. "This. All this." She meant the robbery, but she also meant what had preceded it. Agare. Now this. A Bible-quoting thief. A philosophical thief. Wondrous. Passing strange.

"Indeed it is," Barstow said. "Indeed it is." And just then she felt in league with him, except that he had a deeper sense of absurdity than she. Which was fair enough. Why, after all, should she presume to know about the worlds in which Agare and Barstow functioned?

"All *right!*" Louis shouted. "This is all fucking right. Two hundred thousand K. All right!" He grabbed a package of twenties in each hand and shook them to heaven, brandished them. His gun was stuck in his waistband. "So what are we waiting for? Turn this fucking boat around."

Then, "Who's Agare?" Barstow said. "This Agare?"

"It doesn't matter," Katherine said. "It's of no consequence. I'm going to come about," she announced. "Here is what's going to happen, so you won't be surprised. No one will get hurt. I'm going to come about and then reverse our course. Head back to Mystic. Once we're around, I'll time it so that we get back in the dark. OK?" She explained the procedure. How the sails would move, what they should all do. She instructed Alan to ease off the starboard sheet at her command. She would tend to the lee sheet herself. The foresails were self-tending.

"Ready about," she shouted.

"Wait," Barstow said. "Wait. Keep going. I've got to think this out."

"Think?" Louis wailed. "Think what? We got the money. Let's go. What are you doing, Barstow? What is there to think about? Oh, Jesus. I want to get off this boat. Barstow. Barstow! Don't think, OK? I'm begging you."

"Shut up, Louis. I've got to think. Steady as she goes, Skipper," he said to Katherine.

He walked forward away from them in the cockpit, and he leaned into the slant of the boat. Unconsciously he reached for a handhold at every step. He was learning quickly. He was an adapter, she thought, able to adjust to contingencies. Unlike herself. He stood away from them for five minutes and then returned.

"Now?" Louis said. "I'm telling you the truth, Barstow. I am not well. Let's go back now."

"Listen to me, Louis. You'll get better. You'll feel better. It was being locked up that made you sick. This is smooth sailing. Give it a chance."

"Why? What for? Why should I give it a chance? All I got to do is get back to land. So why not now?"

"We're not going back to land, Louis. We're going for a sail."

"Oh, Barstow, no. Oh, Barstow. Oh, say this isn't true. Calvin, I'm begging you."

"You're going to be fine, Louis. And maybe you're going to be rich. Very rich. You might not have to work again. Follow me. Why are these people here on this boat? Why are they loaded down with heavy money? The lady? Alan? See? All we were thinking was the money. We weren't thinking a lot of money, so much money, right? A big surprise. We were not thinking two hundred thou. But now we have to think why something so unusual should be. Why would an Alan have this kind of money? What would this fine lady and this fine boat be doing with this kind of money on it? My first thought is drugs. They are going to pick up. But that doesn't feel right to me. Even if it was drugs, whose money is it? It can't be Alan's. Maybe the lady's, but that is unlikely. That is very unlikely. A fine lady like this, she doesn't do drug pickups. So this is what I am thinking. Are you following me, Louis?"

"No. Why do we have to think anything?"

"You," he said to Katherine. To Alan and Evelyn. "Are you following me?" But he went on for them all. "Listen, Louis. They were sent to do something, get it? Somebody, maybe this Agare, sent them to do something. Was it that they were supposed to deliver the money? But Alan here has been spending it, so I'm guessing it is Alan's own money. No. The money is a payoff. For something. For what? For what would somebody pay such big money? For something even bigger than the two hundred thousand, a lot bigger, is what. What could that be?"

"I want to go home, Barstow."

"No. Not yet. This is very interesting. What?" he said to Katherine. "Why are you here? What is this all about?"

"We're sailing down to Charleston, South Carolina," she said. "We've heard of a suitable boat. We're sailing down, and if it's what we want, we'll buy it," she said. " 'We' is Agare and us. It's a business deal. Alan is a diver. He's got some good information about some Spanish gold, a wreck. Off Key West."

"Fast," Barstow said. "Fast thinking. But it's desperate. You don't buy boats with cans of cash. At least not legitimately. And if you're going to dive off Florida, on another boat than this, why the equipment?" He pointed to the canisters of air, the generator. "Why not fly to Charleston and buy the boat? Or to Key West? All that cash. It doesn't make sense. Or why not just use this boat?"

"People sometimes strike bargains for ready cash," she said.

"You put money like this in a bank. You take it out when you need it. You don't drive around with it. *You* don't. Katherine Dennison doesn't."

He had called her invention desperate. Certainly.

"It's true," Evelyn said. "It's all true. Every word. What Katherine said."

Barstow smiled at her, then at Katherine.

"Are you going to tell me?" he said. But it wasn't a question.

Katherine told him the story, at least the broad narrative. The gnomes of Zurich. She told him about the airplane in the sea, the disk, that it was important to Agare to acquire, so important that he had paid them this money to retrieve it. For his reasons, which she did not go into, the operation had to be extremely secret. Disguised as a casual sail toward Bermuda. Something that would not attract attention.

"Fine," Barstow said. "Excellent. So here is what is going to happen. We are going to do just what this Agare wants. We are going to get his valuable disk only instead of two hundred thousand, it's going to cost him more. We'll give him his disk, but now he's got to pay for it. A lot. Nice, huh, Louis? How long?" he asked Katherine.

"Originally I gave us four days under good conditions to get to the wreck. However long it takes to find it. Three days back to our closest shore, probably Charleston, South Carolina."

"A week. Ten days. Good. Not bad."

"This is, what you are saying, this is serious? You mean this? Ten days at sea?" Louis Santucci said. "I'll die," he said. "I'll die at sea. You'll throw me overboard in a bag. I seen it in a movie. For what? We've made this great score, and now I'm going to suffer for days and days and finally die anyway and then get eaten by fish? This isn't fair, Barstow. This was not what we thought about. Barstow, you are not even listening to me."

"You're running off, Louis. You're in a panic. You're just making yourself crazy. Now pull yourself together. Lie down. You'll get better. You'll love this. And you'll make a bundle of money."

"But there is a problem," Katherine said. "We can't do it now."

"Good," Louis said. "Tell him, lady. Go ahead. Tell him. We can't do it, Barstow."

"Why not?" Barstow said.

"You've destroyed all the electronics. How can we find the wreck?"

"See," Santucci said. "See, Barstow. You destroyed the electronics. We can't do it. We can't do it."

"How were you going to find the wreck?" Barstow said.

"We had LORAN coordinates." She explained how LORAN worked, the crossing of reciprocating radio beams. "Even with the coordinates, it wouldn't have been easy. And a Fathometer—a depth-sounder. You destroyed that."

"Now it's impossible, right?" Louis said.

Barstow waited, not for them but for his own mechanism to pick up, to catch on to an idea and to see where it might take him. He took out a gun from under his coat, what she had sensed was always there. He did not point it at any of them, but now she knew they were in their greatest danger. "I'm going to ask some questions now, and I want you to be very careful to answer them. Very careful. The right answers too. OK? The first question. Where are the LORAN things, the directions? They are somewhere, right. In your head? Written down?"

"Below," she said.

"Show me."

"Take the helm," she said to Alan. He came forward. "Don't do anything except what I tell you," she said. "Do you understand? Nothing heroic. And nothing provoking. Do you understand?" She looked into him. "Do you understand? Whatever you're feeling about the money, it's important not to do anything. Only what I tell you. Do you understand?" She waited for him to accept what she had accepted: that what was important now was to stay alive.

"OK," he said at last.

"Evelyn. Stay with Alan."

In the cabin below, spread out across the charting table, in a book in which she did calculations, she showed him the LORAN coordinates. He stared at them.

"Show me on the map," he said.

"Chart."

"Chart. Right. Show me." She did. He looked at what she had shown him, then he said. "Simple. If you didn't have the LORAN, how would you get to here?" He touched the spot, the space in which the wreck lay. "Or anywhere? Before LORAN, how was it done?" But even before she could answer or imagine how to deflect him, he said, "What's a sextant? Isn't that what a sextant's for? Do you have a sextant?" His eye swept through the cabin. "What's that?" He pointed to the squared, lustrous case of the chronometer. He went to grab it.

"Careful," she said. "Wait." She opened it for him.

"Clocks," he said. "But an important clock. The way it's taken care of. It's for more than just telling time, isn't it?" Thinking, rapidly, decisive. "And the sextant. But remember," he said, "don't make a mistake. Take your time. Think what you are doing. Don't make a mistake."

"There." She pointed to another case.

"So?"

"You can navigate by sextant. Celestial navigation."

"Right. Yes. I've heard of that."

"But it is not precise. The LORAN could have gotten us to within at least one hundred yards of the airplane, maybe much closer. A sextant can be off by as much as a mile, or two or three miles. Sometimes more. Sometimes a lot more."

"But sometimes less, right? Sometimes a really good navigator can hit it on the button. Get close. Right?"

"Maybe. Under ideal conditions," she said. "But you made the odds very long when you destroyed the LORAN."

"You don't know that, do you?" he said. "I mean, you can't say that for sure. Long odds, yes. But not impossible."

"Very long odds," she said.

"Not so long that it isn't worth four days to find out. Or whatever. Think about it. Me and Louis, we're safer at sea with you than on land. So far we're not even fugitives. So far technically you haven't even been robbed. So what is the problem? What's our hurry?"

"I could deceive you. I could sail for four days by sextant, and you'd have no idea where we were or if we had gotten to the wreck. You wouldn't know anything."

"Right," he said. "But so what? What do I know now? Something could happen. You don't know. We could find it. Then what? And what's it to you? You've got something to do with this Agare? Is he a boyfriend? So maybe not. So all you're doing is working for him. I'll tell you what. Let's be partners. You find the wreck, Alan finds the disk, and with your help, we get more money from Agare. Maybe if it's big enough money, I'll give you back your money, Alan's money. At least a lot of it. It depends upon what Agare gives us. What's good here is that we'll have you to ne- gotiate for us with Agare." He stopped. She felt exhausted by him.

"Look, it's the way things are. You're a famous lady or something. You make books. We found out a little about that, not much, a little, in Mystic. Seems everybody knows you, or knows the boat, anyway. The *Marindor.* But you don't seem to know how things go."

"Is that right?" she said. She felt angry, tired. Trapped not by his gun but by his easy assurance. His confidence. "And how do 'things go'?"

"A lot like life," he said. "You've got to understand, you're arguing with a man with a gun. Two men with guns. Villains, do you under- stand? Real villains. You tell the kids not to provoke, you mean don't try to jump us. Good advice. So don't *you* be provoking. Don't get us lost. Don't try to be ... right. This is a simple act with its own difficulties. Don't make it into something more or something else. Or worse. Just get on with it. Do you understand what I'm talking about? We're all here now to make some money. Do you understand?"

"Yes," she said.

"No," he said. "I don't think you do. I really don't think you do. I'll explain it. I'll make it clear. I've got four days to make it clear to you. But just remember this, if you think I won't kill you if I have to, you're wrong. So now we have a deal. Find the disk, and we all come out of this with something. Now go up and let's start figuring out how we're all going to sail this boat. Go," he ordered, waving the gun. "Go."

She turned to ascend.

"Wait," he said. He was standing over the chart, all of Region I be- fore him. "Look," he said. He motioned her back. "You've got to dive down to the airplane. So how deep can you go? Not so deep. The plane can't be here." He put his finger over six thousand feet of water. "Or here, or here, or here." He jabbed quickly down upon the chart. "You've got to be able to nearly see the plane, don't you? That's it, isn't it? See where you've marked the chart, where you showed me the LORAN crossed? So see how it gets shallow here. That's what the lines show, isn't it? The numbers getting smaller. The water right around the wreck is the lightest blue. Way out here in the middle of the ocean suddenly the bottom rises almost to the surface. A little more it would be an island. The plane is there. So even if you get us close we can sail around until we damn near see the thing. See? It's already not so hard as you're telling me. But you knew that, didn't you? Didn't you?" His voice rose.

"Yes," she said. "Yes. You're very smart to have figured all that out so quickly."

"Not so smart, just not dumb. But I'm smarter than you think. It would probably be better for you if you remembered that. Why I'm here now is to get as much money as I can from your buddy, Agare. That's my business. You don't know anything about that, so get out of my way. But on this boat, this is your business. That's what you know, so I'll get out of your way. So do it. We do what we know. We do what we can. It's simple. For Christ's sake, it is so simple. Don't fuck it up."

On deck she explained to them the routine, the responsibilities of each, who would sleep where. When. Barstow decided either he or Louis would always be awake at one time or another. He had examined the boat closely. When Alan and Evelyn slept, he would lock them in the forecastle. But not much had changed. As before, she would manage the sailing itself. The main difference would be that she would be taking many running fixes, shooting the sun and the stars as often as she could, reading the speed of the boat with a chip log device, constantly monitoring for drift, the weather, variations of any kind. Navigating in the fullest sense. Now, instead of the LORAN coordinates she would have to find 33 degrees, 30 minutes, 15 seconds west longitude and 75 degrees, 40 minutes, 10 seconds north latitude. In certain ways, their lives might well depend upon her skill.

She handed Santucci two ginger capsules from her medical supplies. "Take these," she said. "For seasickness."

"What? How do I know that? Maybe this is something, you know."

She popped one into her mouth and swallowed.

Reluctantly he took the capsules and gulped them.

"Now eat crackers. Dry things like crackers. Keep your eyes on the horizon." She glanced up into her sails. The wind had come slightly abaft the beam. She took the helm and set the boat into the course she wanted. She gave the helm back to Alan. She ordered Evelyn below to open some cans and slice some bread. A quick and easy lunch. She started down to get the sextant and her tools. It would be noon in a few minutes, and she must take her initial fix. She could still get one line of position with a pelorus by reading the last purplish stain of land, the last they would see of it for some time to come. As she started down the companionway, Barstow stood up.

"You're going to have to trust me, aren't you?" she said to him. "You might as well get used to it."

"I don't trust you. That's not the point. The point is there's not much you can do, any of you. But you're right. There's no point in my hanging around everything you do. You've got four days. Go on." And he sat down on the port bench of the cockpit.

Before she went below she looked at him. His skin was covered with a fine netting, a gossamer of filaments that broke the surface into a craquelure surface. Sometimes it seemed as rough as pumice, but in the sunlight it seemed, too, as fine as cloisonné.

6

Growing up at sea with her father or mother at the helm, Katherine would spend as much of herself as she could above decks in the night. No greater magic. The purity of the darkness, the intensity of the stars. The very idea of the ship itself, cleaving the seas, beating into the wind. Her advantage had been that she had come to her wonder directly, had been born into it: her nature and the nature that constructed her were the same. Only later, after she had left the sea, when she had words to describe her thoughts and feeling, to attempt to describe her nature and that nature and her wonder, only then did she understand how words, no matter how glorious, were yet a filter, a deflection. An imperfect substitution. Now she sat again as she had not for many years, reaching across the deepest meridians in the wind's way under the stars and constellations, which she could read as Phoenician sailors had read them two thousand years before—Deneb, Aries, Alpheratz, Arcturus, and mighty Betelgeuse. Polaris, of course, and Antares, Aldebaran and Rigel, Spica, Vega, and Sirius in the colder sky. More. She remembered their names like brothers.

With the last of a usable light, she had taken a sun sight and constructed a running fix. Later she would sight on Antares; she would bring Antares down to the dim horizon at an arc of seventy-five degrees declination and an azimuth of sixty-four degrees. That was her rough estimate. From the almanac and the tables, she would plot the star against Greenwich Mean Time. There would be a late moonrise. At 0100 hours she would shoot it. Tomorrow she would be certain to take a good early fix on the sun and, of course, the major fix at noon. She would navigate with more critical attention than ever and sail the boat more tightly than she had for some time. There was exigency, but pleasure too, in the idea that she was entirely dependent on her proficiency. Dead reckoning. In Slocum's boat, sailing it in Slocum's way.

She sat easily with the boat pushing swiftly on. With the plotting, with the lines of position established, and with her other calculations, she had a good idea of where they were and how they were moving. It pleased her that she had not forgotten her celestial navigation or lost even a little of her skill. She had used it less and less over the years. Eventually she had only dabbled with it as an occasional trick, perhaps, to show off the mariner in her to a guest on board. And in the past three years, she had not used it at all. Now it thrilled her again, as it had when her father had taught her, that with so few tools she could reach out to the stars and find herself with certainty. But what also guided her was her deeper awareness of how the sea created itself. Closer to land, the wind builds and falls quickly, offshore breezes turning into onshore breezes as the sun rises and falls and the air is heated or cooled through the day and the night. Or a headland, even miles away, might sweep a wind ten or even twenty degrees against itself. But at a distance from the shore, the pumping action is not effective, the barrier of a headland, the artificial heat of large cities. Far enough offshore, the winds are free of the land. It is often difficult to sail consistent distances close to shore without tacking frequently to find a favorable wind or an aspect to it, but far enough off, the winds can be unalterable, and then you can move as well at night as in the day.

Like her father, who also had no reliable instruments other than his sextant and compass and almanacs, had only his instincts bred at sea, she sensed where the limit of the shore-affected wind would be and found it. She felt how the long, uninterrupted fetch of the wind coming on the beam was setting them off about five degrees, and she steered the boat against the leeward drift. The sound the waves made as they turned to run in the direction of the wind was nothing you could learn in a book. If the wind held, she would not have to change the tack at all. She could keep the westerlies with her all the way to the Carolina Canyon. Her only problem would be to stay out of the three-knot northeastward rush of the Gulf Stream, but she understood the Gulf Stream and how to deal with it. Often enough with her father, she had encountered it. In the right weather, you could see the Stream far off, the different color of it, the extreme blueness, the absence of birds, the different sky, the frequent squall line that stood like a sentinel curtain at the edge of it. At night you could even smell the Stream if the wind was from the east. So much of those first years she remembered, the kind of knowledge we absorb before we can think about learning it, the way the young can learn a foreign language. And for the past twenty years and more, how much more had she added.

The winds held, and the *Marindor* sped on. Sometimes she would pass through a density of sea plankton and the boat would churn a phosphorescent crease through the sea, a darkness made visible in her wake. Sometimes, at a far horizon, the lights of a tanker or freighter moving fast would interrupt. And in the night you could hear the *Marindor* passing through the water, the loud, sibilant hiss of it, the creak and groaning strain of a wooden hull, the strum of the rigging. Only at night.

She checked the self-steering and made some general adjustments and then lay back into the sound and the darkness and the spiking stars and for the first time in a day thought in isolation about what was and what was about to be.

There was the fundamental terror of the situation and the difficulty in accepting it. Boats all over the western Atlantic were pirated, but not this far north. In the Caribbean and throughout the islands of the Spanish Main and along the Central and South American coast an epidemic of such seizures continued, but these were by drug runners, men who would take a boat for one quick smuggling operation. They would use the boat and sink it. They always killed whoever was on board. But this was so far north, and no drugs were involved. No contraband. That made no difference now. These men had stolen aboard with a reasonable and simple plan: a common enough robbery. The rest was happenstance. But these were not only robbers. She believed that they were men who could have killed before and surely would kill if it became a necessity.

She doubted she could find the wreck. Even with the more accurate LORAN and the rudimentary SatNav, she could see now how much more difficult it would have been than Agare imagined or she had allowed him to imagine. Could she convey that difficulty to Barstow when or if it became necessary? She had to navigate the boat convincingly, from here to wherever *there* was. But she also had to navigate to the convergence that awaited them all, whether she found the wreck or not, for if she should find the wreck, would that be better or worse? It was as if you went to a doctor who tells you that you have cancer, but that the kind of cancer you have is survivable. Then your whole life becomes centered on surviving; everything becomes one-dimensional, narrowed into an abstraction: surviving, a thing in itself. You even lose sight of what is to be saved—the life, the person. The purpose of the surviving.

Barstow had infected her with the fever of calculation. The pressure of her dead reckoning, but more, the estimation of what to tell him, what not, every move on her part a determination, a gauge. Louis was merely an amiable thug. Capable of mayhem, but predictable. Barstow was not predictable. He suggested to her a deep malevolence, an icy belligerence, and even worse, a frightening amorality, and yet a condition arrived at through intelligence. A definition of evil. She walked about the deck of the *Marindor* in the old habit of caution, ceaselessly examining, endlessly testing, pulling at shrouds and lanyards. Satisfied at least with that, unable to do more of anything except to approach, she huddled into herself, drew her sweater and windbreaker tightly around her, and retreated.

She met Tom Lecourt in Newport. The occasion was the sale of the *Marindor.* At that time, in 1971, it was called the *Spray.* The boat was out of the water. High up on the land and blocked up in its cradle, it seemed enormous, but that was not unusual. Most of a sailing craft is below the waterline; in the water it settles in and seems smaller than it is. A boat has to be read in its cubic dimension, not linear, and it takes understanding to do that. A scaffold with steps had been erected beside the boat so prospective buyers could easily come aboard without having to climb a ladder. Katherine had come to Newport with a strong intention to buy the boat.

She had booked into a motel for a week, and already she and Norwood the broker had talked details and terms. She spent the days walking around the boat, over and through it, imagining her life aboard, recalling the old tang.

Since her own coming ashore when her father had gone away, she had not lost contact with the sea. She sailed frequently and cruised in various craft with friends. And with Joseph Mackenzie, who was not a sailing man. Joe was diesels. A fisherman's engine. His crafts were lobster-boat hulls and the like. He had great admiration for sailing craft, but sailing, he had observed, was its own reward. You did not sail to get somewhere. When you sailed you were already there. On his island, he said, he too was already there.

Clambering about on her third day in Newport, she came around the stern cabin to find, propped against the mizzen, a youngish man diligently at work sketching the boat. He did not notice her, or did not pay attention to her. She came behind him but stayed out of his work. He was not so much drawing or sketching as drafting, taking details of the boat with an exquisite draftsman's line. Freehand, yet his lines were as straight as if they had been ruled. His circles were as accurate as if they had been drawn with a compass. The ellipses, the foreshortening, the textures, all were renderings that made the objects feel not more real, but real in a different way. He worked with great speed, extracting delicately with a sharp pencil the essence of a double-sheave block carved out of lignum vitae. At last he looked up.

"Hi," he said.

"Sorry if I broke your concentration," she said.

"No, no. Not at all. I just finished." He misted the drawing with fixative, removed it from his pad, and placed it carefully in a portfolio full of other drawings.

"You've got quite a hand," she said. "I've never seen such marvelous accuracy. Are you going to work all this up into a painting?"

"No," he said. "I make models. Of anything. But mostly of sailing ships." He stood up, tall and sandy haired, rather thin. "Tom Lecourt," he said. "From Providence. Or near it. Do you want a model of the *Spray?*" He smiled. Put out his hand.

"No," she said. "No. I want the *Spray* itself. The real thing. Katherine Dennison." She took his hand. She thought of him as a rival, a competitor for *her* boat. "Is that how you make your living? Making ship models? I should think you could sell those drawings themselves."

"The drawings go with the model. I strive for accuracy. *The Katherine Dennison?*"

"I suppose," she said. "But why should you know me?"

"Children's books. Illustration in general. I've always thought I'd like to take a shot at it, but I can't draw."

"You can't draw?" She pointed to the portfolio.

"I can copy, but I can't draw. Are you hungry?"

She laughed at the lack of sequence but began to like him at once. Then, she remembered, she liked everything these days. Her winning of the awards. The surprisingly lucrative contracts for future books. The idea of buying the *Spray*. Her life, just then, feeling so exactly on the verge, full to the brim of all the promises she had promised herself coming true. Feeling as if at last everything was going to start. And that included men. A man. Not that she had been uninterested or uninvolved. For nearly ten years she had soared and fumbled, pursued and fled. And much of the time she had fought off the notion of Macken Island, of being there forever. But now, more than ever, every man was interesting. Or could or might be interesting. Certainly Tom Lecourt was interesting. Pleasing. Certainly worth a lunch and some conversation. Even if he was after the *Spray*. Or maybe because he was after the *Spray,* even if only at a scale of one foot to the half inch. Eighteen inches.

"I would like something to eat, yes. Is that an offer?"

"Absolutely. Let's go to Pallosa's Diner, up on High Street. Do you know it? Great soups. Wonderful Portuguese breads. My treat."

"Sure," she said. To everything.

At lunch he told her more about himself, what he did, even how he did it. And it quickly became evident that he was not himself a prospective buyer of the boat, and he was not working for someone who was. It was a famous boat. It had a famous provenance. Slocum, Culler, who was next? It was a good chance for him to get on board for detail. Don't tell Norwood.

He was easy, forthcoming. His hair would fall across his face, and he would flick it back with a snap of his head rather than push it away with his hand. And he would look very directly at her. It made him seem so open. He invited her to his studio whenever she was around.

She told him about herself. That she was determined to acquire the *Spray*. He became very excited at the idea and wanted to know more about her reasons. He was not a sailor himself, at least not her kind of sailor, but he had heard so much that was negative about the *Spray*. It was a controversial boat. In a day when fiberglass hulls and aluminum masts and stainless-steel wire had become the perfect materials, why would she want a wooden boat? And why this boat? Fat, slow, and a wallower, at least by contemporary standards. He had read that some considered the *Spray* and the copies of it that had been built killers.

"Culler lived on it for years and sailed it everywhere. And Slocum sailed the original *Spray* around the world alone at the end of the nineteenth century," she said. "No aids of any kind. Dead reckoning all the way. With a sextant and a dollar clock with only one hand on it. He sailed the boat around the world. Around the capes. Think of that! Around Cape Horn and the Cape of Good Hope! What does that say about the boat?"

"But people say it was him, Slocum's great skill as a sailor that did it. He did it in *spite* of the boat. Culler too."

"Then why not me? I'm a great sailor. Not good, great. But the point is that people who criticize the *Spray* measure it against modern boats, which are designed for speed and for racing. You need a crew to sail them in any sort of nasty weather. You don't have many choices with those boats. They're like a thoroughbred horse. They're built to overpower the sea. The *Spray* was supposed to go slow, or rather to go easy. It was supposed to work with the sea, not fight it. To give up to it, go with it. Wait it out. Hunker down," she said. "Look at this."

On a napkin she sketched roughly the logic of *Spray*'s small gaff rig, of the double headsails set up like a cutter, of the mizzenmast pushed as far inboard as it was. She explained how much control you could have with such a configuration of sails, but mostly how easily you could gain that control, fine-tune the boat. Drop the main, put a stays'l up here, use the mizzen reefed. You could sail through nearly anything with that.

And singlehanded. "See?" She insisted that he see. Her hand flew. Other napkins. Suddenly it seemed very important to her that he understand, but particularly that no one defame the boat. "Do you see how easily it can all be done? One person?"

"But even if you're right, why one person? Why do you want a boat that only needs one person to sail it?" he asked.

"I'm only one person," she said, quickly, strongly. Automatically.

As soon as she said that, she wanted to take it back. She had become too intimate, had revealed not only a simple fact, that she was single, un-attached, but had, to her ear, suggested that he might respond to what she had said. Implied. But why not? What was wrong with that? Still, she pulled back.

"It's an old dream that I'm going to make come true."

"Those are the best kinds, aren't they?" he said.

She told him about her birth at sea, her growing up in it and, until she had gone off to college, around it. She thought it sounded like one of those magical tales she might have made a book out of. A sea princess.

"Even now it's what I live near. It's where I belong," she said.

"That's a strange thing to say," he said.

"Why?" she said, feeling safer again.

"Well, you're young, successful, attractive. Most people like you would think about ... would *not* think about sailing around the world alone."

"I'm not thinking of sailing around the world. Alone or otherwise."

"Well, it sounds that way. Something like that. I'm not being critical, it's just that ..."

"You are being critical," she said.

They were quiet. The vapor of the soup, the delicious bread, the breath of the crowded, noisy restaurant rose up in her, made her a little dizzy. Oracular? Delphic? She pulsed. She could not remember ever being called attractive. She was not what she would herself have called at-tractive. She had good features—her bright eyes, her high cheekbones, her fine nose and so forth, her thick auburn hair—that sort of thing. But in her own eyes, all the features had never added up to attractiveness. Not beauty. Not ugliness, certainly. Not even plainness—better than plain. A small kind of prettiness, perhaps; that much she allowed herself. Like the

Spray, not an example of conventional beauty. And she was too long, too tall. And muscular. But attractive? She was fluttering. She couldn't believe it. An inch of an ounce of a compliment and she was coming apart. Well, not exactly apart. Still.

"I'm sorry if you took it the wrong way," he said. "Or if I said it the wrong way. Don't be angry."

"I'm not angry. Really. I'm not going to live aboard her forever. She will just be there. My boat. It's something I want. Something I always wanted. Now it's something I can have." She almost said it was something she needed. "Well, I don't own it yet. Norwood says there are other prospective buyers."

"You'll own it," he said. "You will."

They grew quiet. Not distant at all. Closer, in fact. If she was attractive, that could mean that he was attracted. Isn't that how it worked? They ate their soup and bread. She had a glass of wine, he a beer. Outside it had begun to rain, softly, a little beyond a fog.

"That ends my day," he said. "I can't draw when it's wet."

"I guess not," she said. "So now what do you do?"

"I'll go back to the studio and start working with wood. Finishing things. Starting things. Expanding my drawings. I've always got something to do. I usually work on four or five models at the same time."

She wanted to ask him if there was someone at his studio. Someone with him. Someone waiting. She wanted there not to be. And she wanted him to tell her. She didn't want to ask. She wanted him to be attracted and to act because he was attracted. But he did not. He picked up the check, left the tip, paid the bill.

"Do you have a car?" he said.

"At my motel," she said. "I walked down."

"I'll drive you to the motel."

In the car she said, "Your studio? How will I get to see it?"

"I'm usually there. Just call in the morning, or anytime. I'll make sure I'm there." He turned up Randall Street and stopped in front of the motel. The Jolly Roger. A giant electrified pirate with a cartoon eyepatch leered down at them.

"What about now?" she said. "Why not now?"

He drove across Newport Bridge to Conanicut Island and then across Jamestown Bridge to the mainland and then up the edge of Narragansett Bay to below Providence and a little beyond, back up into the country where the land starts to break away from being a flat shore into woodland with a slight rise and fall to it, scrubby woods but not entirely, pine moving into oak. It took about an hour. She had offered to follow him in her car, but he had insisted. He didn't mind the driving. In the car they told each other more and more about themselves, and each seemed aware of what was happening.

Tom Lecourt's studio-home was enchanting, almost as if it were out of a children's book, Geppetto's workshop, perhaps, or any of the magical workshops imagined in children's stories, replete with elves, only this shop was more intricate, more elaborate and complex, the details of tools and devices more arcane.

The rain had stopped as they had driven inland, and now even a wan filament of sun glowed through the huge window wall that looked out across the buffering acres of meadows and woods behind the house. Most of the wall and a third of the roof were glass. The small light entered and suffused the room and illuminated the ships, which were everywhere. Even the twists in the braids of the millimeter-thin shrouds and stays were molded by the light. The smallest shackle or pin in the fife rail, minuscule hawsers, the oak gratings about the hatchways. The grain of the teak decks. Dumb sheaves and lanyards and even the weft of the furled sailcloth, the polished spokes of the double-wheeled helms. Everything was exactly visible. The smallest marlin spike. The ratchet on the capstan. The hinges on the gunports. All in a Lilliputian scale.

In the room the ships swung their bows into the wind: Drake's *Golden Hind,* the *Endeavor,* the *Indomitable,* the *Repulse,* the *Sovereign of the Seas* and the *Royal William* and Nelson's *Victory.* And more, the *Constitution* and the *Constellation,* a Chinese junk, a Yankee clipper. A mighty fleet, as if the great captains had come to anchor in the roads of Tom Lecourt's studio, summoned up by his irresistible sorcerer's skill. All about, along the walls, on tabletop berths, lesser ships were moored— a small New Haven sharpie, a Chesapeake skipjack, a Jersey skiff. Along

the north wall above the long workbench were mounted highly varnished half-models, solid bisections of hulls fixed to pine planks,
waterlines and frame stations scribed into them.

"Oh." She caught her breath. "Oh. Oh, these are more than just
models. These are true ships. Small ships. Reductions. It's as if you've
taken a ship and pressed it between your hands. Tiny men on little
oceans could sail these."

And that was so. In the lowest bilges of the ships, cobbles of large
grains of coarse sand, nearly pebbles, were laid as ballast. The empty holds
waited for kegs of gunpowder and barrels and casks of water and biscuit
and rum and salted beef. The slotted doors to the cramped midshipmen's
cabins could open and close. The officers' mess waited prepared, the dining table mounted on gimbals against the heave of the sea. At the gunport
stations, where common seamen would live for weeks and months and die
in splintering minutes, the cast-iron hooks for their hammocks stuck out of
true oak beams that Tom Lecourt had shaped with a small adz.

"This is amazing. This is so amazing. I've seen models before, but
nothing like this. Do something," she said.

"What do you mean?" he said.

"Some ... some procedure. Make something. I want to see. I know
how you build a big boat; how do you build a small boat?"

He took up a tool that he had fabricated himself, a long needlelike
tool with a loop at the end with a half circle of bend to it and a twist. Like
many of his tools, he could not have bought it. He took the *Repulse* and
set it in a special cradle on his table and slipped onto his head a band that
held large magnifying lenses. Slowly he tightened the last whipping of
thread around the bitter end of the hawser that made up the anchor rope
for the *Repulse*. With tweezers he took the end of the whipping and drew
it under and through.

"There," he said. He lifted the boat up in his two hands like a votary
making an offering and replaced it on a rack on the wall.

He showed her more. Everything. They walked outside around his
land and came back damp. He started a fire to break the chill, to dry. Into
evening. They cooked a supper together.

There was no one waiting for him, no one coming.

"It's all I can remember ever wanting to do," he explained. "I always made models. My parents went crazy with it, they still do, but I've made pretty good money, so they're happy enough now. But growing up? All the time ... 'Go out and play! Get out of your room! The glue will make you sick! You'll ruin your eyes! Look at your grades!' I was an absolute nerd, only a very, very focused one."

"But you were happy doing it, weren't you? I mean, you chose. You weren't excluded. You chose."

"Happy enough. I guess. I didn't think in those terms. I didn't feel bad, nothing like that. No one gave me a hard time. In fact, everyone admired my models. But I think at some level I was aware that something was missing. Girls, for instance. I never got the hang of girls. Or people, either, for that matter. I guess in my way I've always been a singlehanded sailor. Sailing alone around the world. A little world. A world I made small enough to do it." Then he broke away. "Do you want some brandy, Drambuie? Something?"

It started to rain again, more heavily now. He took a report from a weather radio. A cold front had unexpectedly shifted in toward the coast and was moving up. They were in for a small blow. A cold rain for the end of April.

He had gone to college, MIT, in fact, and had graduated in mechanical engineering, but he had never worked at it. He went directly to work for a small firm that made architectural models. In five years he was a partner. In three more years he owned the business outright. He owned it still, but aside from special design problems and board of directors' meetings, he stayed away. He stayed here and made models of ships.

"Why ships?" she asked.

"No straight lines," he said. "Even the straight lines are an illusion. Everything is a curve, a convexity, a concavity; everything is a compound bevel. Buildings are all square and plumb, rectangular; boats are the opposite, everything rounded and curved. Buildings are more like men; boats are more like women."

"Why didn't you build real boats? Big boats, I mean," she said. "Did you ever want to build a big boat? I don't mean something as big as the *Royal Arc,* but a sailboat, say, a peapod, say? A Whitehall."

"You build a real boat, a boat you're going to use, or someone is, you take a responsibility. At a very early age, I got stuck making models. Not taking responsibility went along with it, I guess. I can't really say, not really. What am I? What's the phrase, anal retentive? If you believe that stuff."

"But you're so good. Your larger boat would probably be as well built as your model. In fact, it's probably harder to build a model."

"It's not that I actually was afraid someone would drown because what I built failed. Boats don't come apart that easily. It must be something deeper. Maybe I'm just a small-boat builder. A *tiny-boat* builder."

"Well, look," she offered. "There's no reason why you should have built a boat or should even want to. It's not a real question, actually."

"It is a real question. I've thought about it, or things related to it. My guess is that I just feel very secure making models. It's satisfying. I'm good at it. I've got no special ambitions. It's safe. Maybe it's as simple as that. It's safe. The way an imitation is safer than an invention."

She had fallen in love with other men in the past ten years, in and out of love, more like in and out of beds. Tom Lecourt was different from that.

And he was different from Joseph Mackenzie. Joe did build real boats. But only for occasions. He built the boat he needed when he needed one. He promised to build for her a fourteen-foot, broad-shouldered, Herreshof-designed sloop, a tough bully of a boat that she could sail anywhere. Already she had plans to hang it from the davits of the *Spray* when it was hers. Joe hovered over her. All her life. From the moment he had saved her in Camden Harbor. She had read how in some African tribes, if you saved someone's life, then you became forever after responsible for that life. It was like becoming a godfather after the fact. Joe, to whom she felt compelled to tell everything, to write without fail. Maybe it was that if someone saves your life, then it is you who becomes responsible for them, as if forever after you have a debt to pay that can never be paid off.

"It's getting so late. We have to leave," she said. "I've really enjoyed this. We must ..." She paused. "We must do this again."

"Why don't you stay?" he said. Simple. Honest. Without evasion or pretending that there was something else in either of their minds, she stayed the night. And the next.

She wrote Joseph Mackenzie to tell him about the *Spray* and about Tom Lecourt. He wrote back to tell her about what was going on in Camden and about the boat-building school that was settling in Rockport. About Naomi Simmons, whose husband had been lost in a fishing boat, taking the two children and moving to Tulsa, Oklahoma, to set up with a sister. He told her about the price of lobster and the sudden lack of menhaden, about the Russian factory ships just off the coast, the Japanese boats that cruised up to Canada and back for squid, which they would catch and freeze, the boats staying in these waters for two years. He told her about Timothy Cousins on Isleboro and the Pacarte family on the Cranberry Islands. About the new road on the shore out of Northeast Harbor. About the suspicious fires in the hills behind Seal Harbor.

It always delighted her that he could make a neighborhood out of so far-flung a region, drawing islands and harbors and townships and locals and "casuals" together. Joe Mackenzie on Macken Island, around which he had made a Ptolemaic universe.

So long ago, she thought as the *Marindor* rushed on. From below, the sound of revelry rose. Through the steel-mesh-reinforced hatch and the sturdy ports, light rayed up out of the cabin and shone against the sails and lit them like a beacon, a good way to be noticed should a passing freighter come down on them. They were still in the narrowing cone of the sea lanes; not for another day at this speed would they be free of the danger, though in so bright and clear a night, it was not much of a danger. And it wasn't the danger out there but the danger in here that mattered most.

Laughter burst upward. Alan and Evelyn were hooting and hollering at something Santucci was telling them. Santucci had healed. He was feeling good. He had eaten. They had all become friends. Now there was music, tapes that Evelyn had brought aboard. Katherine could imagine that soon they would dance. From it all, against it, she turned away, turned back.

Joseph Mackenzie had married soon after she did, to Charlotte Kinsey from near Muscongous Lake. Her family ran a fishing camp of sorts, something between a lake marina and a motel, the old kind of motel that was made up of separate cabins perched on foundations of concrete blocks and shimmed up with cedar shingles each spring to bring them back to perpendicular, or as close as possible. There was a dining hall for those who wanted it. She and Joe had driven up from Camden a number of times to eat there. The food was good. She remembered how odd it seemed to her to eat inland food, she called it, fresh perch, say, pulled out of the large lake just twenty miles away from the seacoast. Two sharply demarcated worlds, yet so close. By the time you got to Muscongous Lake, shielded as it was behind the Camden Hills and Mt. Beatie, the air had turned inland, pine sweet, and the dankness rose from the carpet of needles and leaves and the slow oxidation of the fallen tree limbs. By the sea, tree limbs did not rot; they were scoured into the skeletons of driftwood. The wood broke apart and was polished and then ground down into grains that were finally devoured by plankton. The woodlands were moist with warm dew. If you got wet, you could dry out. You could wear cotton. But at the sea the fog and spray were always salt laden, always damp.

He had married Charlotte Kinsey and taken her away to the island. She remembered getting his letter and the pang she felt. The jealousy. Unreasonable, of course, she told herself. But she did not pretend she did not feel what she felt, that Charlotte Kinsey was a usurper. They had two sons in five years, but then they separated. Twenty miles was too great a distance for Charlotte Kinsey to come, and he could not leave. As much as they moved back and forth between the island and the lake, she could never center in the sea. To her it was always alien. Frightening. She was an inlander. On the lake she understood the steep chop, but in the sea she could not adjust to the swelling waves that broke against the island. And worse to her than the sea storms was the fog, especially the long convection fog that would settle around them sometimes for days, so thick that even the mourning horns could scarcely penetrate it. She told Joseph that it was what she imagined death would be like, an eternity of nothing.

It was a good separation, as such things went. He visited often. Took the boys with him often back to the island. Taught them what he knew. He might never have divorced her had she not found an inlander who wanted her, or if she had not made it clear that she wanted her life to begin again.

It was not like Katherine's divorce from Tom at all.

Beneath her the *Marindor* rode to Katherine's will. The moon would be where she wanted it in about two hours, and she would take her fix. Maybe she would even wait to shoot Betelgeuse, in Orion's shoulder, which was starting to rise higher now as the sky began to slide toward winter and the ecliptic tilted. The chill was not great. The southwesterlies that were speeding them along pumped warm air overhead. The air came across the entire south and had gotten dried out by the land. There was no moisture in it, no rain. Stable air.

She would rather be on deck than below, where the sounds of partying increased. Against the boom and sibilance of the *Marindor* through the sea, the rhythm that a boat can find when running with the wind and the waves just a few degrees abaft the beam, came the artificial rhythms of the tapes from the cassette player that had escaped Barstow. Now that was no danger to him.

Alan and Evelyn would sing along, and often Louis's voice, high with excitement, shrieked above theirs. They would laugh as Louis scratched and struggled with lyrics he did not know and could hardly make out. And then he would laugh, louder than they. Maybe happier, though they seemed glad enough of his company now. What had he told them, or convinced them of? That they would get their money after all? Maybe even more? That they *were* partners now, regardless of how odd that seemed? Was it that, the promise of their money coming back to them, along with the easy possibilities of youth, the inability to deny what for them did not even exist, that made them such good sudden celebrants? She would let that be. It would be better for an easygoing relationship to exist until the moment when it could no longer exist. And she believed that such a moment would come.

7

"You need any help?" Barstow's voice, his sudden appearance, shocked her. Even though she had been thinking about him, she had at the same time allowed him to slip off into the realm of the fantastical and the amazing circumstance. It was a trick of denial. She remembered it from Vietnam. Or from Steven. The odd certainty of something that was happening that could not be happening. It must be like this when after the tests the doctor coughs and turns his head to look out the window as he tells you the cancer has metastasized. The sea at night beyond the land had folded her into it, as it often had. In her life there were no moments more truly magical. As a child she would look up at the stars through the rigging and it would be the stars that seemed to move, to swing and dart about in the sky, not the boat. It was the boat in the night that was fixed and permanent: *mare firma*. And since she had come to live aboard the *Marindor,* the sea at night had become even more of a haven.

In the darkness it was easier to slip back and down into the past, before the cataclysms of death and loss, back to when all her expectations were intact and nothing had yet been diminished. In the darkness, at sea or more often in a cove somewhere on the Atlantic coast, she could turn back the pages of her book, as far back as her life with her parents and her splendid days with Joe Mackenzie on the edge of the bay, the two of them farming the sea with long rakes for the red dulce they would drag out of an ebb tide to dry and sell at a nickel a pound or sea urchins at a dime each for the market in New York; back to then with Joe on the edge of his island, a battlement to protect her against the folly of her demands, the sharp edge of her life just then with nothing but bold prospect before her, all various and new. The battlement over which she felt she had to leap. And did, and was falling, she now believed, through chaos for seven days into pandemonium.

Barstow's voice broke into her, reached down to the chamber into which she had retreated. For the moment she could not remember what had happened. Who was this? What was he doing here? How had he gotten aboard? Alarm spasmed through her. And in the next shattering instant, she remembered everything. It was like waking out of the terrible dreams of the blind, who dream they can see again only to wake into blankness, sightless once more.

"I'm OK. I'm fine," she said.

"I thought maybe you wanted to take a break. Maybe you need to pee. You need to pee?"

"No."

He came fully up from the forward cabin and settled down on the cockpit seat that ran parallel to the centerline of the boat. He was wearing Alan's windbreaker. He took out a cigarette and a lighter and tried to light the cigarette, but the wind blew the flame away. Even when he cupped his hands and faced the wind, he could not light it.

"You have to bend over," she said. "Cup your hands and face the wind, but bend over, way over. The flame will stay straight." He did it. The cigarette was lit.

"Thanks," he said.

It was an odd moment. She had helped him; he had thanked her. Normal enough, a small civility. How could that be in this entirely not normal, uncivilized situation? She thought how quick we are to gloss over the outrageous, to put a proper face upon the monstrous. The flags of truce we wave over battlefields after the dead have paved them with their bodies. The ceremony with which we bury them. The decorum that swiftly establishes itself at bad news as a tourniquet stanches a wound.

"So how's it going?" he said.

"What? The boat? Fine."

"The boat, yeah. The navigating."

"Fine. It's all going just fine," she said.

"At least we're going in the right direction. I checked that. You've got a compass below, upside down over your bunk. I saw. And in this cabin, another compass. We're going almost straight south, just like you marked on the map. The chart."

"You figured that out?"

"It wasn't much to figure. Yeah, I checked it out," he said.

It could have been his own information. He did not have to tell her. He could have kept it to himself, a secret knowledge that could become an advantage to him if he needed it, his checking up on her, his knowing something about what she was doing that she did not know he knew. Except immediately she understood that he wanted to tell her about the compass, to make it a warning, that he was not, say, a Louis, who might be tricked, be turned around. He wanted her to understand that if he needed more than a gun to get her to do what he had decided, then he had the intelligence to meet the demand.

"We're doing very well. At 2300 hours I'm going to take a moon shot."

"What about you?" he said. "How are you doing? Are you doing fine too?"

"Is that important?" she said.

"I don't know if it's important. It's a question. What's important to me in this world isn't the questions, it's the answers. That's why you ask the question in the first place. To find out." Again he was making a point, a warning: he had rules, and those were the rules that counted now. Barstow's rules. And another point. She could do this easily. Go by his rules. There was no real alternative.

In the darkness at sea, when you can hear more because you see less, she listened to the sound of him, unconsciously listening for a hint, an idea of where he came from, to figure from that what kind of person he might be. Louis Santucci sounded like a comic-book bad guy, a television hood. Not a thug, exactly, more like a kid from a street in a Little Italy somewhere. Boston, she guessed. North of Haymarket Square. A kid from Boston who had pulled on a suit of store-bought elegance, or what he mistook for elegance. Jittery with energy, a jivey kid who grew older but never grew up. He would have dropped out of high school at sixteen, probably the tenth grade. He had maybe imagined nothing more than to work for important figures in his neighborhood, but hadn't made it, so he ended up feeding around the edges, picking up the crumbs of small scores. Until now. If she did not know Louis Santucci, she could easily invent him. He had about him the same dimensions as a character in a children's book. But she could not place Calvin Barstow, even though she could hear an oddness in his voice, a kind of offbeat syncopation. He would hold the word just a little longer than it should be, almost as if an extra syllable had been stuffed into it.

"What difference does it make?" she said. "Does it make a difference how I'm doing?"

"See? You didn't hear me. You didn't listen. Questions don't do me any good."

"Well, then. I'm not happy, if that helps you. For obvious reasons. Certainly a smart guy like you could figure that out even without asking. Do you expect me to be happy? Oops. No questions. OK. I'm not happy to be here under these circumstances."

"Good," he said. "Now *that* I can work with. You're unhappy, so how can I deal with that? How can I make you happy?"

She pushed on. "Leave. Go away. Let me put you ashore. You take the money and go."

"You're worried that I'm going to kill you," he said. "So don't worry about that. Louis is not going to kill you, and I am not going to kill you. You are too important to the operation. What I want you to understand is that I know how strange you must feel, this crazy thing happening to you. That would be very normal. What you are feeling. Worry. Anxiety. Fear. That is very normal. What I do, I run into that a lot; people get knocked off their pins by the craziness that this is happening to them. You read about it, you see it on TV. And suddenly it's real. I figure if you know that I know what you're feeling, then you'll be a little calm.

"I robbed a bank once. This is a slow robbery, not a grab-the-money-and-run type of robbery. This way, slow, you get a lot of money, not just a few hundred bucks that you grab from the till. Anyway, it's all going good and then a woman works at a desk, she flips. She starts to scream. She starts screaming, and she can't stop. Right next to me. Now everyone is starting to get nervous. A nice, quiet robbery is getting ready to turn into something ugly. And no matter what I say to her, this woman can't stop screaming. You know what I do? I take a paper clip off her desk and drop it in her mouth. Naturally she stops screaming and spits out the paper clip. You see what I'm saying? Once she gets to do some ordinary thing like that, it puts her back in focus. She doesn't start screaming again. So she was lucky she got me as a robber, experienced. So you see my point? Sure, this is all strange to you, getting robbed. But there it is." He lit another cigarette.

"OK," she said. "Then on a less profound level, it's going to be hard as hell to find the airplane, even if we get as close to it as we can on paper. It would have been a lot better if you hadn't wrecked all the electronics. You can see that now, can't you? So if we can't find the plane, I don't want you to think it's because I'm trying to trick you. I understand that our best chance to come out of this is to get the disk, but you have got to understand how hard it will be. You *do* understand that, don't you?"

Then she took a chance. If it was normality that he wanted, assurance that she was responding normally, then that is what she would give him. "Or maybe I should be sensitive, careful of what I say. Maybe I should tiptoe around you in case you're a psychopath." Her anger had not been prudent, but it rose as much out of her will as against it. She could taste it, this kind of anger. It was a strange taste to her. She had known so little of anger. But it was not a bad taste. Acidic. Pungent. Mordant. A little like an unripe pear.

He did not take offense, or seemed not to.

"Always talk one way and always act one way and you never get confused," he said. "If you get confused, then your opponent gets confused, and that's when he gets scared, and scared is when it gets dangerous. Like the woman screaming in the bank."

"But you could get yourself in trouble that way too," she answered him. "Sometimes if you are who you are, you could thwart your own plans. How people feel about other people has a lot to do with how people act toward each other. The best robbers, the big time, they don't use guns, they get invited to country clubs. They don't use guns *or* tell the truth. They use lies. The robber and the robbee."

"That's right," he said. "Absolutely. I couldn't agree more. But that's only sometimes, like you said."

As they spoke she let her eyes move farther away from the compass, and for longer periods. As she sat there, not far from him, the glow of his cigarette illuminating him slightly when he dragged on it, she steered by the tug of the wheel in her hand, feeling the course down through the wheel into the deep keel of the boat, sensing by the angle of the boat how close to its passage line it kept. Once she had imagined that it was not unlike how plowing a field with horses must feel, the farmer feeling the straightness of the furrow through the plow blade even more than he could see it. She could have set the self-steering, but she enjoyed the helm.

From below there came a burst of laughter, a trio of concord, Evelyn's high trill over Alan's baritone and Louis's tenor. "They seem to be having a fine time. Getting right along. Mr. Santucci seems to have recovered." But he disregarded her.

"It doesn't matter how people feel. All that matters is what you want. Back then, when I wrecked the electronics, what I wanted was so you couldn't call for help. I didn't know which was the radio. Or maybe there was more than one way to signal. So what I wanted *right then* was to be safe. So I did what made sense for that situation *right then*. Then was then, now is now. You think, so how can a smart guy do such a dumb thing, but how can such a dumb guy be smart too? What I did then wasn't dumb. It only looks that way now that we could use the electronics. Life isn't in back of you, it's always in front. That's the difference between people like me and you."

"Oh?" Katherine said. "And what is that?"

"People like you, people who run the world, you make plans, lots of plans. Long-range plans. You think that your plans are going to work out, or that they have a better chance to work out, to get you what you want. Anyway, you've got no choice but to make plans. You live in a world where there is plenty of opportunity to make plans and to see if they work out. You make a plan, it doesn't work, you make another plan.

Me, I don't make plans, not like that anyway. I eat what's on my plate. That way I get more of what I want when I want it. No waiting around to see if the plans work out. No chance to see if there's going to be a second helping. Eat and run."

"What do you want?" she asked.

"You mean more than the two hundred K? More than what what's-his-name, Agare, will pay? Right now I don't have more plans than that, only that's not even a plan. That's just what I'm doing."

"But what about long range? Don't you have any sense of the future? Something you want to happen? Something you can try to make happen?"

My own questions, she thought. I am asking this thief my own questions. Then she laughed. "Or do you just live from robbery to robbery? Do you ever imagine, oh, say, retiring? Do you invest? Do you rob a bank and then put some of the money into a savings account in a bank?" She laughed again. "What are you going to retire on? It's an interesting problem, if you see what I mean. Are you going to go on robbing when you're sixty-five, seventy-five, eighty?"

"What I think," he said, "is the more you're afraid of what is going on in life, the more you plan. If you're afraid of being poor when you're old, you start saving money when you're young. You see what I mean? You eat less now so you won't eat nothing later. So what happens when later comes if you have more than enough? So you spent your only life planning. You never got to eat lobster."

"Do you ever wonder how you got to be who you are?"

"No. I don't wonder about it so much. I just one day looked around and there I was. With a gun in my hand and no problem about using it. I can't blame my parents. They were good to me. I had a good enough home life. Nothing special. But nothing bad. We didn't have much money, but we weren't poor. I even went to college for a year in Idaho. Pocatello, Idaho, and I got good grades, but I dropped out. I drifted around. I got drafted. I was in Vietnam. You see my skin? I got that from a concussion grenade. It went off in my face. A concussion grenade is like a punch. No shrapnel, just a punch. But what a punch. It broke all the blood vessels in my face. It broke the skin all over like an eggshell. But everything healed. I didn't even need skin grafts or any surgery. I just healed. But when I did, this is what I looked like."

"It's not so bad," Katherine said. "It's not a real disfigurement."

"It's the first thing you see when you look at me," he said. "It's what you remember. When you report me to the police, that's what you'll remember to tell them."

"It wouldn't affect your having a normal life," she said. "Getting a job, having a career. It wouldn't have stopped a woman from marrying you. That's what I mean."

"What makes you think I'm not married? Or that I haven't been married?"

"It's none of my business," she said, trying to retreat quickly.

"That's right, it isn't. Of course it isn't. But I started talking about myself, so it makes sense you've got curiosity. You don't have to be so worried about offending me. I'm not married. I was never married."

"But not because of your skin," she said.

"Maybe not. It hasn't given me a lot of a problem. But it was after Vietnam that I found all I was able to do was not be afraid of anything. Was it because of the war, the grenade? Nearly getting killed but not getting killed? I doubt it. I don't believe that. Anyway, not being afraid of anything, it's not much of a marketable skill. And taking what I wanted was easier. You would be surprised how easy it is."

"Yes," she said. "I would be surprised. But maybe not surprised either."

"Whatever that means," he said. "I'm glad we are having this nice conversation."

"Like a paper clip in my mouth," she said.

"Yeah," he said. "Something like that."

Then they were silent. She was surprised at the intimacy of the encounter. What was her frame of reference? Like everyone else, she imagined violence out of the violence of the movies and TV or the most lurid accounts of street crime. But this was altogether different. There was no place for violence here, and no apparent necessity, even though it was as close as it could be, she had no doubt. What else could they do? Either be separate and silent or talk. People, whatever they did for a living, meeting and talking. Once again, like the venture itself that Agare had proposed, like the unlucky advent of the robbers, what was odd was not. And how often did the executioner talk with the condemned, because until the final command on the final hour of the final day comes, he is not something else, only someone on the other side of a gun or an issue or a paycheck? They spoke to each other as they had because that was who they were, even though all along she knew he had his strategy, a subtext.

He lit another cigarette. On the eastern horizon, slightly below it, the faint glow of lights from a passing freighter glimmered, rising and falling with the sea. She could tell the dark sea at the horizon from the equally dark sky because there were no hard and sharp stars in the sea, only the shimmer and smear of their reflection.

His expansiveness had been sudden and unexpected. He had sought her out to talk to her, to calm her and to warn her, as he had said, and to intrigue her, she was sure. A tactic. And she admitted she was intrigued, the rough-cut blend of the man and his thinking, or was it really condescension on her part, a contempt for his pretension to thought, a refusal to accept the idea that a man such as he could have an outlook? Still, she could not resist. If he was working her, so what? One way or another, he was right. These *were* his rules, and she must adhere to them. If he wanted to talk this way, to be engaged, then why not? And for all the oddness, after the fact—or within the fact—of what was happening to her, nothing was much different than what she had actually started out to do: sail a boat to a tiny dot in the eastern Atlantic. They would retrieve the disk or not, and more would follow or not, and eventually the robbers would be gone, and Alan and Evelyn would be gone. Agare would be gone. And almost certainly all the money. And these revels, as she had already foretold, would end, and all she would have would be one hell of a story to tell Joe. It had turned into far more of an adventure than she had bargained for, but then, she had bargained for so little in these recent years that any profit, no matter how little, was a significant gain.

"What about your life, the day-in, day-out part of it? What do you do when you're not robbing?"

"You eat, you shit, you fuck, you die. When you have money, you do more of it. Sometimes you go to prison. You play the ponies. Or you go to

Las Vegas or Atlantic City. Or St. Thomas or Cancún. You watch a lot of TV. Sometimes you even read books, crime, detective stuff, mostly."

She waited to hear if he would laugh at his own words, their brittle inventiveness, but he did not. It was a description after all, not a commentary. She doubted that he was given to clever laughter.

"And love? What about love? Did you ever fall in love?"

"Maybe. At seventeen. I can't remember now. Sure. But later? Love is something you expect if you live in a certain kind of world, your kind of world. In the world I live in, people don't fall in love. Or if they do, they don't stay in love. Maybe that's true for your kind of world too. Read the papers. So who isn't getting divorced anymore? What about you? You're alone on this boat. You divorced? You got any friends who're divorced?"

"Yes," she said.

"So who do you know who is happier than Louis Santucci right now?"

Again from below the sound of the three of them billowed up, a party building upon itself. And what, after all, was the difference between the intimacy of her talking with Barstow and the kids howling with Santucci? How quickly all of them in their equal ways had come to grips with each other! If anything, it was she who was at a disadvantage. It was her assumptions that had been shaken, not Barstow's, she was certain. He would talk or not as occasion or purpose required; he would do what he wanted. Now he wanted to convince her that he was always who he said he was, and this was who he was. At least he had a purpose. She talked with him because it was at least prudent to do so, but also because she had never come this close to this kind of nether being before, not one whom she could speak to or hear.

That she should be sailing now as she had on many other occasions, talking with friends this way, even about such subjects as these—the form and shape of life, the forces that compelled it—struck her sharply. Perhaps, indeed, it doesn't matter what company we keep. She remembered one sail with friends five years ago, a sail as good as any she could remember, the wit of the people aboard, the ease of the boat, the certainty of the *Marindor* as it slid up the coast of Maine. The transfiguring gaiety. And she remembered exchanging recipes for pesto with Nancy Kelly, who was, even then, her husband's lover.

Later, he would always protest the word. "We were never lovers," he would say. "It was just a physical thing. There was never affection." She thought she might prefer it had there been affection rather than not.

To Joe Mackenzie she wrote: "If he had fallen in love with her, or even loves her still, if he had desired her for that—because his heart would burst without her—I could have found in that something admirable, something that I could separate from my pain. But he makes it sound, or tries to make it sound, as if that makes the offense less, makes the action less offensive, but to me it makes it worse. I could have understood his loving two people. I love you, have always loved you, and not only as my oldest and deepest friend, but we never touched each other after we married. I never even reached for you. When I married Tom I loved him, even though I loved you, but when I married him I made a covenant, and to me that is worth something.

"But what I find to be truly at the heart of the matter is that his adultery has made me feel that I can no longer be vulnerable with him, and that is what love is, the only chance we have in life to be unguarded and yet safe. He has robbed me of that, and for that I cannot forgive him."

"So how long you going to stay up here?" Barstow asked. "What happens at night?"

"That depends upon you, doesn't it?"

"I figure this first night I'll lock up the kids, and Louis can sleep first. They'll be plenty tired. You don't seem so tired. Me? I'm never tired. I can go all the time. I'll stay up with you. Anyway, when you get tired, I'll wake them and Louis, and you can sleep and I'll sleep. During the day it won't matter that much. Whoever gets tired can sleep."

"But not you and Santucci at the same time. Why is that? What do you think will happen?"

"I don't know. I don't even think about it. If one of us is awake, then nothing that I don't want to happen will happen. That's all I care about. So this seems the best way to do it. What do you think?"

"It should work. In weather like this, we could all sleep. In fact, in a little while, I'm going to set up the self-steering so I can take the moon shot. I'll leave the *Marindor* to take over. We could all sleep."

She watched him consider, but she could see that he could come up
with no reason why not. There was nothing for him to work with, and
nothing she would give him. She would take his store. She would remember all that he showed he did not know about making a passage.
Maybe at some point she would be able to use it against him, if it came
to that.

"That sounds all right. Leave it that way, then. Maybe tomorrow
night we'll change it. I'm getting cold. You must be cold."

"I'm OK," she said.

"I'm going below. How long are you good for? I'll send them to
bed soon."

"You won't be able to turn them off. That party's going too strong."

"I'll turn it off. Don't worry about that." Before he went below, he
looked off to the horizon and saw the lights of another freighter or oiler.

"How far off is that?"

"About twenty miles," she said.

"Can it see us?"

"No."

"What about all the sails? Couldn't it see light reflected on them?"

"It would have to be a lot closer, and even then it might not. That's
the danger in here, within the shipping lanes. You could get run down."

"They get that close?" he said.

"Sometimes. The man who designed this boat, the first *Spray*, was a
man called Slocum. He probably died that way. Run down in the night.
But now the freighters all have radar, of course, and I carry a reflector up
at the top of the mast. It could happen, but not likely on a night like this."

"So it can't see the sails, but it can see us on the radar?" he said.

"Yes. Probably, on a night like this. But there are ships all over. You
would be surprised how busy this part of the ocean is. Freighters, oilers,
boats sailing to Bermuda or down to the Bahamas even."

"If one gets close, you could maybe signal it, get its attention."

She was silent.

"Don't," he said. "It would be bad for all of us. You understand that,
don't you? So, you have any cigarettes on this boat? I'm almost out. I

didn't bring any extra, just what I was carrying. I didn't figure to be on this boat more than a few minutes."

"No cigarettes," she said. "Do you want me to head into the nearest port?"

"I don't need cigarettes, I just want cigarettes. It's what I've been telling you. It makes all the difference."

They both settled back again into the silence.

"Listen," he said. "I don't expect we should be friends. And there is a lot that's unpredictable here, so what I'm saying is, for what you can make of it, think what I'm saying, don't make plans. We just do what's possible. Am I making this clear? I'm telling you a little about me so you'll see that I'm reasonable. I think we've got a job to do together. And it could work out. There's no reason that it can't work out. Nothing bad has to happen here. I figure if I can get that across to you, then it is all going to work out—if it can work out."

"You said before that what's central to your nature is that you can't know fear."

"Yeah. That's right."

"Well, I can."

"That's my point," he said.

"Which means I can worry, I *have* to worry, about what's going to happen. And be frightened. Surely you can understand that."

"Sure. Yeah. So what I'm trying to do right now is make it easier for you."

"What you're saying is that I should be more like you, is that it?" she said.

"Yeah," he said.

"But maybe what frightens me is that I'm more like you than I should be. And that hasn't worked out so well."

"Yeah, well. I'm not sure what that means. But for what it's worth, this can work out. All we have to do is do it, like what I've been saying." And then he dropped down through the companionway.

8

"What a night; what a great night. Do I feel terrific? I feel terrific. I can't believe this. Yesterday I was dying. Last night I felt good. No pain. But this morning? This morning? I'm telling you, I can't remember when I felt so good. Maybe I never felt this good before in my whole life. Go figure," Louis Santucci shouted.

She heard him from her berth deep in the stern cabin. He bellowed out of his ebullient pleasure and the happy surprise of it, the whoop and holler you give after diving into the cool water on a very hot afternoon. She heard him thump over to the companionway and clamber halfway up it. She could imagine him popping halfway out into the cockpit like a jack-in-the-box, a jackanapes, bells ajangle from the point of his floppy hat, a buffoon out of the commedia dell'arte, but a deadly jester, she must not allow herself to forget, as the others seemed to have already forgotten.

"Hey, Barstow, can you believe this, this is so great? And good morning to you, Alan, my friend. How you feeling?"

"Good," she heard Alan say. "Really good." The boat followed on stiff and certain. Even with someone at the helm, she had set the self-steering. She left the helm engaged, giving the appearance that the helmsman was in control, but in fact the boat was sailing itself. It was an old precaution and a procedure from all her singlehanded work. It allowed her to leave the helm quickly if she had to without the need to set up the self-steering each time. Now, if the helmsman did turn the wheel, the ship would come back to its predetermined course, as if a small wind shift or a large wave had pushed it off course and now it was pushing back. It was an old-fashioned mechanism constructed out of blocks and wind vanes and counterbalanced weights. Her father's innovation on the classic design before the electronic machines that were coming into more common usage, smooth hydraulic arms driven by machines that read the stars even when you were asleep, satellites that could guide you with a precision measured by centimeters. It was all coming; it was nearly here, but not on the *Marindor*, which she had mostly sealed off from the future, much as she had sealed off herself. And now, of course, with all the electronics gone, her father's wisdom prevailed. As had the sextant and the chronometer. And human skill so far, although she could never forget to think about how far that skill must take her. Them.

Louis pulled himself up onto the main deck and babbled on.

And who, indeed, was setting the course, driving the good ship *Marindor?* She had slept more deeply than she was used to when alone, but not because she could rely on her crew. Hardly. And it was not her habit to sleep deeply while on board ship, even at anchor. There was always something that could go wrong, or less right than you wanted. But now, in the midst of all the truly dangerous turmoil, she had slept, perhaps exhausted by vicissitude. Or maybe because for the first time in the three years since she had weighed anchor forever, she had unveiled herself. For three years she'd had so little contact with others that she had been overwhelmed when the contact came again. Like a person on the edge of starvation who finds food, who must eat small portions and slowly until the body readjusts to sustenance, even if it is only the gristle of Barstow and Santucci. There was so little lubricity in her life that when she reengaged she found the gears had grown rusty. The transmission had exhausted her. The metaphors were everywhere. Like my life, she thought, laughing out loud. What Joe had said of her so long ago. "Instead of living your life directly, you make a metaphor of it," he had said, not without some anger. "It's like looking at life through the wrong end of the telescope. It makes life smaller than it is. That's why you're always expecting life to mean more than it can. You don't have enough faith in the surfaces of things," he had said many years ago on Macken Island.

Would he have included Agare, Evelyn, Alan, Barstow, and Louis? And how could she imagine this, any of this? And yet this was what went on all the time. The newspapers, the television. All the time. The difference was that it did not go on, was not supposed to go on, aboard the *Marindor*. Nothing was supposed to go on aboard the *Marindor*.

As she came more fully out of sleep and back into life, the enormity of what was happening expanded in her. She had not believed that people like herself were betrayed by a husband, or that they could lose a son to nothing. Even less could she believe in people like Agare, but least of all in falling captive to Barstow and Louis. But that was because the life she had believed in, and sought, didn't exist at all. What had she believed in—the marvelous creatures like the *Marindor*, the sleek and unparalleled loveliness and dignity and ultimate valor of the creatures she had created in her masterpiece? She had believed in mythic creatures and had sought mythic possibilities, but truth, which was preposterous, truth itself was beyond her, had always been beyond her.

She looked up at the pilot's compass on the overhead. The boat sailed on as if the lubber line had been drawn in ink across the compass card: the boat did not vary in its eastward or westward motion enough for the compass to measure it. It made her think of *The Rhyme of the Ancient Mariner*, how enthralled she had been by the poem when her father had read it to her when she was eight years old. Even now she had it by heart.

She lay in the berth, slowly rising out of the trance of the past day, but sinking back into it as well, just like a ship rising up and falling down over the swells and into the troughs of the sea. That this should be! Above her, through the deck, she heard the scuff of Louis pacing the deck, the muffled jabbering.

Now there came a banging on the forecastle door from the far end of the forward cabin.

"Hey, hey," she heard Evelyn shout. "Hey. Let me out of here. I got to use the john. The head. I got to pee. Hey, hey. Somebody. Come on."

"All right, all right, all right. Put a cork in it," Louis shouted down. "I'm coming."

Katherine heard him move forward and work at unlocking the door. She heard him fumble and curse lightly.

"Hurry up, Louis. I'm floating a kidney," Evelyn said.

At last he opened the door. The girl stumbled into the head. When she emerged, she said, "Do you remember how to flush this thing?"

"No," he said. "I don't remember either."

"So what do I do?"

"So when Katherine wakes up, ask her to flush the toilet. Right now I need coffee. Breakfast. What's for breakfast? Sea cruising, look at me. I ain't sick even a little. I feel great. I got an appetite. I could eat."

"I can't cook so good. Me and Alan, we just *eat,* you know, whatever's near us."

"You don't cook. *I* cook. That's what I live for. Good food. But you got to know how to do it. I'll cook, so where's the food? What have I got to work with? Last night for supper, what'd we eat? Canned crap? But then I wasn't feeling so good. I ate whatever it was. Never again. And not now. I'm the new me. The new Louis Santucci."

"Katherine knows where everything is. Ask her. I'm going up on deck. Then I want to take a shower. If there is a shower. Do you think there's a shower? And I want to change my clothes."

"OK, I'm going up top too. We'll wait for Katherine."

"To start breakfast," Evelyn said as she mounted up the companionway.

"Yeah, and flush the toilet," he said, following her. They both laughed.

"Ouch," Evelyn said. "Don't do that."

"Well, move it then. Move it!"

Katherine did not hurry out of her berth to start breakfast or flush the head. She stayed tight, firm against the starboard heel of the boat. But in twenty minutes more she felt the slight shift in the pattern of the waves. The compass heading was the same and the angle of the boat was the same, so the wind had not changed, but the wave pattern had. She could hear the different rhythm on the hull and feel it too, the nearly negligible but not insignificant shift. In rough weather and heavy seas, you don't feel small patterns, but in weather like this you can, and they mean something because there are no small cyclonic disturbances to account for them. This kind of pattern comes out of the sea itself rather than out of the wind. It was what the Polynesians navigated by, the wave patterns, the eternal vibrations sent out by islands or off the contours of the ocean floor, the spinning of the earth. More even than the stars, those sailors in their seagoing canoes navigated by the matrix of the pressures out of which the sea was made. It wasn't a skill exclusive to Oceania. Sailors had always known and used those rhythms, and sailors like her father and her had never lost the skill of reading the heft of the sea. Even with nothing but her immediate senses, even without a compass, she could take a boat to a landfall.

The shift in the tattoo of the waves on the hull raised her. The only quick explanation she could make of them was that the boat had progressed farther than she had estimated it would, that it had already reached the point where the Continental Shelf finally dropped away completely and that they were now truly off soundings, well into the blue water over the abyss. How had they gotten here so quickly?

She got out of her berth and went to the chart flattened down on the pilot's table. She checked her watch. 0800. If she was right, then they were already in the high fifty degrees of longitude. It meant that they had made good distance over the sea bottom, about 210 miles in less than twenty-four hours. Which meant that they were doing better than nine knots, exceptionally fast for the *Marindor,* more than her hull speed. Working over the chart and considering the line of fixes she had taken through yesterday and into the night, she saw what had happened. They had picked up the West Gulf Eddy, a backward swirl off the Gulf Stream. The Gulf Stream went north and east; the Eddy split off like a spume of water and reversed, flowed south by west. If you could find it in the sea, for it shifted constantly, then you could be moved with it. The actual sailing speed of the boat would stay the same, but the water you sailed through would be moving as well, sweeping you with it. That is what had happened. Maybe that is what had happened to the Ancient Mariner as well, no mystery, only the currents in the sea, though they were mystery enough. She would take sextant readings, especially the critical noon sun shot, to bear her out, but she was confident that she knew where she was, nearly halfway to the Carolina Canyon. For better or worse.

Her plan from the start was to sail more or less parallel to the coast inside the Gulf Stream and avoid its strong northward and northeastward current. When she was below the mark of the point that she was looking for on the western ridge of what formed the Carolina Canyon, she would swing perpendicular across the Stream and use it to push her on a ferrying angle toward the ridge. If she was right now, in about two hours she would swing from a southerly course onto a more east-southeast course. She would try to make the transit of the Gulf Stream boundary, always turbulent, at its narrowest point.

It was good for her to be thinking about the management of the *Marindor* and not the rest of what was happening, this adventure that had become so outlandish and ominous, though the serious danger could never be far distant from her mind. Still, the decisions about the boat, those were her purpose and not theirs, whatever the larger outcome might be. Maybe there was even some validity in Barstow's jejune philosophy that you dealt only with what there was to deal with at the moment, that plans were only a defense against the fear of what might not happen anyway. Good enough, then. She would manage her boat as she must; let him manage the rest, as, of course, he would.

She pulled herself into fresh clothes and made her way to the head, where she washed and brushed her teeth and used the commode and flushed it. Maybe she would have to write out instructions for the crew and tape them to the door. Before she went up on deck, she thought again of Barstow's attitude. Yes. That is what it was, not even a simplistic philosophy, only an outlook. A stance. Her last three years, which seemed so unplanned, so "escaped," were after all just such a defense as Barstow's, as careful a construction against the life that had failed her as were the exact formations that Nelson had constructed for his fleet at Trafalgar. So in that sense Barstow was wrong. We plan even when we do not plan. We plan not to plan. After Tom, after Steven, after the very breath of her life itself had gone out of her and she had ceased to aspire or to be breathed into, she had planned to avoid the danger of any failure again, to keep moving. A moving target is hard to hit. To reject henceforth all annunciations. But look what had happened! Look what even now was happening!

She patted her face dry and rubbed a protective sunblock into it and thought of the unfortunate Admiral Byng, the only admiral in the history of the British Navy ever to be executed, and that for the offense of having broken out of formation at Minorca and having crossed the line of the French battle fleet contrary to traditional principles of engagement. It wasn't even that the result was a disaster, nothing like that at all, even though the French did escape. What Byng had really done was break the rules, go against the plans of his superiors, plans that had been determined by the ministers in London, hundreds and hundreds of miles away from the scene, abstractions determined by theories of naval conduct rather than by the present necessities that Byng faced. The ministers in Greenwich had planned all battles once and for all, as if all the battles were the same. Byng had thought otherwise. And for that they hung him, not for the failure of the mission but for the audacity of his challenge, a maddeningly foolish kind of admiral's *lex talionis*. When she had read the story of Byng's fate, it had amazed her that he should have been hung. It seemed so severe. But not now. If there are rules, you do not break them with impunity. If there are no rules, then what you do does not matter to anyone but you.

As soon as Katherine came up on deck, Barstow pointed out to her the change in the waves.

"That's very observant of you," she said. "It really is. I'm impressed. Maybe you could make a sailor out of yourself."

"Maybe. So what does it mean? Anything?"

She explained about the Eddy and what effect it had on their speed. She told him they would change their course in two or maybe three hours.

"At the rate we're going, we should make the general area of the Carolina Canyon the day after tomorrow, probably early in the day." She looked around her, tested the nature of the light, the color of the sea, gauged the pressure of the air on the back of her neck and the density of the wind. She looked aloft to see how taut the rigging was. She ran her hands across a sail and then rubbed them together. "This weather will hold," she pronounced. "Today and tomorrow at least, but probably even longer. So far we've had good luck. When we pass into the Gulf Stream, we'll get bounced around a little, but not for long. Mr. Santucci seems much recovered."

But Barstow was looking aloft, looking to see what she had seen. The sun, still low enough to be warm, lighted him. His fractured skin glinted in the sunlight like a shimmer of mail. He wore his skin, she thought, as if it were something he could shed.

"What were you looking for?" he said, dropping his eyes. From the sunlight in the sky and radiating off the sails, the irises had constricted to points nearly too small to see. It made his eyes look robotic, blank, like the eyes of Grecian statues. Nothing that could be read.

"You see the topmost sails, the smaller sails? You can tell a little about the moisture in the air by the way they set. Even Dacron sails will respond to moisture a little, even the running lines. When I was a kid and sailed with my father, the sails were canvas and the rigging was still hemp. The moisture in the air could change them so much you could have measured it with a ruler. Wet air or dry air aloft is information. You add it to other things." Now she had told him something more about herself, that she had sailed with her father. She must be careful, but not so careful that she alarmed him.

"It could be a good life, I guess. It looks like it agrees with you," he said to her. "What's it take? How did you end up on a boat all alone?"

"I got lonely," she said. "My life suddenly got very lonely, so I decided to be lonely in a setting where I could be left alone. If you want to be a sailor, you've got to be willing to be alone."

"I could handle that part of it," he said. "When I was inside, a couple of times I got locked up in solitary. It wasn't so bad for me. Some guys go crazy. They come out messed up forever. Not me. For me it was easy. The lonely I could handle."

The boat sailed on tight and smooth. Behind it, its track in the sea was level as glass and straight. She turned away from him to examine it.

Arrow straight. Unnaturally straight for a ship under sail. *The air is cut away before, and closes from behind.*

"Steady as it goes, Mr. Sonderson." She smiled at the young man, but he looked confused that she had called him mister.

"Yo. Miss Katherine," Louis yelled. "Show me what you got to eat; I'll cook you something good." He was sitting back near the wheel on Alan's side. He and Alan and the girl were warped together. They had become good friends.

"Come along," she said. "I'll show you."

He was as good as his promise. She showed him the larder, where she had put the packages from Agare and what she had added. She showed him how the propane stove worked and how to let it swing on gimbals if he wanted or how to brake it. She showed him how to use the special stove fitting for the coffee pot, though she had no coffee other than instant. She showed him pots and pans and dishes and how to pump the water, and then she went back topside. He could hardly contain his excitement.

The day had brightened and would grow brighter still. It was a phenomenon of the sea. Light became like a lens to itself; with nothing but the absolute dome of the sky, the sea became a mirror. The higher the sun rose, the more the light all over increased. All they could do now was sail. But for the sailor, people such as herself, that was the place in itself. Unlike her crew, which had a destination and a purpose, she was already here. Sailors like herself understood that, but how would this day and the next bear upon Alan and Evelyn, upon Louis Santucci? But mainly upon Barstow? If the weather was as good as this, the others would settle into the cruise, lulled down into the timeless empyrean of the sea. But Barstow was as taut as the *Marindor.*

Soon enough Santucci handed up a mixture of Dinty Moore stew and eggs that he had somehow compressed into a kind of pancake. He had oiled and pan-baked the English muffins so that they were like something else, something *not* packaged. He had found a can of thinly sliced chicken and had floured it and seasoned it and lightly turned it in a film of hot oil. He put it in a bowl along with a sauce that he had whipped together out of milk and lemon and dried rosemary and dashes of paprika.

The *Marindor* sailed itself, and they all ate with gusto.

"Quite a feat," Katherine complimented him. "You're very good. The food is so good, and how you did it in a galley in such a short time. A marvel."

Louis beamed in the praise. His dark hair fell back away from his eyes. Yesterday she had thought he was in his forties; now he looked ten years younger. His two-day growth of beard darkened him attractively. It filled in the pallor of his skin. And he was full of color from the sun. Too much so. Soon he would have a burn. "Eat, eat," he urged them. From the chef, now he had turned into the maître d', hovering, offering, directing, gently insisting. "Nothing," he said. "This is nothing. Wait till I get a chance to plan something. Wait till I really get to know what you've got down there. Of course, the coffee is a real disappointment. You can't make coffee without the coffee, you know what I mean? Instant Taster's Choice? It's something I can't believe I'm even drinking. On the land, wherever I am, I take my coffee with me. And a little machine. I can do anything with it, ain't that so, Barstow? Ask Barstow," he said to them. "Espresso, cappuccino, regular brewed coffee, steamed or boiled, drip. You name it. It's a great little machine. This machine, you got to order it direct from Italy. From Milan."

Barstow nodded. He ate slowly, deliberately. He did not show whether he understood how good the food was, or whether he cared. He finished before the others and took out a cigarette. "I'm down to eight cigarettes," he said.

"Break them in half," Alan said. "Sixteen smokes."

"No," Barstow said. "No rations. Eight smokes."

"You could have a restaurant," Evelyn said. She was eating without restraint or inhibition. "I mean it. No fooling. You could have a very successful restaurant. Did you ever think of that?"

"Yeah, I did. Sometimes I do," Louis said. "I mean, actually, like it's something I would like to think about, something I've been meaning to think about. I just never got around to it."

"So?" she said.

"So?"

"So why don't you think about it?"

"Yeah. Well, so maybe I will. Think about it. Think about doing it. But it takes a lot of money to get started, I mean, if you're going to do it right. Otherwise, what have you got, a diner or maybe a chop house on a side street where the guidos come for red cooking? What have you got? A restaurant like that? Sicilians is what you have got. Neapolitans. You can't cook for people like that. All you can feed them is garlic and tomato sauce. Na. You got to cook for Rome, or better, Milan, Florence, Venice, the north. Como. Bellagio. You know, the Italians taught the French how to cook? That's a fact. Isn't that a fact, Miss Katherine?"

"That's a fact, Mr. Santucci."

"But with the right money, you could get the right location, you could start right in cooking the best and just wait until you get found. You could start right out without no trouble about getting your garbage collected. Yeah, I'll think about it, but you need the money."

"Garbage collected?" Evelyn said through her stuffed mouth.

"Very important," Santucci said. "And expensive."

"But the city picks up your garbage," Evelyn said.

"This is special garbage," Santucci said. "This is the kind of garbage that you pay for to have picked up so you don't get a bad fire or a brick through your window."

"I don't understand," she said.

"Protection," Alan said. "It's a way of paying for protection."

"Protection?" the girl said. "Protection from who?"

"From guys like me," Louis said, and howled. "From guys like me." He laughed hard and slapped his hands on top of the forward cabin. "From guys like me."

The money brought them back to where they were. It was never far away, but it had been submerged. The money for Louis Santucci's restaurant would have to be the money for Alan and Evelyn's boat. There was only so much capital available in the world, just as Agare had explained it. The dreams for its use were infinite.

Now they were silent, busy enough at their eating. Katherine wondered what Evelyn and Alan could be thinking. That they would all strike a deal with Agare, that Louis and Barstow would actually give them back their $100,000? That this would all end happily for them all? Were they incapable of doubt? she wondered. Or fear or outrage? But had she been capable of doubt at their age? Had Steven? Sally? All Sally doubted was her, Katherine. So what alarm bells could she sound for Evelyn and Alan? And to what avail, anyway? They liked Louis. They were *like* Louis, though not violent. So they believed him. Alan would retrieve the disk and they would deal with Agare and everything was going to turn out fine. Perhaps, like Barstow, they had only planned as far as they could reach with their fingertips. Even the idea of their boat in Florida probably had no more substance to it than their life this past summer. She remembered Evelyn after her boat sank, pounding on the hull of the *Marindor,* how she could easily have died but could not truly imagine that. It was so like the young, for whom death is an abstraction, a shadow on the wall of the cave. The girl had known she was in danger in the water in the cove that night, just as she knew that she was in some sort of danger now, even on this bright and beautiful day. But she could not imagine it. A future for her could have no more substance than her past. No wonder the girl and Louis had bonded so easily. Unlike her, who dragged a past around with her even though she as well had no future into which she could move unencumbered.

"You've gotten your sea legs quickly, Mr. Santucci," she said.

"My sea stomach," he said. "That's what you mean. Yeah. I feel good. Last night, it was great, right?" he turned to the children. "We did a lot of talking. We did a lot of relating. Me and Barstow, our line of work, we don't get to meet such nice people too much, if you know what I mean. It's a pleasure, let me tell you. Now I feel so good. Yesterday at this time, I thought I was going to die. I *wanted* to die. Now I think I'm going to live forever. I *want* to live forever, it stays like this."

She thought how unguarded he was. Or seemed. How simple it would be for Alan, say, to overcome him; Alan was so much larger and stronger. She wondered if he was even carrying his gun. But there were two of them, and of course Barstow would not be surprised. He would be eternally on guard and somewhere armed. The thought passed quickly. They could not take back the boat; they could not overcome Santucci and Barstow with conventional force.

"Katherine, if there's a shower, can I take one? I'm itchy from the salt."

"There's a shower," she said. "I'll show you how." She stood up, as did Evelyn. "Take the dishes," she said.

Going down below, the girl handing the dishes to Katherine, Louis shouted after, "You need some help? You need someone to scrub your back?" And hooted.

Her calculations were correct. At ten o'clock and then again at eleven, she confirmed their position. She would make the turn and at noon shoot the critical sun shot and realign the boat. She showed Barstow where they were. At 1100 hours she stationed them all on deck to maneuver the boat farther off the wind. Now they would be on a very broad reach, nearly before the wind. In the near distance, maybe only ten miles off to the east, she could see the curtain of purple squalliness that marked the edge of the Gulf Stream, but she could see through it as well. It was only a narrow lamination today. There would be some turbulence, but they would pop through it in no time and be in the river of blue water that was the Gulf Stream. Already the countercurrents at the edge were setting up a rip of waves. Along the edge now she could see a clearly defined line of debris, plastic bottles and torn-out fishing nets and water-logged timbers. The line was formed by the two currents, which pushed the litter and detritus of the sea into a scum line. The *Marindor* began to rise and fall and smash away the small but persistent seas. It was like riding a horse over a flat but rough terrain, where the gait of the horse was always just a second off the stride, like a syncopated misstep.

The warm, moist air of the Stream reached out over the sea, licked over her crew. She ordered them to put on foul-weather gear. Louis had given Alan back his waterproof windbreaker and put on an older yellow slicker, and Barstow did too. The chop worsened. Now they could look into the bordering area and see the disturbed seas, the waves smashing into each other so that the water broke upward like old-fashioned sheaves of corn or splashy fountains of water. But it looked far worse than it was, at least in a large boat. The crossing of the waves dissipated the energy in each of them. The wave action could take no hold upon the boat. The

Marindor sailed over the tumult easily, steadily. The wind was not a factor. Once well into the Stream, she would bring the sails across and sail on a port tack.

In less than an hour, they were through the boundary and into the Stream, and here the wind freshened. Rather than jibe, Katherine chose to come about through the eye of the wind and fall off in the new direction. Barstow wanted to see what she had done, where they were now on the chart. She took him below and struck a pencil line on the chart marking the new position and a new course.

"On this course, we come right across the airplane," he said after examining her line. "That's too good to be true."

"You think I'm playing a trick on you?"

"That's a question," he said. "Just give me the answer."

"It's nothing unusual," she said. But he wasn't satisfied. "It's an old racing trick. Very basic. To make a mark, in this instance the airplane on the ridge, you have to come abeam of it, and then you make your turn. With the wind anywhere abaft the beam—behind the middle point of the boat—you can aim the boat on any course you want. So look. If I draw a line from the airplane down to where we are, then it's an easy matter to turn where the two lines meet. I could have turned here or here or here or anywhere and the line I drew to the wreck would go directly through it as long as I adjusted the sails to keep the right angle to the wind. Or from the wreck the boat would have to go directly to wherever we are. See. It's not such a trick after all." She showed him.

"So why did you turn here instead of here or here or here?" At each "here" he poked his finger down on the chart at what could have been a juncture. "Why did you wait to *here?*"

"Because I'm figuring in how much the current in the Gulf Stream will set us off. For every boat length forward, we'll slide about this much off in this direction. It's called leeway." Again she showed him. "As much as three degrees eventually, and maybe even more. So to get here," she pointed, "we actually have to try and sail in this direction. We're sailing above the mark in order to be brought down right on it. Do you understand?"

She waited, and she realized that he was not thinking about the explanation she had given. That was simple enough, as clear as the lines she had drawn on the chart. What he was weighing was her. Had she told him all there was? Was she taking an initiative, taking a small action now that would add up to something important later? She sensed his problem. He had to think about what she was doing in case she was doing something bad for him, but he had no way of understanding what that might be. He would have to trust her, but he could not trust her, of course. That was absurd. Trust was not possible for him. The best he could do was get as much information as possible and see what happened. That is what he was doing. She must try to reassure him.

"You've got to understand," she said. "You've got to accept. Besides the celestial navigation, we're using a lot of dead reckoning. We check our speed and our distances and then we make a guess. From here on in we're going to—I'm going to—have to guess more and more. And better and better. It's not an automobile. We're not on a highway. We're not a train on tracks."

"Right. But you've got to understand that you've got to get us there. I mean, you *do* understand what I'm saying, don't you?"

"Yes. I understand. If we don't find the wreck ..."

"You're way ahead of yourself," he said. "You're way ahead of me. Don't do that. I told you before, don't do that. Just get us there. Don't think, 'what if.' Just think, 'get us there.'" But that had already been her own conclusion.

The Gulf Stream, once they were well into it, picked up between two and three knots. With the wind now on the port quarter, Katherine estimated their speed over the bottom as high as eight knots, or maybe even nine knots. The *Marindor* was flying. The Gulf Stream was serving them well. For an hour after the noon sun shot, she settled the boat down. She adjusted the sails, curved the boat into its steady, lilting motion. Lilting. It was her father's word. What he meant was that a boat would tell when it was being well sailed or not and that you should pay attention. Feel for the struggle the boat made against what you were making it do. Too much weather helm. A shudder as you bucked directly into a stiff sea rather than easing through it. A graceless wallow that exhausted you if you rode the boat up a beam sea and rolled it down on the other side. A well-sailed boat was quiet, and a badly sailed boat was not. It made all sorts of noises like complaints. Tight noises, he had called them, unlike the easy creaking. A well-sailed boat sprang into its task, happy. Lilting. He made the boats he sailed lilt. He was a lilting man. Even in foul weather.

The boat can take more than you can, he had told her, if you give it a chance. And it can take care of itself if you let it. If you help it.

She would always remember the first time she and her father had come into a storm that had frightened her forever. Years later she thought how that had been her catechism and the confirmation that brought her out of her childhood—the discovery of precise fear. What she learned was that fear was always about what was going to happen: fear was about "what if. ..." Her father had always made it his rule to think, "what now?" rather than "what if." *Now* is what matters, he had explained. You might never get to *if*. And pay attention to the omens, he had advised. Trust the gulls, he had told her, but not the shearwaters. Gulls were survivors. Scavengers. Shearwaters were hunters. Shearwaters counted on the storms to beat the smaller dazed fish up to the surface. Shearwaters flew into the storm-shaped troughs, and sometimes the waves broke on them and caught them and they died. Gulls waited for the killed fish to float into shore. They waited for the aftermath.

Like the gulls, his rule was to sail in the aftermath of storms, later rather than earlier if he could, to delay, to avoid, to dodge. Wait out foul weather rather than try to outrun it. Stay well off a lee shore, as tempting as it is to cut across the miles-saving line. Sail in the aftermath of storms. Watch what the gulls do. What he told her was that time made no difference at sea. Space did, but not time.

But eventually you will get caught out, he had explained to her, caught without options, and such a time it was off Long Island, only twenty miles from land but nowhere they could run to, no harbor of refuge, nothing but the blank shoals of the Hampton beaches. They had been headed to Block Island, and no one could have predicted the squall that hit them, but squalls were not uncommon and there was nothing in them that his experience was not superior to. They saw it coming, black and quick, so he got the sails down far enough, made the important decisions, and was ready.

If you cannot sail around a squall or if you cannot run before it until it overtakes and passes you, then you punch through it. You get through it quickly. There is a lot of wind in a squall but seldom significant waves. Large waves take time to develop; they depend upon the long fetch, the distance they have run. Squalls are windy and wet and quick. Local. He had brought the mainsail down and would power through with a small jib and the mizzen sail, itself reefed. But the squall seemed to grow thicker as they plowed and bucked into it. It began to turn itself into a true storm that surrounded them, generating itself, intensifying itself. If he'd had the sea room, he'd have lain down into the storm, dropped all sail, and let the storm push across and under. But he had only the twenty miles, and every minute he had less. He took the reef out of the mizzen sail to give a little more power and better balance, but it made no difference. The storm would not move past them; it only enlarged. All he could do was have faith in his tactic. They might die. But not because he had failed. If they were blown onto the shore and broke up, there was the smallest chance, if they grounded near enough, that they could be washed onto the sands, but that was unlikely. He stayed at the helm and tried to find furrows into which he could dip, find the backs of the waves that he could hide behind. He tried to dance the fifty-foot gaff-rigged yawl through the worst of the gusts, heading up or falling off. But all he could really do was stay with his decision.

Then the squall broke up. It seemed to explode, blow itself apart, a victim of its own energy. An hour from the start, it was gone entirely. Then it was sunny again, pleasant, nothing left but the brightening day. They were less than four miles from the shore. Fifteen minutes of space-time before the deep-keeled boat would have grounded out. But it had not, and here in the aftermath, even in less than an hour, the decks and all were steamy dry again, all sails set. They would make Block Island by early evening.

She was eleven years old when this squall happened. It was the greatest danger she'd known in the eleven years she had been at sea. Now she was here in this other kind of danger, this human squall, and with no options. All she could do was make her decision and keep to it. If she stayed with her determination to do what she had agreed to, then maybe this squall would exhaust itself as well, destroy itself by its own energy. Again, she lived in her metaphors. Small comfort now, these metaphors that could instruct but not save her.

Well into the Gulf Stream now, they sailed quickly along the course she had plotted. She had calculated the movement of the boat and the push of the Stream perfectly. They were sliding down upon the Carolina Canyon. If all held, they would slide across and out of the Gulf Stream. This day was sailing-good. Tomorrow would be tomorrow. They would arrive in their general destination area maybe early on the fourth day, as she had predicted.

An easy lassitude descended upon them. Alan at the helm, and sometimes even Evelyn. Or she would sleep, and then at times Alan would sleep. Barstow, forward of the main cabin on the foredeck, appeared to sleep, but Katherine was certain he did not. Maybe it was that he could sleep at one level but be awake, alert, at another, not unlike herself at sea. Louis, sitting up on the cabin roof, would be silent for long stretches and then suddenly burst out with lyrical descriptions of food. The idea of his restaurant had taken hold of him. He sang to them, to the sea, the breads that he would bake in his own ovens, the rough peasant breads of the hills of Tuscany, of Voltarra on the road to Pisa where his grandmother had come from. He had never been to Italy himself, but now, soon, that is where he would go. Maybe that is where he would be when the police were looking for him in Boston or wherever. He would be in the mountains north of Milan gathering information for his restaurant. Then he would fall silent. He was like a bird in a forest. Suddenly disturbed by ideas into song, Santucci sang.

The *Marindor* drove on, hovered, effortlessly it seemed, like the great albatross seems to fly, a long glide. The wind had freshened from the southwest, pushing them even faster. She had expected the wind to shift from a more northerly direction, a continuation of the high-pressure that had given them this weather, this gift between two high-pressure areas, one over the Atlantic, the other over the eastern United States. The more southerly winds suggested that the Atlantic high was beginning to move.

It would move slowly, she knew. But it would move. And when it did, they would have to sail in different seas. It would not be tomorrow or the day after when they reached the Carolina Canyon. But the day after that?

They sailed all the rest of the afternoon. She took as many shots with the sextant as she could. Alan stayed by the helm, but only languidly, a happy indolence. Evelyn sunbathed and slept. Even Louis, unable to stop, moved slowly, and for an hour sat before the mast thinking, who could imagine what, or maybe not thinking at all. Barstow prowled relentlessly, though without sharp effort. He examined, read the boat, every fitting, the arrangement of davits that held the fourteen-foot boat over the stern, the arcane conglomeration of peak and throat halyards, outhauls and downhauls, reefing lines, stoppers, vangs. Katherine watched him place a hand on a line and follow it with his eyes to a block or a spar, follow it to its function. What would he do with his information? She did not think that he could have answered that, but if there were something to know, then he should know it.

Eventually Louis bestirred himself. He went down into the galley, and in less than two hours, waving two bottles of wine in his hands, he announced the evening meal. He stood up on the canted cabin roof and called it out to them. Something to do with sardines and lemon zest and a pasta that he had found in their stores. Also pieces of a canned Polish ham from one of Agare's baskets. Sautéed in garlic butter. A simple but remarkable salad. Anchovies.

"Santucci cooks," he shouted to the sky. He tossed the bottles to Evelyn, who had come toward him. She shrieked but caught them both. He clattered down to the main deck and moved to the companionway to return below. "Come on, Evelyn, give me a hand getting this stuff up. Alan," he shouted, "open the wine." Out of his pocket, he produced a corkscrew. "Here."

Katherine thought about the squall she and her father had been caught in and about the idea of death. Then. The possibility now. The black squall bred in the sea. Barstow. Santucci. How odd to think about death on such a day as this! She did not believe that in the moment before we die our entire life flashes before us: the image was too melodramatic. But if you die slowly, if you decline into death, slide down into it on a certain but barely perceptible incline, then perhaps your life does return. When you have no future, and are therefore stalled in a static present, only the past has the possibility of movement, and it is unrestrained by the vectors of time. Memory can go anywhere it wants, and in any direction. And it can be protean, taking shapes it never had. For three years, in what Joe Mackenzie called the coffin she had made of the *Marindor,* her past had become her only companion, sometimes stiffly articulate like well-rehearsed vignettes, sometimes as inert as the dumb show in medieval pageants.

"Ta-da," Evelyn said, rising up with a casserole in her hand.

The food was playfully elegant, touched with delicacy and surprising brio. Katherine had always eaten well on cruises with her friends over the years, but it was mainly an eating off the sea: lobster and mussels in Maine, oysters and crabs in the Chesapeake, shrimp in the Carolinas and Georgia, and everywhere whatever fish was in season. Good food and hearty, the kind of food that didn't need much done to it—simply boiled or steamed or grilled. But Louis had invented and contrived. His sensibility was European; what they ate now could have come out of the Dolomites.

"Your friend, what's-his-name, the disk guy, his stuff, very good, very, very good. All right, so it's in cans, but there's cans and then there's cans, you know what I mean?" Santucci waved his fork at them, a conductor. A tutor. "Of course, nothing can touch fresh food, that's the secret. But even with cans, with anything, you can always do something. You know what I mean? You take a can of tuna, see. So you squeeze it good, really hard, so what is left is the juice, and even that, what is it, some kind of sunflower juice, not even good olive oil. Still, it's got something in it, something that you can work with. The trick is, I heat it, I thicken it. And some spices, whatever I got to work with, but paprika I use. Yes!" he shouted. "Paprika. You would never think about that, would you, and then I soak some dry dill in it. The best I can. Miserable stuff, dry dill, but with the tuna and paprika thickened—you see what I'm saying? Something is starting to happen. You see what I'm saying? A recipe, you know what is supposed to happen from the start, but me, it's a ... it's a ..." But he got stuck.

"It's a search," Katherine said for him. "A discovery. Like marching is different from dancing."

"Yeah! Yeah! That's it," Louis said.

But he seemed suddenly confused by his own enthusiasm, that it had come out of him. He stalled. His language had gotten in the way of his instinct. "So who knows what is going to happen?" He finished standing, flung about by his lyrical excitement.

"An adventure," Katherine said.

"Yes!" he actually screamed. "Yes! Exactly! An adventure! That's it, exactly right. An adventure. So OK, now, everybody. Eat. *Manga, manga.*"

She looked at Barstow, but he was looking aft again at the davits from which the small boat hung. He ate quickly, with necessity but not savor.

"How did you learn to cook so good, Louis?" Evelyn said as she scraped her plate clean. With a piece of hard bread, she polished the plate with serious intent, her brow creased, her long hair dropping down across her shoulders like a shawl, the low sun's warming rays burnishing her. It was an endearing action. Katherine remembered how often she would tell her children to clean their plates, and they would scrub them with bread as the girl did now.

It was marvelous to Katherine that the girl could be so certain of her life. Had she ever been this way? She did not think so. Evelyn Kinski seemed to live with total liberty, compelled only by the urgencies of her body, which sanctified her. Katherine liked the word: *sanctified.* She marveled, allowed herself to marvel. Certainly the girl must have a history, and therefore a complexity that the simple ardor of her senses seemed to belie. Or maybe not. Maybe, whatever her small heritage, she had escaped its gravity and had lived all of her short life as insubstantial as a spirit. Or as substantial as a spirit. And Alan seemed her counterpart, quiet and stolid; he seemed impartial, a willing participant in whatever events came along, as much an observer as an actor. More an observer. Again, how unlike herself, both of them, when she was their age. But would she ever get to know more of them than what she could infer from so little now? In the midst of an amazing crème brûlée that Louis had manufactured out of nothing, Katherine looked into a blackness that made her clench, and she knew, she *knew*, what the children did not, no more than did Santucci or Barstow. If they should survive this hallucination, all or any of them, no one could ever again be as *uninformed*.

"You know what would be a great idea?" Louis said, leaning back from his food. He had eaten little, his pleasure taken in the pleasure of the others who ate. "Make a restaurant on a boat just like this. You know what I'm saying? Very limited serving, very limited offering. And very, very expensive. Everybody rich would come because it would be so hard to get into the boat. And because it was such a kick, the boat part. Or maybe on good days you could sail out from the harbor and eat under sail just like now. Huh? What do you think, Katherine? Is that a good idea or not?"

"I think that's a great idea, Louis," Evelyn said.

"What about it, Katherine?" Louis said.

"It's a good idea. Something like that is done already. There are husband-and-wife teams that take out charters in the Virgin Islands and elsewhere. The team sails to different harbors and coves, and each night they make a feast for the people who chartered the boat."

"So see?" Evelyn said. "It's so good an idea other people are doing it. Listen, why don't we do that?" She looked at Alan.

"We can't cook, and we can't sail," he said.

"I mean as partners. We could learn it. Louis could cook, Katherine could sail. You could learn. I'd wait the tables, wash the dishes." Now she looked at Katherine and expected an answer. Katherine could tell that she did, could tell that the beautiful girl could compute nothing, that she and Alan had maybe even forgotten why they were here. Or maybe they thought that they were simply going on to do what they had been paid for, once by Agare, now by Louis.

"And what about Mr. Barstow?" Katherine said. "Where would he fit in?"

Evelyn had not thought about that, about Barstow. Now she looked into her empty plate to not see him, as if not seeing him would make him go away, or at least become something else.

"Perhaps the maître d'."

And then they were silent, the wind so perfectly taut that it did not rush singing through the sails and rigging. The hull was heeled so tightly at fifteen degrees of inclination that the mast and the great heavy spars did not work in the step or against their fittings, did not squeal or grind at all, which is the way of even the most well-founded wooden boats. The *Marindor* sailed quietly, only the susurrous hiss of the hull rising around it, but that sound was so constant and unvarying that it dissolved into the air and the sea, just as in the gloaming the sky and the sea dissolved into each other. Even Louis was silent, perhaps considering Evelyn's idea, or at least struggling with the larger idea that there could be a life beyond the one he had lived. Not just a restaurant, or the even more exotic idea of a restaurant on a boat, but the idea that there could be dimensions to life, any life, even his own.

Katherine hoped that this was so, that Louis was struggling with fear. He could rob a bank with equanimity and quite possibly commit mayhem of a random sort, but the idea of a sustained and committed existence baffled him. How could he live that way? What could it mean to live that way? Maybe she should say yes, to Evelyn's encouragement. Encourage him. Sure. Partners in the Caribbean, the Leeward Islands. St. Croix or Antigua or Guadeloupe. As far as Trinidad. Perhaps she should draw him into his own muddled dreaming and destroy him. Be careful of the dreams you dream because they will come true. Look what happened to me.

Barstow was the first to speak. "My last cigarette," he said, holding it up to them.

"What do you do now?" Alan asked.

"Do?" Barstow said. "After this, I don't smoke, that's what I do."

"Does it make you crazy?" Evelyn said. "Is the craving bad?"

"It's not like that for me," he said. "In Vietnam on a break on a patrol, the sergeant would say, 'Smoke 'em if you got 'em.' So that's the way it is with me."

"Like," Alan said, "if you don't have them, you don't want them."

"No," Barstow said. "I can want what I don't have; I just don't need what I want if I don't have or can't have it."

She did not want Alan to respond. She did not want him to press Barstow in any way or to engage him. He would not know how to talk to Barstow. Barstow would not know how to talk to him. But Alan did not go on. He leaned back into the self-steering helm and watched the night rise up over them as Louis expanded on cooking and how he had come to it. Again, Katherine sensed Louis's confusion, the paradox that the more he talked about a restaurant, the further he would push it away. The thought fascinated her, Louis's terror as he approached the possibility of achievement.

"You grow up in a house like mine, it's in the air. It's what the women did. All the time. It's not a new story, right? So all the time I'm hearing a pinch of this, a pinch of that. All the time I'm stirring something. There is never something not cooking, never nothing to smell. Taste this, taste that. Don't even swallow it. Keep it in the front of your mouth. My mother, she'd take me shopping with her to carry the stuff she bought, so she'd show me how to feel things, a tomato, a pepper. She'd show me how you run your finger over a piece of meat, you can tell what it's going to cook like, tender, tough, greasy, dry. This is all not so long ago, but where I grew up, it was like Italy a hundred, two hundred years ago, right? So you learn, you don't even know you're learning, and that's the only way." And he went on, the recitation of his novitiate in his mother's kitchen. And Katherine thought that quite possibly it was a story he had never told before. No one had asked.

9

Once again, in the darkness Katherine huddled in the cockpit of the boat. Again, like the night before, Louis and the children made a party. Soon, she knew, Barstow would appear. Soon he did. In the first of the true dark, she had shot Venus and Polaris and Deneb, and he appeared, as though by touching the stars she had conjured him.

"We should talk about tomorrow," he said, settling down in the cockpit as low as he could. "And some other things. Are we on schedule?"

"I've taken some new shots," she said. "I'll plot them when I go below. But I think, yes. We should get to the vicinity of the ridge either very late tomorrow, probably in the night, or else early the following morning. We're making incredibly good speed. Still, don't count on it. You're in the sea. Don't count on anything."

"I don't count on anything," he said. "I think I made that clear. But I expect things. It's not the same."

"You make distinctions that are not real distinctions," she said. "In the old days, when all the lines were made of hemp, sailors would pick and strip the lines and smoke them in their pipes."

"What about the weather?" he said.

"Now the lines are all Dacron or nylon or some form of plastic. You couldn't smoke that," she said.

"What about it?"

"Maybe I could find some old-fashioned fiber line, some hemp."

"It's been good to us, hasn't it? The weather?"

"Yes," she said at last. "Very good. Amazing, even. Maybe. But September can be like that."

"Will it hold? What do you think?"

"Who can tell?"

His question just then, against the clattering from below, forced her for the first time to a specific decision. The weather was his greatest vulnerability. She saw him know that. She saw that he understood the limited possibilities of a boat in the sea. More than just finding the airplane and diving for the disk. More than getting to shore to deal. There was the overall vulnerability that he had come to understand as he had all that day considered the boat, walking about, understanding moment by moment the predicament a ship at sea is always in, that it is never safe. That vulnerability was all she had that she would be able to use against him, though how or where she did not know, only that this was the last knowledge she could withhold from his scrutiny, but maybe the most potent knowledge. She and the *Marindor*. It would be the only advantage they would have. If it came to that. When it came to that.

What she had decided was to think about beating him. Realizations codify; they devise themselves into a design. She did not yet have a design, but now she felt that a deterioration had begun, that the shock that had battered her since Barstow and Santucci had captured them was going away. The good wind and the good behavior and the bizarre civility would not contain them. Eventually everything changes. What bound them now was the quick rituals of the sea. It was like when ships sailed to battle or to seek whales. Mutinies did not occur during the certain motions of sailing a ship, only at the end when the act was no longer so certain and contained, and the chaos of gunsmoke or the rage of a wounded humpback whale unleashed the rage that motivated us all. She had sailed with people who had been the epitome of courtesy, models of propriety, for as long as the ship itself demanded them, but who shattered into shouting fights and near blows, friendships and marriages cracking and fractured, as the anchor paid out and the perfect harmony and grace imposed by necessity ceased. Now in the night of the second day,

Katherine's perspective was returning. Under the tough reasonableness of this passage, lurked the truth of wrath.

"It will hold at least through tomorrow, and another day, I'd guess. But it could go on, maybe even much longer. There is nothing to indicate otherwise, but nothing so good as this lasts. Weather is always developing; it's always happening, always moving. You understand that, I'm sure."

"But you will know that," he said. "You couldn't do this if you didn't know that." Even in the darkness she could see his hand wave across everything.

"Lots of people sail. What they use are radios."

"Not you," he said. "I watch you; I figure you. You couldn't do this if you didn't know whatever you needed to know. You can't do what you're doing if you don't know it all. You can't know just enough; you've got to know it all. I don't know how you got to know it so good, but you do. Sailing with your father? So listen to what I'm saying. I'm going to work on that assumption. That you know exactly what you are doing. You've got to make everything happen just the way it's supposed to—I mean the way you would make it happen if it was just you and not because of us. Do you understand? It is something I've been thinking about. You are going to have to take the responsibility."

She did not have to answer. It had not been a question.

"Tell me more about this Agare," he said.

"I don't know much. He represents people who need the information on the disk in the airplane. He's involved in international finance. What's on the disk represents a lot of money, or at least the power of the money to get something done. He didn't say what."

"Why you?" he said. "Why this way?"

She explained what Agare had explained, the perfect cover that she and the *Marindor* would provide. Above suspicion, beyond it.

"From the Coast Guard," he said.

"From that, yes. But maybe even more from other people who are involved in the transaction."

"He paid you well. You and the kids."

"It didn't seem to be a matter of money to him. To him the money wasn't a large sum."

"That's good," Barstow said. "If he paid you all what he did, he'll pay us more. I don't see that as a problem."

"What will you ask for?"

"I'll ask him what he'll give."

"And how will you ask him?"

"You'll ask him."

"Me?"

"He's waiting to hear from you. It would have to be that way. You've got a number or something. You must have made some sort of arrangement. We'll get to that when we have to."

"And suppose he won't give more? Suppose what's on the disk doesn't matter to him anymore, or enough?"

"You suppose," Barstow said. "That's going further than I need to bother with. But anyway, so what?"

The noise from below grew louder still. Then he said, "Tomorrow, I want you to tell the girl to cover up more. Maybe she shouldn't even wear a bathing suit."

Katherine waited.

"It would be better coming from you," he said.

And still she waited.

"Louis is very excitable, you see what I mean? He's already gotten the wrong idea of what is going on here. He's nearly forgotten about the money. Everything."

"He's your buddy. You'd know him better than I."

"I haven't known Louis forever. We come together and go away and come together again. But I know guys *like* Louis. He's forgetting what's going on here."

"Maybe we all have," she said.

"You haven't," he said.

"So why don't you tell Louis what you're trying to tell me? If he's so dangerous ..."

"I didn't say he was dangerous."

"That is exactly what you're saying," she insisted.

"What I'm saying is that we are all going to do what we're going to do, and we're going to do it my way, only we can do it easy or hard. If you

tell the girl, you don't have to say Santucci to her, you see what I'm saying? That's the difference between hard and easy. Coming from you, you
talking to the girl, it would be different than me telling her. And different to Louis as well, me telling Louis to stop—what? Thinking about the
girl? You're smart. You've been very smart so far. So stay smart."

The boat sailed itself. If she closed her eyes, she could be anywhere
else, the boat was still so firmly rooted, its speed unslackened. They said
nothing to each other for half an hour. She watched the time change in
the movement of the ecliptic and the major stars. In the heavens she could
tell the seasons, even the months, and thereby in the night the hour. Sirius
twenty degrees above the horizon in apposition to Aldebaran in Taurus
would mean September, 2300 hours. Without her instruments, she was
returning to her first knowledge. She must hone it on the whetstone of
this need. How would her father search for the wreck? How would she
calculate the drift of the *Marindor?* She might have to take soundings
with the lead line and steer the boat at the same time. If the wind held as
it was, she would drop all the sails except the smaller yankee on the
forestay, which she would back, and then put the helm down, effectively
heaving to. She could do this. And more and other things.

"Do you think of yourself as a victim?" he said out of the darkness.
And his voice, the odd elongation of his words coming out of the privacy
of the dark cockpit, surprised her now, she saw, more than ever. She
was awakening.

"A captive, do you mean?"

"They're not the same," he said.

"All right, then. I'm a victim of my enthusiasms."

"Which means?"

"Do I have to explain? Will you kill me if I don't?"

"What's your point?"

"I just made it. The difference between victim and captive isn't so
great as you think it is. If I don't do what you want me to do, you'll
kill me."

"I'm not going to kill you. I'm not here to kill."

"The point is, you could," she said. "I'm here not because of you but because I tried to get to something I shouldn't have. I was working on false assumptions. You," she said. "You. Louis Santucci. Our captivity. That's just one more accident I set myself up for."

"You're way beyond me," he said.

"The readiness is all," she said. "But I'm not ready." Did recognition flicker in him? In the blackness she could not tell.

"I'm not following you. You're way beyond me," he said again.

"You bet I am, Mr. Barstow. You bet I am."

And then he said, "You had enthusiasm. You had dreams. I never did. In the hospital after I got my face blown up, in the bed next to me there was this guy, he lost an eye, and the other wasn't too good either. At night he would have nightmares. You could tell. He would call out names. I never knew who. His girl, maybe? Or what. But it was something. Somebody. I always wondered what that must be like."

"There's never been someone in your life, in your memories?" she said.

"No. No one. Nothing." He waited. "So you probably think that's how I came to be what I am. But that doesn't interest me. What interests me is what it must be like."

"To have a name to call out in the night?" she said.

"Yeah. Something like that."

She could tell him about that, but of course she would not. She was managing to deal with what was happening to her, this mugging in slow motion, by doing what would have been done regardless. Sailing the ship. Getting there. Managing. She could handle her fear by keeping it focused. What her father had taught her was to keep tight to the task because it was the panic that would kill you before anything else. Now she saw how she had counted on Barstow's own restraint, and even Santucci's, his manic screeching aside. So Barstow's talking now was more unnerving than the clearer danger. If he grew anxious, and she sensed that he was, what paper clip could she throw into his mouth? This intimacy. Last night he had told her about himself as he was, as an operator, a robber. So she wouldn't miscalculate. He was establishing rules of engagement. Now there was more peril. Just as it had been for Admiral Byng. If he turned her into more of a friend than an adversary, it would be dangerous in other ways.

It was, she thought, like the Stockholm syndrome in reverse, the other side of what was happening with Santucci and Alan and Evelyn, when the hostages become sympathetic to the captors. Was Barstow drifting that way? Why?

She thought it was because, like Santucci, he had never been so long engaged with his victims, and had never considered, been forced to consider, anything but his life's smallest tactics. Never a strategy. Like Santucci, maybe Barstow, faced with so much money, was unnerved by the idea of an existence that he had never truly experienced before. She wondered if this was what was meant by a criminal mind, not simply someone born or made into pathological anger but someone who might not be able to consider *actual* existence, to comprehend that the world was not flat. Santucci had never truly touched his restaurant, for all his babble, but when he did, it frightened him. Maybe Barstow was like one of those people who were born without the capacity to feel pain, who could break his leg or cut himself severely and not know it; maybe he had lived so narrowly that he had never known what he knew now. "Welcome to the universe," she might have said. "Let me show you how much danger there really is."

"Where do you keep your guns, you and Mr. Santucci?" she said. "I don't see them. No holsters. Nothing sticking out." She would give him something exact to hold on to.

"Ankle holsters," he said. He raised his leg to show her, but it was too dark.

"I'm going below to put these fixes on the chart," she said.

"Come back up, then," he said. "We've got to talk about tomorrow, the day after."

Below decks at the chart table, she entered her figures and looked for her parallel rulers to strike new lines of position, but they were not there. She would not have misplaced them, and nothing that did not belong here would have been here. The weather had not been rough enough to displace the tool.

She moved into the bright forward cabin. To keep the lights she had run the diesel during the day, recharging the batteries. She had not allowed them to use the oil lamps. In the forward cabin, the party rattled on. The music thumping. They sat playing cards.

"This is pinochle," Santucci was shouting above the music. "I can't believe it, kids these days, they don't know pinochle." Evelyn sat attentively, her head swinging with the music, her shoulders dropping away from her head alternately, her golden head bobbing like a doll's. On every other beat, she thrust herself forward. All of her seemed to be moving at once. Alan sat heavily, but happy, the cards nearly hidden in his large hands. They had all been drinking; last night some and now much more. They had gotten into the stores, what Agare had brought, what she had carried abundantly, old cargo from old days when there had been people in her life. Wine.

"After pinochle, casino. You know casino? No, I bet not. Kids. Kids today. It's all that television you watch, you got no time to play cards. So, OK now, put your cards down. This is just a show-how hand." He fanned out his cards.

"Have any of you seen the parallel rulers?" she said, but no one answered.

"Have a drink, Katherine?" Santucci said without looking at her.

"Someone must have taken the parallel rulers from the chart table. I must have them. And no one is to go into the stern cabin."

"The stern cabin," Evelyn said. "Th-uh sterrr-n ca-ca-cabiiin," she sang along to the music. "Is this good?" she asked Santucci. "The queen?"

"A queen is always good," he said. "Always, always, always a queen is good."

"Except in hearts," Alan said. "The queen of spades in hearts, that's not good."

"It can be good," Evelyn said. "You got it, so you can lay it off on someone. You can lay it off."

"Lay it off, right," Santucci said.

"Listen to me." Katherine raised her voice. It was late. They should have been asleep. And the drinking was a bad idea.

"So let me tell you this story," Santucci said, turning away from the pinochle lesson. "This is a true story. This happened in Chicago to a friend of mine; he wouldn't lie. This is a true story." He started to laugh. "This is such a good story; this is so funny." He laughed on.

"So come on, Louis," Evelyn said. "Tell it. Tel-el-el iiiiit."

"This guy is with this bimbo up in his hotel room, OK? And he has got her pants down, you know. They are ready to go at it, and he says to her, 'I got some coke. I'm going to put some coke on your pussy and eat it up. You'll love it. OK?' And she goes, 'Sure, OK, but can you use 7-Up? Coke don't agree with me.'" He laughed and pounded the table. Evelyn and Alan laughed too. As strongly.

"That's good," Alan said. "That is really funny."

"Listen to me," Katherine shouted over them. And then the lights went out.

"Wha ..." Santucci said.

The lights came on. Barstow was standing in the companionway, his hand on the box of switches that controlled the lights. He turned the lights off again and then on.

"We have a problem here," he said.

"Ah, Barstow, we're just having a little fun. I seen on the TV, people go on cruises, they eat, they play around, they have fun. You want something to drink? We got wine; we got enough wine to go us for a week. Two weeks." He reached for a bottle. The lights went off again, and stayed off. After a time, maybe a full minute, still in the darkness, Barstow said, "We have a problem here, but we don't want a problem. Now is not the time for problems." He turned on the lights. "What are you looking for?" he said to Katherine.

"The parallel rulers," Katherine said.

"These?" Evelyn said. She reached behind her into the fiddle. Pushed in between the arms of the ruler were wine glasses. Some drops of wine were on the arms. "See? These work just great. For when the boat is going, so nothing spills?" She looked at Katherine. "I'm sorry, huh?" she said. "I guess I shouldn't do this." She worked to pry her glass free.

"You must all stay away from the charts," Katherine said.

"I'm sorry, Katherine," Evelyn said.

"Yeah, Katherine, I'm sorry too. We won't do that again."

"Turn off the music," Barstow said. "You two," he indicated Evelyn and Alan, "go to bed. Louis, lock them in. And get some sleep yourself. Tomorrow's a big day. Tomorrow night, even, we get to the canyon."

In the cockpit Katherine resumed the helm. The night had darkened. At sea the stars are so bright, with no other light to deflect them, that they come together into a general light. On some nights when there is no moisture at all in the air, the stars together make it possible nearly to read by them. Now they were not so bright. Even in the last hour, they had dimmed. Beyond the *Marindor,* somewhere to the south, clouds were forming. Already they had drifted here but were still too thin for any but the likes of her to know that, or to think of what the dimmed stars might presage. But clouds were forming in some quadrant into which they were sailing.

"Did they break the ruler?" Barstow said. Again, it surprised her, his voice out of the dark. Even though she knew he was there, she always forgot. She was living now on two levels, one close to what she had imagined her actual life to be and the other in this inconceivable situation.

"No," she said. "It's not broken, just twisted a little. It's nothing I can't compensate for. Or even improvise. It's not a big deal. It's not nearly as much of a problem as getting rid of all the electronics." But should she provoke him now? "What's done is done."

"What's done is always done," he said. But he had darkened too, as had the night. She was good at reading him, reading his weather, sensing the quadrant he was in.

"That was not good," he said.

"They drank too much," she said.

"I'll get rid of it. Over the side. Like the electronics," he said.

Was he now making a joke, small as it was, at her expense? If so, it was more than she could afford.

"But it's not the drinking," he said. "That's not the problem; it's not the main problem."

"The girl?" she said. "Santucci?"

"That's part of it," he said.

"And the other part?" she said. "The other parts?"

"That's nothing that we can talk about now. Maybe it's nothing that we can ever talk about. Maybe its nothing that can ever be said."

"So cryptic," she said.

"I'll take the helm," he said. "You go and get some sleep."

10

And now the third day had come. She awoke and watched the compass over her head. Tightly as ever, the *Marindor* clung stiffly to east-southeast, hard on 120 degrees. She had sailed continuously down from Mystic between a close and a broad reach, but when she crossed into the Gulf Stream, she had brought the boat onto an increasingly broad setting of the sails. And the *Marindor* had moved faster still, all unopposed. Her tactic was to keep heading 120 degrees east-southeast even as each hour they sideslipped northward because of the Gulf Stream current. Eventually the boat would be turned back to a close reach, the sails drawn in as she headed farther and farther up into the wind. But the heading would stay the same, one constant in the midst of all the variables. If she had calculated right, she could get to the Carolina Canyon without being forced directly into the wind that had come steadily out of the southwest. That way, she could avoid a slow and possibly thumping beat. Now, in the bunk, she watched the compass, the barest tick of the needle as the *Marindor* accepted her command. And already she could sense the slightest response of the ship to the current as it was pushed back by the ridge somewhere in the Carolina Canyon. The current would grow stronger as the boat drew closer. The Gulf Stream would cleave upon the ridge, nearly split itself in two. The volume of the Stream, compressed between the ridge and the ocean through which it traveled, would increase and thus speed up. She would read this and use it to get them there.

From where they were now, she thought it would be about 150 miles to where the ridge rose up to a depth of ten meters, to the pinnacle upon which the small airplane rested. She would find the Carolina Canyon and the ridge, had almost certainly already found it; that was never the central difficulty. But to find the precise point might be an insurmountable problem, though that is what she must do. Must. She thought about how her father would deal with this. How would he find the airplane?

She heard Barstow in the cockpit. At least she heard someone, but she knew it would be he. The children would still be asleep, locked in the forecastle. And Santucci would already be planning and preparing breakfast, inventing lunch and supper. Barstow would be looking outward, thinking what to do now. He would be thinking about what she would do and how to anticipate her if he could. It was not like the anticipation of a chess match, where black and white played by the same rules. She knew that Barstow did not, or could not, play by rules, only by intuitive moves, structures that he devised moment by moment. She thought again of how his current dependency burdened him. He could conceive of trust only as an abstraction. Trust was nothing he had ever experienced, and he could not know what it felt like any more than someone could know the taste of a coconut who had not eaten one. So he could not trust her, although he must depend upon her. She sensed the tension of his dilemma, and how dangerous that could make him. He had no patience, only the capacity to endure waiting if the waiting were part of a tactic. But patience and the ability to wait were not the same thing: a child could wait for Christmas morning because he knew when it was and what would happen. He could wait because he must. In the morning he was certain he would get a toy. But patience itself was a condition, a way of observing life. Patience was not waiting for something to happen; patience was an acceptance of ambiguity. Patience was what Joe Mackenzie was all about—able to live in what might never happen. Unlike her, who had *never* been able to live in what might never happen. That is why she had brought herself in the last three years to make a circumstance and to live in it, a circumstance in which nothing could happen, nothing more. Now all this had happened.

Barstow would try to learn as much as he could to diminish his dependency—learn how to operate the diesel engine or how to trim a sail, how to tie a square knot or a bowline—but the rest, all of the craft that was beyond him and required her, that would trouble him.

She lingered in the berth, thinking about what Barstow would do if they did not find the airplane and retrieve the disk. That was easy to understand. With or without the disk, they would have to return to land. And with or without the disk, there would be a reckoning.

She had earlier translated the LORAN coordinates to compass headings, and with all her celestial navigation skills, she would be able to construct the smallest triangulated zone of possibility. Even so, if she came within even a mile of the airplane, which would be small miracle enough, much less half a mile or a quarter of a mile, finding the small sliver of the airplane in ten meters of water would be as much accident as skill.

But accident was her métier, was it not? Her profession? Her calling? No, she thought, only her curse. She did not believe there was a providence in the fall of a sparrow, only gravity. Before you had an apple that fell on Newton's head, you had to have a Newton, and that was no accident. But the apple falling, that *was* an accident.

When the time came, she would send someone aloft, certainly Evelyn. She expected that tomorrow would still be reasonably even, the sea and the ship firmly met. She would drop the mainsail and use the main halyard to haul Evelyn up in a bosun's chair to look for the telltale change in the color of the water. Over the ridge it should lighten significantly. Out of the dark azure of the Gulf Stream, the water over the ridge would become a thin viridian. Then what? And as she thought, she saw that of all she had learned from her father—for all the exact lessons, the mathematics of navigation, the analytical skills—mostly she had learned his intuitions, the feel for the situation. After knowledge, there was a grace beyond the reach of art, and in her most sublime moments, here on the *Marindor,* she had touched it.

What she had was what Barstow and Santucci did not have. That could be her advantage, might be her only true advantage when she might need one. For all that it had been mangled and cracked, she lived in a continuum, always had. Barstow and Santucci had not. Barstow especially had only lived in the instant. She remembered reading how the zebra in the lion's jaw actually died before its neck was broken. For the animals there was only the instant life and the instant death. That is why Barstow could not fear.

Once, she and her parents had borrowed a small and ancient fishing boat, about twenty-five feet, a pinkie. It had been built in 1885 in East Boothbay, and it was one of the first boats that had tried to trawl under sail for bottom fish in New England waters. At that time all northern fishing, from the Grand Banks down to the inshore fisheries off Maine and even to Massachusetts, was long-line fishing. A long line, maybe as much as a mile, was paced out with a baited hooked line from three to five feet long suspended about every forty-eight inches. On each end was an airtight barrel that floated the line. The fishermen, two in a dory, were put over the side of a large mother ship, and they would bait and play out the line and then row back to the beginning of it and haul in the abundant cod, one by one. And then they would return to the mother ship to be hauled aboard, dory, men, and fish.

But a trawl worked differently. A wide, weighted net was dragged along the bottom in shallower water, and fluke and yellowtail flounder and halibut, even striped bass and bluefish when they moved inshore and along the bottom, and all sorts of trash fish would be taken, the single net hauled up with a large cranked winch turned by a capstan. It was an effective way to fish the bottom, but it had come before its better time. Under sail power alone, for in 1885 small engines were not truly possible, the difficulties were very great. The drift of the boat could not be adequately controlled if the wind veered or backed even slightly. And with the heavy sunken net, it was hard to drive the boat across the productive waters. And in the time when they had borrowed the boat, even updated with a small engine on deck to haul the net and a small diesel to drive her, there was still not enough power.

What her father thought to do was to heave to. He would back the jib and release the main, and he would put the helm down in an opposed direction. It was a classic maneuver—every sailor would know it, but it had not been applied this way before. It worked very well, allowing the boat to pull the net across the bottom, slowly but thoroughly, and especially without twisting the net, which then could take a day to untwist. And something else. From time to time, her father would put the boat into "irons"; he would set her directly into the wind and stall her so that the boat would slide backward. Doing this, he could ease the strain on the net and let it do its work until he reversed the helm and let the boat fall back into the wind and begin to move again. It was a master's touch, not only thinking to do it but being able to do it as well as he did.

For a month they hauled fish and made some hard cash. They might have stayed at it, but after the month it was clear to the three of them that they were sailors first. Always. Not settlers. And not hunters.

These were the maneuvers she would use now. She would sail to about the middle of the Carolina Canyon, which was about fifteen miles in length, and, heaved to, she would slide across it, like ferrying. Then she would come about, reverse the set of the headsail and the rudder, and traverse the canyon now from west to east until she crossed the ridge. Then, almost literally, she would back down it until they crossed over the airplane. It would be a slow process, but it would give the most coverage. If there were enough time, she could repeat the passage, sliding back and forth across the bottom half of the ridge. With each passage she would drop down a quarter of a mile, narrowing the band where the airplane must be. She would have to sail the *Marindor* as tightly as if she were carving the furrows of a plowed field, each passage overlapping the last. But she could do this. She could make the *Marindor* do whatever she wanted. With enough time.

There would be no guarantee of enough time, she knew. At sea there was always the chance that there might never be enough time to do anything again. As her father had taught her, you only get the one chance: you should always think that way. Their kind of sailing, like life itself, was divided into a single opportunity that was followed by another one, and that by another, but the certainty of sequence was an illusion even though you could work with the illusion most of the time, just as she had for most of her life worked with illusions. Life itself was linear, not circular: nothing came around a second time. Joseph Mackenzie had lived—lived still—without illusion.

They would need at least another day of these flattened seas to find and then to dive for the disk. But she smelled the roughness coming. If only it did not come too soon. As long as the odds had been, they were longer now. She got out of her berth to go up on deck and tell Barstow her plan to give him time to absorb it so that he could accept it even as she put it into motion.

At breakfast, eggs Benedict (gin instead of brandy sprinkled through with capers), she explained to the girl.

"Up there?" Evelyn said. "You expect me to climb up there?" She pointed up to the top of the mainmast. "No way, Katherine. There's no way I'll do that. I can't do that. I'm not going to do that." Katherine explained about the bosun's chair, how Evelyn would be hauled up, that she didn't have to climb the mast, that it was a safe procedure. The view would be spectacular. The seas were gentle enough even though they had begun to show movement.

"Let Louis do it," she said. "I just don't like that. Louis, you do it."

"OK," he said.

"No," Barstow said. "Louis will have something else to do."

"What?" she said. "Let him do this, and I'll do what he's got to do. You mean cook? Lunch? I can make lunch. Tell him, Alan. I can cook. I mean, you know, a little. Sandwiches or something. Coffee. Or we can make something the night before."

"No," Barstow said. "You go up the mast. Louis has got something else to do."

"Like what?" Evelyn challenged him. "What does he have to do?"

Katherine watched Barstow darken. As his face flushed, the hundreds of threads of his cracked skin did not. They were white, or appeared that way against the darkness, as though he were wearing a fine net over his face. And when he spoke, the elongated enunciation returned, what she had noted that first day but which had mostly subsided since then. She realized that this quirk in his speech was connected to his tension; it was a kind of stutter. She would remember this.

And she understood that Barstow was angry not so much at the girl but at himself, that he had not gauged the consequence of the last two nights of partying. He had stood by while they had forgotten. He had allowed them—Evelyn and Alan and Santucci—to slip into a sociable condition, into an amiable benevolence toward each other. But now his anger, a useless thing, subsided quickly. He had allowed what made sense at the time, in the past days and nights. It had worked to advantage. Now he would put them all back into where they were.

"Evelyn. Alan. Come here." He motioned them to the edge of the forward deckhouse. "You remember why we're all here, right?"

"Sure," the girl said.

"So tell me," he said.

"Oh, you know," she said.

"So go on, tell me."

"To get the disk out of the airplane. To sell it to Mr. Agare." She flounced her hair, already straw-whitened in the days of ocean sun.

"No. Not quite right." He reached down and came up with his gun out of the holster around his ankle. He held it high so the fullness of its menace could weigh on them. He slid the top of the gun, cocking it, chambering a round. The sound was more emphatic than the gun itself. Through the wall of television violence that Evelyn and Alan had established as their idea of mayhem, as innocuous as the cartoon their own lives had so far been, the sound of the gun broke. Katherine watched, attentive to this baptism, so rich with irony. They *knew* the sound well—all those television guns that they had heard—but it had never been connected to anything, only the flickering on the screen. Barstow was real. You could smell the oiled steel of the gun.

"So let me remind you. You are here because I am here with this gun."

"I thought we were friends," the girl persisted.

"No," Barstow said. "Not friends. You are like a hostage."

"Louis is my friend," she said. "Louis," she called to him. But Barstow had said enough.

"Now, or soon, tomorrow morning, Katherine will send you up the mast to do what she tells you to do. So that's that. Alan has to get his gear ready. So that's that. Is this all clear? Good." But now he was looking at Alan. The girl was not important. Alan was important. It was necessary that Alan understand what was going on.

"But it's so high and ..."

"Just do it," Alan said to her. "Just do it, Evey."

"But Alan ..."

"Just do it, OK?"

"Jeeze," she said.

"Good, Alan," Barstow said. "That is very good."

Barstow bent down, and when he stood up, the gun was not in his hand.

"OK, Alan. Let's start to get ready."

That is how the third day went. Alan, Barstow, and Santucci moved the generator to a centered position in the main cockpit and started it, making it run perfectly. The air tanks were emptied and filled, the regulators checked and double-checked. The lights and the batteries, the wet suit, the weights measured and attached, all the necessary paraphernalia. Alan tried on various masks and made adjustments. Barstow saw the diver's knife attached to the wet suit and removed it.

If the doors of the airplane did not open easily because of the pressure of the water on them, or if the fuselage had been crushed when it hit the ocean, Alan would have to cut his way in. And the growth of sea organisms was so quick that even in the time the airplane had rested on the ridge, the hinges might have become jammed. Agare had not said when the crash had taken place, but even in three or even two weeks, even one week, the fecundity of the sea life near the surface would be great, everything that lived seeking a hold. Small barnacles could start in a night; anemones begin to bloom in four days.

Alan set up the cutting torches and tested them. At one point he put on his equipment and tied a line to himself and went into the sea to test the torches under water. He adjusted the flame to cut aluminum.

Once he got into the plane, he would have to bring up the disk. He had already rigged a wire basket that would be closed and secured so he wouldn't risk dropping it. The person in the inflatable would bring it to the surface. He attached the basket by double lines against the chance that one of the lines would break or be cut.

To another line he attached a slate and a special marker that would work under water. He would use this to communicate with the surface if necessary.

The three men brought the inflatable across the forward deck and pumped it tight and checked for anything that could become a problem. Katherine herself went over every line and fitting and knot that might be used. And more attentively than ever, she sailed the *Marindor,* drawing it down to the Carolina Canyon and the ridge. She would begin the search for the airplane in the morning.

The sky had lost its lustrous brightness. The slight mist that had darkened the stars the past night had come even farther toward them, making the sky more opaque. The sun became a pearly disk. It would still be bright enough to illuminate the airplane, and without full sun the glare of the sea itself, like a tarnished mirror, would be reduced.

Imperceptibly the day dulled, which did not alarm her. A darker day tomorrow was better. But she felt the waves and the newer motion of the *Marindor,* and even at times a shudder that the others would not feel and certainly would not understand. The tremble she felt told her that far south of them some turbulence had begun. It could easily be nothing more than the normal variations of the sea, of weather at sea. Against the perfection of the past days, any alteration made sense. Calm was *not* the normal condition of the sea, but neither was storm. It was the motion itself that troubled her. If it became too strong, then it would be difficult to dive for the disk.

The busyness of preparing was good. It would distract. Barstow would notice less, would have less to ask of her, for she understood that though he could comprehend what she would have to tell him, how the motion of the sea could prevent them, it was not his nature to accept such consequences. But equally, she thought, he could give up a venture, suddenly stop what he saw could not be done. Who could read such a person? And even if the weather became bad enough to prevent them from retrieving the disk, what had always been more important would not be resolved: How were they to free themselves from each other?

Evelyn sulked, every so often looking up to the point on the mast where the high yard of the gaff attached, the point where tomorrow she would go.

At the end of a small lunch they sat in the cockpit around the generator. The sky continued to soften into an opaline filminess. The cast shadows lost their edges. The dulling contrasts drained the light everywhere. Alan said, "The people in the airplane?"

"One or two?" Katherine said. "Or more? Agare did not say."

"Two, he told me," Alan said. "The two pilots." Then, "They'll be there. The dead men."

"Yes," Katherine said. "Or what is left of them. Have you ever seen death, Alan? Dead men?"

"No," he said.

"Will you be bothered by that?" she asked.

"Yes," he said. "I mean, I guess so."

"Then let me prepare you."

"You've seen dead men?" he said.

"Yes," she said. "Dead men and women and children and lots of animals. In Vietnam. A long time ago."

"What about you?" he said to Barstow.

"I've seen dead men," Barstow said. "Not many, and not for long. To me they looked like they had just gone to sleep. Or been knocked out, like in a prize fight. But not like what she is going to tell you."

"The first thing is to prepare yourself for how the gas has bloated them. So much that in many cases the skin will have split. It's like an overinflated basketball. Prepare for that. The next thing is the eyes. The eyeballs will be gone."

"Gone?" he said.

"Eaten," she said. "It's the first thing that gets eaten. They're so soft, even the smallest plankton can absorb them. I'm telling you this so you won't be shocked when you get to the bodies. You've been thinking about it, right?"

"Yes."

"That's if the windows have not been broken. If the windows have been broken, and they probably have been, or if there are any holes, then the crabs and the fish will have by now eaten most of the men. What you'll find probably are their clothes floating on their skeletons. There won't be much left, more than likely. This is good."

"Good?" he said.

"There won't be much left to attract sharks if the scavengers have done a good job," she said.

She could be this explicit not because of Vietnam but because of Steven. However he had died, this is what had happened to him. The idea that he had been returned to the elements of the sea had not comforted her at all. None of the people that she had known had ever thought well of dying at sea. None thought of the sea in gentle terms. They all had wanted to be ashore at their deaths and to be buried there in earth, where they belonged. In Mother Earth. There was no Mother Sea. She had never heard of a fisherman who wanted to be buried except on land, or who wanted to be cremated and have his ashes flung into the wake of his boat. That was only the lyrical myth of those who did not know the cold hunger of the sea.

"Yes," he said. "Well, I'm glad you told me. It's better to be prepared." Forward, at the absolute end of the boat, the girl sat and silently wept.

"You'll have to go into the cabin of the airplane, won't you?" she said. "Do you know, did Agare tell you, where the disk will be?"

"No. He said I'll have to find it. But he said he didn't think it would be in the luggage compartment. He said he felt sure it would be inside the plane somewhere."

"How long?" Barstow said. "How long will you be down?"

"It's hard to say."

"So say it anyway," Barstow said.

"Well, ten meters, I should be able ..."

"How much is ten meters?" Barstow said. "How many feet is that?"

"A little over thirty feet, close to thirty-five feet. I can get down to that pretty quickly. Coming up I should come up as quickly. Thirty feet is nothing much. There won't be any problems with the pressure. I can go down a hundred meters and up without a problem."

"What about air?" Katherine said. "Will you have enough air?"

"One tank should be plenty, but to make sure, to save time, I'll take a spare tank down with me. If things work out, if I don't have to do too much cutting and if I find the disk quickly, I should be able to get down and up in an hour. Piece of cake."

Forward, Santucci stood next to Evelyn, his arm around her, comforting her.

They would use the inflatable and not the boat on the davits. The inflatable was too small for the two men and the diving equipment, the extra air tank, the cutting torch and the tanks for that, other tools, but it would do, and it could be managed by Barstow alone. He could not have managed the little sailboat. There was no motor on it; it would have to be rowed and kept in place. He wouldn't be able to do that. Katherine could, but not Barstow.

In the afternoon, soon after lunch, they would launch the inflatable, and she would show Barstow how to operate the outboard motor, how to move through the waves, should there be any. With the inflatable they could pinpoint the airplane and tie off right on top of it. It would be easy to tie off with a line to the wreck itself once Alan reached it. And if the airplane should shake free when Alan was working on it, she would have put a slipknot onto the inflatable, so all Barstow would have to do was pull the standing end of the line to keep the airplane from taking the inflatable down with it.

"Why not anchor the *Marindor* over the wreck?" Barstow said. "Or near it. We could work off the deck of the *Marindor*. Only Alan would have to leave the boat."

"You couldn't tie off on the plane. The *Marindor* would rip it loose easily. And to anchor you need scope. You need to let out the anchor line for the ship to hold. With enough line out, we would be a couple of hundred feet off from the wreck. And with any wind at all, we'd swing. If we set an anchor straight up and down into the ridge itself, the first small wave would pull the anchor right out. It's better to keep sailing around, drifting nearby. With the diesel running, I can get to you right away if you need something. It's the only way to do this," she concluded. "If you want to stay aboard the *Marindor,* send Santucci in the inflatable, but that's probably not the best idea. He doesn't strike me as able. So what are your options? Alan goes alone? I go in the inflatable? Evelyn?" She was pleased to narrow him down. She wanted to see how he would react, or if he would react.

Barstow calculated all this but said nothing. He would go in the inflatable, that was obvious, but he had revealed nothing more except that something important had occurred to him, she could tell.

How odd that we can come so quickly to some knowledge of others, she thought. Unlike the animals, our threshold of perception has been so coarsened that we seldom see what they can see—the merest tightened muscle, the slightest shift in the angle of an arm, the darkness of the narrowed eyes, even the odor, the excretion of action—whatever sign will help them to survive, and maybe only when our own survival depends upon our perceptions can we sense sharply again, at least for an old, vestigial instant. Something had flickered in Barstow just then. Something had surprised him.

Then, as quickly, she knew that eventually he would tell her what that was. He could not trust her because he could not trust anything, but if he told her what he knew, what he thought, then she would trust *him*, and that would be enough. Both of them could make do with that. She had no share in this project. He had raised her, and at the end he would let her fall back into her slough. It irked her to think that this was true, that if she could understand him, at least some small part of him, he could even more easily read all of her. It angered her that even her fear had so small a dimension, and that instead of fury all she wanted was to live.

By 1600 hours Katherine had brought them to the proximate area of the Carolina Canyon. The airplane would be in the upper half, on the north half of the ridge, actually maybe even the north third. But she would cover a full eight miles, narrowing down like a cone as she moved across the ridge, narrowing down as in a funnel to the airplane, as in a vortex, to the intersection of the coordinates of latitude and longitude. What little would remain of the sun would be behind them, shining through the water and not reflecting off it like a mirror. And the extra distance they sailed would make an angle that would allow the sun to go further into the sea. The extra distance, the four miles, would give them all a chance to see how the *Marindor* and her plan would work, the chance to make the procedure methodical. Tomorrow she would send Evelyn aloft to look for the light streak that would signal the highest point of the ridge upon which at some point the airplane rested. She would position Santucci out on the bowsprit, right over the water. There he would be in a good position to spot the airplane itself if they passed over it going forward.

But it was too late in the day to do this now. It would all begin at first light. For now it would be enough to rest and wait, though she would have to work all night to keep them where they were instead of sailing straight away. She would have to turn the boat in a great circle around the canyon.

In the midst of preparing supper, Santucci was the first to announce what she had felt for the past two hours.

"This boat is tipping," he said. Evelyn was below helping him. He popped up into the cockpit and shouted to them. "I can feel it. The boat is tipping more."

"Yes," Katherine assured him. "A little more than yesterday. And it will heel—tip—a little more and a little more. It's to be expected. It's nothing to worry about."

But he was not assured. "It's going to get rough again? Is that what you're saying? Barstow? Are you hearing this?"

"What are you making for supper?" Barstow said.

"That's it? That's what you've got to say?" Santucci's voice was tightening with his first returning memory of seasickness.

"Alan," Barstow said, "what would you like for supper? Tell Mr. Santucci. Mrs. Dennison, what about you? What would you like?" But neither she nor Alan answered. It was clear to both that this was not the point he was making, that it was Santucci he was aiming at.

Santucci dropped back down into the forward cabin and to the galley, but in five minutes he was up again, a moment after Katherine had brought the *Marindor* a full ninety degrees into the southeast, nearly east, and the boat leaned down onto its starboard side for the first time in over three days.

"What happened?" Santucci screeched. "Jesus, everything is going the other way down here. What are you doing? What's happening? Are we sinking, for Christ's sake?"

She explained as simply as she could: she would be sailing in a wide circle from now on, through the night. And every time she made a move, the ship would feel different. What was up would cant down, down would turn up. And at every new direction, the sea would feel different because the waves would come at a different angle. And there might be more wind. The boat could begin to pitch and yaw as well as roll. With her hand she made the motion.

"Stop," he said. "Stop. I don't want to hear this. I don't want to know." He was gone again.

But Barstow did want to hear. He asked her to say it all again, not because he did not understand but because he wanted to listen for something between the lines, inside the cracks. What advantage she had would be in this, her knowledge and command of the *Marindor* in the sea. He knew this and knew that she did as well. She saw in him that realization, and that he wanted her to see it. He wanted her to know what was in him, that nothing was getting dealt from the bottom of a deck. If you could convince the victim that there was nothing more than what was happening, then nothing more than that had to happen.

For supper Santucci had mashed sardines and crumbled crackers and chopped onions and garlic and assorted spices all together and had gently roasted the mixture. To the scrapings of the pan, he added lemon juice and an egg and olive oil, mustard and cayenne and just enough flour to slightly thicken the sauce, which he spread over the sardine mixture. He had also made a salad with the radicchio and endive and leafy lettuce and a French dressing to which he had added curry. He had sliced hard sausages into wafer-thin slices and sautéed them in oil.

"It's all I could do," he said as they ate. "I had to use the mustard in the jar; I had no dry mustard. It makes a difference. It's all I could do. I'm in no mood."

"It's a good sign," Evelyn said, still eating with vigor, sucking on her fingers, swallowing wine like a Viking. "You're, like, temperamental, you know? Like an artist? Right? Like the guy who cut his ear off. Or all the movie stars? You're always hearing stuff about them. So it's, like, well, *you're* like that, Louis. Sensitive. I can understand that. It's a good sign. Just look, just look what you could do even feeling temperamental. Everything is so good. I can't remember ever eating so good as these last three days, no fooling. Someday you'll have to show me how to do it." And she ate on.

But Santucci was no longer happy.

In the still darker night Katherine sailed the *Marindor,* wheeling it like a great black palfrey. It felt good to her to be in the action of sailing. The three days of perfect weather and the nearly unaltered bearing had thinned her. Except for crossing the Gulf Stream, the boat had sailed itself, had plodded through the sea like a plowhorse, blunt and thudding. And she had sat too long with nothing to do but absorb the absurdity of the situation. The weather had been so gentle that none of the gear had shown the slightest wear, no chafe. But she was worn and chafed. Now in the night at work, she felt spiky and craggy, with angles and aspects to her again.

It was an old feeling, this alertness in the body. Not unlike what an athlete felt the moment before the game began, not fear but the embrace of purpose and the confidence of success, the feeling that she sought before she began to draw and paint, or to write poems, or to make children's books, but it was a feeling she had never found there or anywhere else in her life. Only in this sailing, in the adversarial sea. And she had given up even that over the past three years. But not now, not in this night.

Now she was certain that weather of some kind was approaching. And Barstow was also certain.

"Soon?" he said to her when she had settled down after putting the *Marindor* on its newest heading, which she carefully recorded at 2300 hours. It would be harder for her now to keep to where they were, in the dark and with the water beginning to twist and slightly curl around them, far more difficult than it had been to get here from Mystic.

"Soon?" he repeated. Again, as all along with him, his questions were not really questions so much as assertions.

"Do you know what you remind me of?" she said. "Have you ever heard of the temples at Karnak, the Egyptian temples that the pharaohs built?"

"The Sphinx?" he said. "The pyramids?"

"Right. Those pharaohs."

"No," he said. "I never heard of the temples of Karnak. Johnny Carson. He does this Karnak routine. That Karnak?"

"Sort of," she said. "That's where he got the name. But what I'm saying is that way up at the top of these huge columns in the temples of Karnak on the Nile in the middle of Egypt were statements, histories of wars that told about how the pharaohs had won one battle after another. Only it often wasn't true. The pharaohs would have it only the way they wanted it, like saying it was thus and so made it thus and so. That's what you're like."

"Me?"

"You," she said. "Everything you say is like saying it will make it the way you want it to be."

"I don't know what you're talking about. Do you think I believe I can make the weather what I want it to be by saying that?"

"Yes," she said. "That's what I think. Or nearly so. You can't make the weather do something, but you can disregard it, make the weather do what you want by acting as if it wasn't there."

"That's crazy," he said.

"Is it? You've got no room in you for what anyone else thinks or wants. No room for anything. Why stop at the weather?" She waited. The boat was full of small noises now, small but sustained as the boat worked its way into the different seas that were building.

"Maybe you're right about that," he said. She did not expect that he would answer her, that he would go on. "But it's not the same thing as the pharaohs, what you said."

"You are what you are," she said. "Nothing less, but nothing more."

"That's right," he said. "I am what I am."

"Corinthians," she reminded him, with enough sardonic irony in her tone that he should hear it, or maybe imagine more. "At the last trump,"

166

she said. "There's always more, always the possibility of change. Didn't your mother teach you that too? It's also in Corinthians. I am what I am. But what does that mean?"

"Popeye," he said.

Lucifer too, she might have said. Mephistopheles. The exact same words. But she did not want to think in literary terms about an experience that could not be mediated by poets. That, at least, is what she had discovered in Vietnam. Now, unlike Vietnam, the danger and the fear were personal, not like a universal destructiveness at all, where you could curse God and all humankind but not the single rifleman. Poetry makes nothing happen, and certainly it does not *prevent* anything from happening. Here in the night she sailed with Barstow and thought again of Joseph, who had told her all this.

She had lost all his letters, but why had she kept them in the first place? Why would she sometimes reread letters that he had written to her five or fifteen or thirty-five years ago? She had asked herself that often enough over the years to have come to a response, but not an answer.

We save ourselves by saving what we were.

"What is that?" Barstow said. He had stood suddenly, and she could see where he was looking. About two miles off, the sea glowed and shimmered in a long pulsing line, pointing like a finger. "What is it? Where is it going?"

"It's not moving, we are. It's the ridge," she said. "The light is coming from the plankton that are being washed over it. The motion ignites a kind of phosphorescence."

"Have you seen that before?"

"Yes," she said. "Usually much closer to shore, where the waves move the plankton strongly. It's very unusual this far out, but of course the ridge is not far from the turbulence it is causing. It also tells us that the turbulence is increasing. That's why it's able to move so much plankton. But it's a good sign too. If it were really getting rough, the huge raft of plankton would be dispersed. You wouldn't get the lighting action."

"So we're somewhere between good and bad," he said, and sat down.

"More good than bad," she said. "It depends upon how soon we find the airplane, how quickly Alan can get to it. Or maybe the weather will come at us sooner. Listen," she said. "Listen to me. You can't make things happen, what you want to happen."

"I know that. You keep harping on that. You think I won't know if the weather's too bad against us?"

"Yes," she said. "That's what I think."

"Well, you are absolutely wrong." And then his voice firmed up, took a grip. "What you get confused about is that I only think about one thing at a time. You think about what if the weather is good or bad, as if it matters. To me it doesn't matter. *Not now*. Maybe tomorrow, when it *is* tomorrow. When we have tomorrow's weather. Why can't you understand that? What can't *you* understand?"

"You are full of contradictions," she said.

"No," he said. "You're wrong. You are the one who doesn't understand."

They sailed on in silence; occasionally she would move to turn the ship. With the glow over the ridge, it was easier. The ship was moving up and down now, into a trough, depending upon its angle to the wind, and the glow would momentarily be lost, but she would find it again. The plankton had been unpredictable, a lucky stroke. Still, she couldn't rely on it. At any moment a deep subsurface wave could come out of the south and wash the plankton away.

"Are you going to stay up all night?" he said.

"Alan needs as much rest as he can get. Louis and the girl can't do this."

"I can do it," he said. "You should get some rest. You'll need it tomorrow too."

"And you?"

"I don't need rest."

But she said nothing.

The air was warmer, another sign of south winds coming up to them, increasingly southeasterly. Not a good sign. If it were a tropical depression, the low would circle more and more to the east. If she had been alone, the master of her ship, she would have turned for Charleston now and used the easterly winds to outrun whatever might be heading at them. But that would not be something Barstow would do: to him prudence was a plan. And she thought this, that if some time came when she would need to defend herself, her only weapon would be that she *was* the master of this ship. It was all she had, and perhaps—or certainly—it was not enough. Still, she would not squander any of it now. She would tell him nothing more than what he could see for himself.

"They're much quieter," she said to him.

"Santucci is very nervous. He's afraid he'll get seasick. And I got rid of most of the booze. I saved some champagne for celebrating when we get the disk."

"You surprise me there," she said.

"That's because you think I'm a piece of wood."

"No," she said.

"It's OK," he said. "I don't take offense. We find the disk, we all feel good. So we have a drink. It's like winning the championship of something. You squirt champagne all over. And it will help Santucci not worry too soon about getting sick. Or if he gets sicker."

"He might. The boat will get jumpy, with all this maneuvering. And in his head. He'll talk himself into it."

"I'll feed him ginger," Barstow said. "And crackers. You got enough ginger?"

She could hear Santucci jabbering below nonetheless, only now his words came in sporadic bursts, aftershocks of his exuberance. The lull of the past days had broken, and now he was falling through. He would not be able to adjust to what would happen. She did not hear Alan, perhaps he had gone to sleep, as she had advised him. From time to time, she could hear Evelyn croon something, a piece of a song or some plaint to Santucci. None of them, those below, were fit for this, or for what was going to happen. Only herself. And Barstow; to him it did not matter.

"Are you going to use the sextant tonight? You've not done any of that?" he said.

"We're as close as the sextant can get us. I'll see if there's sun tomorrow. There are no stars tonight."

"That's right," he said, looking up. "I hadn't noticed. I hadn't thought about that. No stars."

"And that annoys you, doesn't it? That you didn't notice something important?"

"What annoys me is your questions. Don't ask those kinds of questions. And the pharaoh stuff. You're getting into mumbo-jumbo, at least from my point of view. So can it, OK?" They sailed on until he said, "Tomorrow. In the inflatable. Me in the inflatable, Alan in the water. You could sail away. You could leave us."

And now she knew what had flickered through him earlier that day, and that he would tell her this so that she would trust him.

"Why would I do that?" she said.

"So you would be sure that you'd be safe."

"But Santucci? If I tried to sail away, wouldn't he shoot me before he left you?"

"What for?" Barstow said. "If he shot you, who would sail him back to land? Evelyn? He might more likely order you to leave us and just get him to land so he could take off with the two hundred thousand. He might even just as soon do that."

"So you're worried about what he might do? That he might betray you?"

"No," he said. "If I was worried about Santucci, then I'd do something about it now. Maybe I'd shoot *him*. But what I'm pointing out here, because here, *now*, is when I can do something, is that it occurs to me that you could leave us, and I want you to know that I've had that thought. That is all. *That* is what I'm doing. *That* is something. I'm making sure you know what I'm thinking."

"If I left you and Alan in the inflatable over the airplane, then surely you would both die. Alan would die. And you would die."

"Exactly," he said. "Now we are getting someplace. This is my point. Now you listen carefully to me. Good. *I can die, but you can't kill.*"

It was as if he had slapped her in the face.

"Here is what to do," she said at last. "Sail on this heading for one hour." She wrote it down on a waterproof pad by the light from the binnacle. "Then come onto this bearing for another hour. And then this third bearing. And then wake me up. At that point we'll need to get the sails over to starboard. You can't do that. It will be getting light by then. Now do this. Each time you come onto the new heading, let the mainsail out. Take the mainsheet. This line. And let it out about two feet.

Keep the mainsheet snubbed around the winch while you do this so the sail doesn't get away from you. Don't worry about the headsail, even if it flops around. And I've dropped the mizzensail. Just tend the mainsail. Do you understand all this?"

"Yes," he said. "I've been watching."

"I'm sure you have," she said. "I'm going below. Three hours of sleep will help."

But she did not sleep, not well, only fitfully. It was not that she was specifically concerned, but rather that she felt she should be. It felt wrong to sleep. An Evelyn Kinski could sleep. An Alan Sonderson. Even Louis Santucci could sleep. If she could not sleep, it was because maybe she was coming to the grand climacteric that all her life she had sought. But what kept her awake, she knew, was her anger that even now, even *now,* after all her life, she could still think in such terms. She had come no further than this. And worse. She had wasted Joe Mackenzie. All his counsel and admonition. And yet, where else could she be?

11

It was barely first light when she got out of her berth—0400 hours. The clothes she had slept in were clammy. The air was changing. The gauzelike film, the highest cirrus that had been working over them since yesterday and through the night, was dropping lower. Soon it would turn into stratus. And then into nimbus and touch the sea. The warm front was coming, and with it would come a blow. Would it be more? In September it could be much more.

Light at sea, dawn far from land over blue water, comes earlier than to the land even at the same latitude, or so it seems. Her father's idea was that a boat far out from land was as if at the top of a dome so that the horizon line, which surrounded it completely, was lower than the boat, which meant there was more sky and more light, and that is what made you think the light had come sooner or stayed longer. He said it was as if you were looking downhill, over the normal horizon of land people. As she grew older, she learned that this explanation was not accurate, but because she could not explain the earlier light, because no one else could either, she accepted it as true because she had learned from her father that sailors could know things beyond reason.

Below deck it was still dark. She turned on the lamp over the chart board and began the measurements to see if Barstow had held good to the course she had left for him to keep on his watch. She thought he would be good at that. She smiled inwardly. If there was intention in the universe, at whom was it aimed, Barstow or herself? Who had killed the albatross? She leaned back from the table and stretched and laughed aloud. Laugh before breakfast, cry before tea, her mother had always said. These fragments I have shored against my ruins. Now we come to the breaking day, she thought, and she laughed no more.

The *Marindor* had held its steady pace through the hours. From that speed now she calculated the leeward drift the boat had made as closely as she could estimate it. She computed everything twice; the margin of error had shrunk to nothing. On the chart the early evening before, she had constructed around the ridge a diamond out of the bearings she had set. These were the bearings she had given for Barstow to sail. Now she drew a second diamond over the first to see how close the two of them came. Close enough. It was her dead reckoning that would determine their course now.

She dressed for the day. It would be warmer yet, at least until the front arrived. When. If. From cottony sweats she changed into expensive Gore-Tex pants and hooded shirt. By the end of the day, they might know some weather. She would be ready at least for that.

On deck she saw Barstow working on the compass. There were more waves now than ever, still small but steeper because they were so near the shallowing rise from the ridge. The ridge was causing them, but their frequency was from energy coming from afar. From their angle she could tell where she was sailing. She saw too that he had tightened the foresail as the boat came more and more onto a reach. He had figured that out for himself.

"You've done well," she said to him. "We're not too far off, not too far off at all. I couldn't have done better." That was not true, but it was what she would tell him. "After some coffee, and in about an hour, I'll start the search. Go wake Santucci," she said to him. "Get Evelyn and Alan up here." She had put on the face of command. He started toward the hatch of the companionway. In her new clothes she seemed to have grown larger, nearly as large as Barstow, her cropped hair nearly as long as his.

"Wait," she said to him. "Wait till I bring us up on the other tack. So you don't get knocked down by the shift." He hung on to the companionway.

"Ready about," she said. Then to him, "Say 'ready' if you're ready. Then I'll know and you won't get your head knocked off or be thrown about. Of course, here in the cockpit we're well below the boom when it comes across. Nothing to worry about. Still, from here on, it's important that we understand each other. It's important that you do what I tell you to do. That's clear to you, isn't it?"

"Of course," he said.

She let the *Marindor* fall off the wind to pick up speed. The warm southerly moved the boat briskly.

"Ready about," she said.

"Ready," he said.

"Hard alee," she said, and spun the helm, and as the boom came through the eye of the wind, as the sail collapsed and slatted and the fittings all jingled and clanged, she threw off the mainsheet from where it was cleated into the traveler to let it run a little and absorb the shock but yet not lose the boat's speed. Almost instantly the boat bore down into the water and onto its new heading. She had kept it moving losing less than half a knot, and even that for only a few seconds. "Hurry along, now, Mr. Barstow. With this good wind we'll make our final turning point in less than an hour. And then we'll search. Hurry along, now. And change your clothes. Something dry. You must be very damp. And borrow suitable boat shoes from Alan. He has an extra pair. You'll be moving around a lot today. You'll want firm footing. Go along, now. Time means a lot to us from here on in."

She could not hear them below. The wind and the slap of the waves washed anything else away. A windward beat was always the direction most full of sound, but sound that could be interpreted. Her father had taught her how to close her eyes and tell her speed from the sound of the boat in the sea and from the kind of sound the gear and rigging made, and of course from the kind of pressure in the helm that a beat created. And deeper still she could feel through the boat the weather coming. And in the light she could tell that as well. And now in the taste in the air.

In different regions of the sea, air tasted different. The north was saltier than the south except in storms, when the swirl of the warm wind made the air more dense. There was more to taste in it, a greater concentration. At the helm, Katherine leaned the boat further into the sea, shouldering it in so that it began to boom, but maybe only to her own ears. She had come alert to contingency. Old knowledge shook itself free. She licked her lips and tasted storm now more certainly.

Within the hour, when she came to where she wanted to be, she dropped the mainsail down onto the deck and roughly furled it, then hauled it up just enough to lower the boom into the gallows and lash it all together. And then she began the search of the ridge. She used the mizzensail for balance like a weathervane. She had already taken down the foresail; the large yankee. She backed the cutter stays'l against the wind and put the helm far over in the opposite direction. Almost instantly the boat was heaved to. She established her headings, calculated the drift, and set a stopwatch around her neck going. On paper she had worked out the distances she would move across the ridge, shortening them each time she came back across until she would be sliding down the ridge as if on the edge of a knife.

"I don't want to do this," Evelyn whimpered. "Oh, Katherine, I really don't want to do this." But already Barstow had strapped her into the bosun's chair. "I don't even know what I'm supposed to do."

"I've told you. You look in this direction." She pointed without turning her eyes to the girl. "And you look for something shiny. You look for the airplane. Shout if you see something."

"Oh, Katherine. Please. I just can't. I just can't." The girl gripped the straps of the canvas chair and began to sob.

"You sailed your little boat to find me in the cove. You weren't afraid then, and that was far more dangerous. This isn't dangerous."

"That was different," the girl said. "I wanted to do that, to sail over to see you."

"Don't hold the chair," Katherine said. "Use your hands to keep away from the mast. You won't fall. You're strapped in. And the boat's hardly moving. Use your hands to keep from bouncing off the mast. Up," she said to Alan. "Slow and steady on the halyard. Take two turns of the halyard around that winch and keep pressure on the line," she said to Barstow, who was standing by. She had shown them both what to do. "Lively now. Lively." To Santucci she said, "Go forward to where I showed you to stand. Look down. Look for the airplane."

Already Santucci had lost his color, even though now, with the boat essentially before the wind, heaved to and barely moving, the sea was calm enough. The boat weighed down the small, steep waves, ironed them out as it slid nearly sideways over them.

"I'm not feeling so good," he said.

"We're barely moving," she said. "Go forward."

"Jesus," he said. "How did this happen to me?"

"Wait," she said to him. "Take your shoes off. If we get any water on the deck, you'll slide around in those."

"What are you talking? These are very good shoes. You know what shoes like this cost?"

"Quickly, now," she said. "Quickly. Take them off. You'll slide with them on. You'll slide off into the sea. Look at it. Is that what you want? Do it! The decks are teak. You'll like the feel of them. Take off your shoes. Take off your socks. Do it!"

"Haul," she ordered them.

Soon enough the girl was aloft. Even thirty feet above them, they could hear her whimper.

Katherine made adjustments, resetting the tension of the sail and the angle of the rudder so that the *Marindor* moved a little more quickly. And the cone became tighter. At the apex of the cone, she put the *Marindor* in irons and slipped down nearly backward along the ridge until she turned the boat across the ridge and repeated what she had done.

In two hours they found the airplane. Santucci had seen it, a glimmer. Evelyn had been useless. For two hours she had hugged the mast and kept her eyes closed. Quickly Katherine started the diesel engine and brought the boat over the wreck. It shimmered and undulated. If it had been even a few meters deeper, they might not have seen it at all, or not easily. If it had been a sunny, bright day. Or if the sea had roughened. If there is intention in the universe ... Immediately she threw markers, floats on long weighted lines, over the side of the boat.

But before they could launch the inflatable, Santucci screamed, truly screamed, in the highest tenor of fear, and awoke Evelyn, who also began to scream, a shriek.

"Oh Jesus, mother of God," Santucci shouted, even as Katherine heard the first cannonade of thunder behind her. Without even looking back, she spun the boat to face the sound. The diesel labored against the configuration of the sails and the set of the rudder. She released the wheel.

"Take the helm," she said to Barstow, but he was also stiff with wonder. "Come now, Mr. Barstow. Move along. Take the helm. Steady as she goes." She released the cutter stays'l sheet and then that sail's halyard. "Bring down that sail," she shouted forward to Santucci in the bow, but he was locked into the sight of the dark purple smear of the squall already bearing down on them, the tinge of wind, the fleck of the rain. The crack of lightning.

"Bring down the girl," she said to Alan. "Slowly. Keep the halyard around the winch." But he was frozen too. She slapped him across the back. "Go!" she said. "Slowly." It was as if all of them were caught in a tableau, dazzled stiff. It was by her that they were brought into action again; she was the principle of energy. She went forward and seized the downhaul for the cutter stays'l and hauled the sail down to the deck. Immediately the boat no longer strained against the diesel. Back in the cockpit, near the helm, she brought the diesel up to 1,800 rpm. Against the wind that would soon be on them, they would need at least that much power merely to jog in place. She checked the mizzen and brought it amidships. Already the girl was halfway down the mast. She was screaming. Unable to move, she twisted and bumped against and away from the mast. Then the rain came, even though the sight of the black smear was still far enough off to terrify. And yet thrill. Forward again, she dragged Santucci to the cutter stays'l and forced him down on it. She wanted to use him to keep the sail from blowing about. She returned to the cockpit and to the wet-locker near the stern end of it and drew out slickers.

"Put these on. Good, Mr. Barstow. Good. Steady on."

Evelyn was almost to the deck. There were some small abrasions on her arms.

"Easy now, Alan. Don't rush it. Easy." And then the girl was down.

And then they were into the squall, where the rain and the wind mixed into each other, into nothing, and nothing could be seen. She took the helm from Barstow.

"Go and help Alan get her unstrapped," she shouted into his ear over the wind. She felt certain that none of them had ever seen a black squall, and none of them had experienced such wind.

It is always better to be inside a black squall than to be looking at it. She had sympathy for Santucci and for the girl. Few spectacles are as frightening as the sight. A black squall always reminded her of a tornado, the blackness of it against the white calm on either side. Inside a squall it was a stinging gray. Inside a squall, because the wind comes so quickly, there isn't time or fetch enough for significant waves to develop. And inside a squall, if you are prepared—or if you are me, she thought—there is nothing more to do but go through it, outlast it. Ships are not lost to the sea and the wind, they are lost to land, and above all they are lost by the failure of people. But she had been here a thousand times. And it was only a squall; to her and the *Marindor* this was incidental. But from the outside, a squall is darker than invention. And it is amorphous. It is the cast of our nightmares, of chaos made immanent. Outside the squall you think to escape it, so there is hope. But inside a squall, you cannot, and so there is acceptance.

And as quickly it was gone.

As it passed beyond them, raced north, it assumed again its startling blackness. Behind it, where they were, the sea had calmed slightly. The squall had beaten it flat, had even given them a small advantage. The air also had cleared, the squall sweeping the sky clean. But it would not remain so. Katherine brought the *Marindor* back to the airplane.

"Get below," she shouted at the girl, who was still locked up but drenched and shivering. She had worn only a t-shirt. It was wet and clung to her, her breasts sculpted, the nipples protuberant as if aroused by a lover, her skin pink and glowing beneath the skim of cloth wherever it touched her. "Get below. Change." But Evelyn could not move. Alan went to help her, to take her down.

"No," Katherine said. "Go on with the inflatable. You've got only a little time now to get to it and to anchor it to the wreck. Mr. Santucci, take the girl below." But Santucci himself was frozen.

Barstow stepped toward the girl and shook her, but she didn't respond. He went forward quickly and pulled Santucci by the arm and shook him to some degree of life.

"Get below," he said. "Take her below. Change. We're here, Louis. We're here at the airplane. Now we've got to get the disk." He pushed him toward the girl.

"I'm going to die," Santucci said. "Holy Mary, mother of God," he said, and sank to his knees. He crossed himself. Barstow pulled him to his feet.

"Not yet," Barstow shouted into him. "Not yet. First you're going to get rich. After that, I don't give a shit. Move." He pushed him harder. The girl screamed.

"Evey," Alan said, "it's all right. It's going to be all right." He put his arms around her to keep her from breaking into pieces.

"It wasn't like anything before," she said at last. "It was so black. And I was up there, Alan. I was up *there*. And it was so black."

"Go below, honey. Change. Get warm. I'll be back soon. This is a piece of cake. A piece of cake." He kissed her forehead.

"It was so black, Alan. And I was *up* there. I was up *there*."

"We're over the wreck," Katherine said. "Near enough. I'll keep us over it until you launch the inflatable. Downwind, remember. In the lee of the boat. You'll get some protection. Remember what I told you. Load it slowly. Now's when things get dropped overboard. People too. Slowly. Remember to put a line around the tanks when you lower them. And check that there are no lines around your legs. Check that twice. Mr. Barstow, put on your life preserver."

In fifteen minutes they had gotten the loaded inflatable over the wreck, and Alan had dived down and secured it. Santucci and the girl were gone. Katherine eased back the throttle of the diesel, brought it down to a slowly turning five hundred rpm, the deep thump of the diesel reassuring, even the lingering exhaust reassuring. How the act redeems us, she thought.

It was good to be here on the deck alone. She kept the *Marindor* about a hundred yards from the inflatable. Barstow sat in the inflatable and waited. She thought about the squall and what it foretold. Auguries. That it would be a strong storm, now she knew. Even now, against the southern sky, she sensed the front advancing. It was not too far away. What had happened, the squall, was a confirmation. At sea, in a phenomenon not clearly understood, her father had explained how a very strong front will generate a sharp squall line as much as a hundred miles ahead of itself. Like a probing line of a massive attack. There will be the squall line even in a field of calm weather and then a field of level weather immediately after it, and then in two or three or four hours the storm. What it was or what it would be—a gale, a full gale, a tropical depression, a hurricane—she could not yet tell. Or it could variously be all of that, shifting itself. But it would punish them.

The *Marindor* shuddered. Beneath the deep churn of the slowly turning prop and the thunk of the diesel, she felt the boat respond to the hit of the new wave. These were not the local surface waves but something that had come from many miles away. And in the air was a kind of bristling. And then she saw that the color of the sky was changing, the merest tint of raw sienna. The color came from dirt, from the dust of Africa or the Yucatán. What they were going to face was a storm that had either begun in Africa or passed over the Yucatán.

A hurricane.

She had been in hurricanes before, but with her father. There was only one strategy in a boat like the *Marindor*. In the very worst of it, if it came to that, lower all sails and batten down perfectly and then lie ahull. Turn yourself into refuse. Give up to the sea and the wind. Let the storm bend you down. If you did not capsize or pitchpole, you could survive. And the *Marindor* would be good at this. Slocum had moved the boat in worse conditions around the Cape. He had sailed the *Spray* through worse than a hurricane, and alone. And for days. Now she would do this too. Sail until she could not, then lie ahull. And give herself up to the *Marindor,* her well-founded ship.

She looked across to Barstow, who had not moved. He had no idea what was coming, what he would lose and what she would win.

If only she could tell the direction of the hurricane. Then she would sail away from the dangerous quadrant. Every storm had quadrants. On a more or less northward track, the low pressure of the storm swung its energy counterclockwise. The energy entered in at the southwest quadrant and moved counterclockwise into the southeast and up into the northeast and exited in the northwest quadrant, the dangerous quadrant because that was where the great power of a hurricane was unleashed. Hurricanes that hit the land hardest hit with the dangerous quadrant, a scythe of wind and the sea driven by it, the ending crack of the whip. If she could find the main direction of the hurricane, she could try to sail as long as she could away from the dangerous quadrant.

If only he had not destroyed the electronics. Would they be here now at all? She had gotten them here as perfectly as if they had used the LORAN. But they would have heard the predictions. They would have headed into land at once. The storm had formed so quickly. Before she had sailed, she had checked the weather maps and found only the usual patterns, not particularly ominous even for September. If you did not sail against any possibilities, then you never sailed at all. And if a fast-moving storm quickly developed, you could race away from it. Even if yesterday she had made toward Charleston, she could have beaten it. She pictured again the weather maps before she had left—how long ago? on the other side of a lifetime? And she saw nothing to indicate a mid-Atlantic disturbance of this size. A storm coming up over the Yucatán was an oddity. It had been hiding out in the jungles of the Yucatán, and when it had been born into a tropical depression, it had veered into the Atlantic rather than staying in the Gulf. And because it had stayed at sea, it would have gathered power and with it speed. With a radio they would have known this. A radio would have kept them away.

Or would it? Would it have mattered to Barstow? Short of sailing into the actual storm, would merely the possibility of destruction have stopped him? He could go into a bank where there were men with guns who would shoot him; would he let the idea of a storm stop him? She could not say. He was not a fool. Perhaps, like Santucci, he lacked imagination. Maybe when he left Pocatello, Idaho, at nineteen, he had exhausted whatever ambitions he might have had for a life. Or maybe he had never had any. He had an *amoral* imagination. The thought came to her suddenly, the phrase. What a wonderful phrase! An amoral imagination from which could come only his perfect indifference to hope or plans or justice or fear. But he was no fool. Santucci was a fool. Santucci would run from nothing but would also run into anything. Barstow could not free himself to choice, he could only prevail, which did not mean that he could prevail over an event like a hurricane but that he could prevail in the act of confronting it. It was the kind of will that allowed someone to act without regard for victory or defeat or any kind of profit or gain. Or deeper than will, beyond it, he was that rarity of pure instinct bedecked in the costume of a man.

Charleston was three hundred miles due east of them. Waiting, the *Marindor* slowly circling Barstow in the inflatable, she pictured her course, the line she would draw upon the chart. She envisioned how she would set the sails, the exact shape she would give to them given the increasingly easterly winds. She accounted for the order in which she would raise them, and in what order and in what degree she would reef them, and then, as the winds strengthened, how she would drop them until at last all that would drive them would be the wind upon the masts and the cabin structure and the hull of the boat itself. She had been in many storms, some severe, and always dangerous. But she knew that she would survive this one because that is how mariners thought; the greatest concern was not dying but screwing up. Against the rogue wave that could rise up and shatter you, there was no defense; you accepted that or you did not go to sea. She thought that you were somehow born with that. And she pitied those who had never been in a storm at sea, those who soon enough would be with her in this one.

She circled Barstow. After the storm had blown over them, she would have to find where it had driven them, how far from Charleston. Perhaps they would strike off toward North Carolina, somewhere below Hatteras. They would not be able to get around Hatteras unless they sailed farther out to sea. And that would be too late for Agare. Agare. She had forgotten about him until now, even as they searched for the disk. How irrelevant he had become! After the storm, depending on where it left them, they might strike for Moorhead City, Beaufort, Georgetown, or

Cape Fear. She pictured each precisely. She had sailed into these ports, first with her father and then with the *Marindor,* all her life. After the storm, as they neared the coast, she would move to charts of smaller scale until at last she would use the harbor chart. With her eyes closed, she pictured again what she already knew. Even without the charts, once she was over soundings again, she knew that she could bring her boat safely to an anchorage.

That was what she knew. Now with her eyes opened, she looked at what she did not know. If the storm was coming in from the sea, they would escape from the dangerous quadrant. If it was coming up along the coast, then they would not. Eventually she would know this, but by then it would be knowledge that she could not use.

Where were Evelyn and Santucci? It had been nearly half an hour. But what difference did it make? There was nothing they could do now, nothing that she needed from them. Nothing she had ever needed from any of them. Over the sea, rising and falling down in the great swells that were building now, the inflatable rose up and fell into troughs. The great swells smoothed out the small vertical chopping waves caused by the ridge. The great swells would increase as the storm came closer. They would rear higher and higher until they could not hold themselves up, and then they would break and become the white rolling combers that crashed into you and did harm. The breaking waves. Even at this moment, she knew the waves that would pummel them were already racing toward the *Marindor.*

Alan surfaced and rolled into the inflatable. He signaled her to come to them. She brought them together and took a line from the inflatable.

"The whole wing is crushed up against the door," he said to her. "I've been cutting around the door, but that's not going to work. I'm going to have to try and take off the wing."

"Can you do that?" she said.

"I can do it, but it'll take more time. I might need the other tank of gas. Let's put it into the inflatable now. And a different torch head. I'm going to need more heat. Where I'm cutting, it's not just through the skin. I'm probably going to have to go through the actual structure. The other torch is right there in the red box."

"How long?" she asked.

"Can't say exactly. If I have to go all the way through, maybe an hour. But maybe once I'm mostly through, the weight will take the rest of the wing off. And I've got to watch out I don't go with it. Can you handle the tank?"

She looked around for Santucci, but he was not there.

"I think so. Yes," she said.

"I'll come back aboard," Barstow said, and hauled himself up. The two of them wheeled the tank of acetylene over to the rail. She tied it off with a rolling hitch, and after Barstow was back in the inflatable, she lowered it to him. She got the other torch head and handed it down.

"There's not much keeping the plane on the ridge, Katherine," Alan said. "When the wing does go, the plane could lose its balance and slide off." She had understood that from the start. As did Barstow. But what he was really saying was that once he was inside the airplane and searching for the disk, then it could slide down off the ridge, and it would go more quickly than he could get out. Or when he did, he would be too deep to come up without the pressure of those depths breaking him.

"Would a line around you help?" she said. "Or extra lines onto the plane tied off to the *Marindor?*" But that could make it worse.

"No," he said. "Take my chances. Earn my money." She saw that he was not afraid of this, just as she was not afraid of the storm coming at them. Just as Steven had not been frightened of his ventures.

In fifteen minutes he had resurfaced.

"It's what I thought might happen. I'm cutting off the wing, or a good part of it. And the plane is starting to shift."

"How bad?" Barstow said.

"It's hard to say," Alan said.

"So say it anyway," he said.

"It's shifting, but it might not go down. There's a secondary ledge about another five meters lower. If the plane shifts, it could still get caught up. Maybe. And I think there's maybe an air pocket still in the plane. The plane is shifting around, but more like it's floating. So what I'm going to do is take off the wing. I'll cut straight down from the top.

It will give me more of a chance if she goes. What about it, Katherine? Have I got the time? The weather, I mean."

"It doesn't matter," Barstow answered for her. "We're here. The weather doesn't matter yet. Go." For a moment Katherine thought he might push the younger man, but Alan quickly sank on his own.

Back on her patrol, she circled the inflatable. The waves had increased considerably. It was not a question of how deep the waves would go. When waves got higher at sea, unlike along shore, they also got deeper. She did not think they were ten meters deep, but already she knew that the plane would feel what was above it. She saw that Barstow waited with his hand on the slipknot that could free the inflatable from the plane in an instant, at the first sense that the plane was going down.

She circled the inflatable and turned her mind away from what she could not see. She had imagined the scene, and now she knew the situation. She thought how it was easier to face danger alone than for another. She turned away and defined her tactics. After the champagne with which they would celebrate his success.

At first she did not see Barstow waving. How long had she stared off? But then she saw him waving, and then he held up the wire basket. Alan had found the disk. She took the *Marindor* softly toward them. Slowly, now. Easy. She brought the *Marindor* near, but she did not want to close on the inflatable with her prop turning and a man somewhere below her, maybe still inside the precariously perched airplane. But now there was enough time for this, for this kind of caution. To be quick was not the same as to rush, as her father had taught her. As Joe Mackenzie had also taught her about her life. Why, when she had learned so much, could she use it only at sea? Then Alan broke the surface and pulled himself into the inflatable, and now she brought them together.

She left the helm and from over the port side took the line to the inflatable and made it fast to a belaying pin set into the rail. Still attached to its own line, Barstow tossed up the wire basket in which the case with the disk rested. The case was small, probably brushed titanium, untarnished by the seawater. She thought how small treasure chests had become since the days of Captain Kidd. How could Wyeth have romanticized this scene? Except for the *Marindor* itself.

"You're sure it's in here?" she said. But she did not care. That was not her concern.

"It's in there," Barstow said. "At least, some disk is in there. But it doesn't matter. Your friend Agare will have to pay for it, whatever it is. If it's not the right disk, then that's his problem." He was speaking to her as he climbed the ladder she had left secured, his voice growing louder as he came up and over the gunwale. His face looked black and golden, his eyes like blue marbles, like a satin matte upon porcelain, a sheen deeper in, beneath a surface. She thought that this was how he must appear when he made a robbery, sleek with a luster of victory, the achievement of booty, the mastery of circumstance. Winning a high-stakes game. Perhaps he was not so unlike Agare and his group as at first it might appear, not unlike other corporate lords. Or maybe not unlike long-distance sailors, either, who risked their lives for a paltry silver cup, or mountain climbers who clawed themselves up K-2 because they could. Maybe Barstow was like these, and the money was secondary, only an excuse to live in the intensity of *what if.*

On deck he took the case out of the wire basket and gave it to her. "Put this somewhere safe. Put it under your bed. Put it in with the money under your bed."

He looked about. She saw him think about the weather. In the inflatable he must have been thinking only of Alan searching for the case, as if he were going down to do it himself. To be certain. Only one thought at a time. Now it was time to think about the next thing, about the weather. That is the way you won. You did not plan. You did what there was to do.

"A storm is coming, right? So let's get going. Where's Santucci?" he said.

Alan shouted up, "Hey, we did it. We did it. Once I got the wing off, it was easy. I cut an opening. I didn't even bother with the door. The plane shifted, but it jammed itself into some rocks." He too was alight with his success, but his brightness haloed him; unlike Barstow, who compressed himself into a dense star, the boy-man burst out in a universalizing light. "And the bodies, you were right. Nothing left. Only the clothes waving around on the skeletons, except the skulls had come loose.

The heads were in their laps. No eyes, like you said, and no flesh, but it was weird. There was still a lot of hair left. Weird. Hair on a bone. It was kind of like a horror movie, you know. It wasn't real. I mean, it was real but not real. Wait till I tell Evey; she'll flip. Jesus, I wish I had a camera. Who will believe this? OK, let's get this gear into the boat. All right, all right, *all right. Yes!*" He raised his arms and shook his fists at the sky. "Yes!" He turned to the task.

"Forget it." Barstow went to the rail and shouted down. "Get up here. Let's get this boat moving."

"Forget it?" Alan said. "What do you mean? This is all good stuff. What do you mean forget it? This is the best gear you can get. Come on, take this tank."

"It's nothing we need now," Barstow said. "Dump it. Forget it. Let's go. Get up here."

"Now, wait a minute," Alan said, but Barstow had already turned away.

"Louis," Barstow shouted.

At the rail Katherine looked down at Alan. "Leave it," she said to him. "At least leave it for now. Come aboard. Maybe we can get it later once we're under way. Leave it. Do what he tells you."

"No way," Alan said. "The hell you say. Leave this? No way."

"Do what he says, Alan. Just do what he says." She wanted to remind him that he was expendable now, that Barstow would not need him. All Barstow needed now was her.

"I'm not leaving this gear," he said. "No way am I leaving this gear. This is the best stuff there is. This is the best stuff I've ever worked with. I'll use this in Florida; it will be terrific."

"Alan, please. Listen to me," she said down to him.

"Alan," Evelyn Kinski shouted. But barely. Katherine turned. The girl was bruised, in places bloody. Not from her descent from the mast. "Alan," she shouted more loudly, but more like a bleat. "Alan."

Did he hear her?

"Come aboard," Katherine said. "Something has happened to Evelyn." He looked up at her, and then he came quickly up out of the inflatable.

"He raped me," Evelyn said to all of them. Behind her Santucci appeared, slowly emerging from the companionway, himself beaten, scratched. "He *raped* me, the son of a bitch. He beat me up, and then he raped me."

"Now wait a minute," Santucci gasped. "Who beat you up? I didn't beat you up. Not exactly."

Already Alan was moving toward him, his black wet suit still glistening like a sea creature's skin. Katherine saw his hand go down for the knife that would have been attached to his calf muscle, but it was not there.

"Back off," Barstow said, his gun out. He stepped in front of the girl and fired past Alan's head. Then he stood quickly in back of the girl. "Tell him to stop," he said to Evelyn, "or he's dead."

But all she could say was that Santucci had raped her.

Katherine threw her arms around Alan and pulled him against her.

"You're dead," Alan shouted at Santucci. "You're dead, man. You're a dead man." Katherine felt the threat rush through his body. She held him tighter, held him back from dying, held him back from all he could not understand.

"Listen," Santucci said, "I got a story about this too. ..."

"Shut up, Louis. Shut up, you stupid son of a bitch, or I'll shoot you myself," Barstow said.

The first true wind of the storm swept through the rigging. No sails were up. They had all been brought down while Katherine maneuvered the boat around the inflatable with the diesel. Without the sails up, the rigging, waiting for use, was soft, without its tension. The wind swung through it, shaking it all. Unlike the wind song of rigging under proper stress, this was an ugly sound, only noise, no music to it, a banging and clatter.

And how could they move, each poised for his or her own battle, like armies surprised or diverted and not at attention? What was there to fight for now?

"Listen to me," Barstow said. "We're going to get this boat moving." To the girl he said, "Mrs. Dennison is going to take you to her cabin, and after the boat is going, she'll come down and help you. Do you understand?"

"He raped me, the son of a bitch," she said. Alan lurched, but Katherine held him.

"We are going to do this," Barstow said. "We've all got to realize that." Katherine listened for the tension in his voice, for his words to separate, but there was no tension in him: he was as certain of himself now as she was when she rode the *Marindor.* "Alan, you are going to go into the room up front. What, the forecastle? You're going to spend some time there until we work things out."

"I'll kill the son of a bitch," Alan said.

"Yeah?" Santucci said. "Well, maybe I'll kill you first." He had taken out his own gun. "What about that, huh? What about that? You think I got nothing to say in this matter? Is that what you think? Is that what you think?"

"Shut up, Louis," Barstow said. "Shut up, I'm telling you."

Another gust of wind came across them, and then another gust and another, and then the gusts gathered up into a single wind. The *Marindor* began to swing into the wind, to head up into it. Now the shaking of the rigging was all around them.

"I'm going to kill you, you son of a bitch, you fucking bastard," Alan said. Even with her weight against him, Katherine felt his anger begin to pull him away from her.

"You can't kill him yet, Alan," Barstow said. "We've got to do the rest of what this is all about. We're going to do what I want. You want to kill him, then kill him. But not now, not yet, not here." He looked at Katherine. "Talk to him," he said. "Explain to him."

It was Barstow again, his fundamental self. He would tell her his mind because by now he believed she would understand that he was telling her his mind, all of it, and that was as close to trust as he could come. He knew what she would tell Alan. She would tell him that Barstow would kill him before he would be stopped from delivering the disk to Agare. And Barstow knew that she would tell him it was not worth dying for, this fury; Barstow did not judge Santucci, he only did not care about Santucci or the girl or Alan. He did not even care about Agare and the disk. What he wanted was for Katherine to sail the

Marindor. Nothing would stop that. He looked at Katherine, and she understood that it was up to her to save Alan. And maybe to save them all. He could trust her to understand that.

She managed Alan down into the forecastle, but there was nothing she could say to him. From the exhilaration of the dive down to the airplane and the retrieving of the disk, the return to this human destruction was nothing that could be leveled out in their few minutes.

"Tell me about the dive," she tried. "What else did you see? What else did you have to do? How did you find the case? Tell me about it. Tell Evelyn about the skeletons without their heads." But that did no good. All of that was gone out of him. Only furious vengeance was in him.

"Did I ever tell you about Steven?" she said. "My son? Who died three years ago?"

"No," he said, forced by what she had said to respond, but could he hear her?

"Steven was my son. He died in a sea kayaking accident a little more than three years ago. He was close to your age. And I have a daughter, Sally, who's getting ready to get married in a month. I want to tell you about them, but especially about Steven. It's important to me that I tell you about Steven. About all of him, not just his death. Will you do that for me? Will you wait to hear my story? Will you stay alive for that?"

He said nothing, but she felt his body accept her. Now she could say more.

"I can't tell you now. It will have to wait. I've got to get us back to land. We've got to live so you can hear my story, OK?"

Still he was silent.

"You've got to say it," she said to him. She waited. He would not look at her, as if to look at anyone would be too painful because he would have to give up his anger if he looked away from it, but at last he did say it. "I'll wait," he said. "But I'll get him."

"There's something else. Evelyn will need you now. More than ever, she'll need you. You understand what I'm saying? Will you love her? At first she'll think that you'll not love her anymore. If you still love her, then first you've got to think about that. Revenge is something else. The love has to come first. Revenge is for yourself; love is for her. What do you want now, love or revenge? Choose love, Alan. Choose love and stay alive for both of you."

Now he turned and looked at her. Now he could look at her.

"I'm going to kill the son of a bitch," he said. "But not yet."

"Good," she said. "Now I'm going to bring Evelyn here and lock you up, and you take care of her. And after the boat is going well, I'll come and sit with you and talk to both of you and tell you Steven's story."

"Yeah. OK."

In her cabin she cleaned the girl and tended to her and murmured, but whatever she said was not important. That she was there with her was enough. She put her into the sweats she had first given her when Evelyn had swum across to the *Marindor* when her own boat had sunk. Then she put her into the forecastle with Alan and locked them in.

On deck she moved firmly. The wind was strengthening, which was good, at least for now. She could use all of this wind. With the diesel she kept the boat straight into the wind so she could raise all the sails. The strong wind slatted the sails as the *Marindor* pranced and shook. There was too much noise for anyone to hear, but it did not matter. She put Barstow at the helm and told him to keep into the wind, and then she brought all her well-designed contrivances into play, all that Slocum had devised for the *Spray* that had helped him sail her alone around the world, all that Culler had incorporated and added to this child of the *Spray,* and what she herself had invented as well. She had sailed the *Marindor* far longer than Slocum had sailed the *Spray,* and even longer than Culler had sailed and lived aboard. She needed no help in sailing this boat. But now she would have to save them all.

At last she reined in the mainsheet and the mizzensheet and the sheets of the two foresails and turned the *Marindor* before the wind. With one last shuddering heave, the *Marindor* took the wind and moved and in less than a minute was at hull speed and beyond. And silent. All that could be heard was the sea through which they swiftly passed.

She took the helm back and set Barstow the task of doubling the lashings down on everything that required it. It would occupy him, keep him away from anything else he might be thinking. He had gone into the inflatable when she was below with Alan and had thrown everything in it into the sea. Now the inflatable streamed along with the *Marindor,* not on a long line in the wake but tight to the port side. "Bring that in," she told him, but he would need help. She would not include Santucci, but Barstow did. The two of them got the inflatable aboard. Then she motioned him to her at the helm.

"Deflate it," she said. He stood there. It was not his decision to deflate the raft. He might use it. He waited for her to understand him. Trust.

"It wouldn't do you any good in seas like this and what we're going to face. That's what you're thinking. It's not a life raft, it's an inflatable. You wouldn't last two minutes in what we're going to go through. Deflate it. If you don't, then the wind can get under it and blow it around the deck. It could be dangerous."

"I'll get rid of it. I'll throw it over the side."

"No," she said. "Do what I tell you to do. I can't be explaining everything I tell you. I might need it to use as a sea anchor, like a drogue. Don't argue with me. Do what I tell you." The *Marindor* had outsped a following sea; now it had slipped off it, then fell back heavily. The sails shook the wind out of themselves for a few moments and then snapped back sharply under pressure. The entire boat shuddered. "Damn you," she said to him. He had distracted her. She turned to examine the sea behind her. It was starting to crosshatch itself, the wind itself becoming confused, but soon it would not be confused, and then it would strengthen more. She put the dominant wind onto her quarter until the wind got straight. "Damn you," she said. "Do what I tell you."

"Yes," he said.

She described the valves on the inflatable and how to open them. She pointed out where on the forward deck he should take the flattened skin and how to fold it and how to tie it down.

Sometimes she could see him working at tying down.

"You can't tie a knot worth anything," she said to him when he had finished and was standing with her in the cockpit.

"I'm not a sailor, that's for sure, but nothing will come loose," he said.

"That's the problem," she said. "You want a knot that won't come loose until you want it to come loose. What you tied, we'll have to cut everything free when the time comes."

"And when is that?" he asked.

"Why, Mr. Barstow, I do believe you asked a question." But she did not push him; he had no levity in him. And his contradictions would not matter to him either.

She explained their situation. They had three hundred miles to go to the South Carolina coast, and they were going quickly now, but when the storm caught them, then she would have to drop the sails one by one until there were only bare spars and eventually wait for the storm to pass. That would depend upon the direction and the speed of the storm. "You can't tell that from the storm itself once you are inside it," she explained. You could only read that from the eye of the storm, which she felt certain would not get to them. They would not get that far into the storm. "But once we are in the storm, you cannot tell anything at all. If we had a radio, we could tell more. But by now it's too late anyway. We're heading westward. Toward land."

"So if we don't sink, eventually we get there. Somewhere," he said.

"Right. Then I figure out where is somewhere and where to go from there. And we won't sink. Boats like the *Marindor* don't sink. And I won't let it sink. We'll get to land. In fact, maybe our greater problem is if we get to land too soon. If we get to land with the storm, then we'll have the worst problem of all."

"What's that?"

"If the storm is driving us, it will drive us right up onto the land. We'll smash to pieces. What we hope is that the storm runs over us. By the time we get into the storm, it is bad enough; then there is no more sailing to be done, only waiting it out. Lying ahull, it's called, Mr. Barstow. We drop all the sails and just wait. We'll be nearly on our beam ends—on our side. And then you'll know what suffering is."

"I know what it is," he said. "It's like solitary in prison. Just lying there."

She glanced up again and again at the sails and astern. The cross-hatching was disappearing. All the waves were running together now, and the wind was well over thirty knots, with higher gusts. The sea was turning white.

Her tactic now was to ride on the solid cushion of wind the prevailing force was creating. It was like surfing. The power of the storm-generated wind was compressing the air it was moving into, making a kind of thick band. Eventually the storm wind would scatter it, probably in an hour or two when the wind could get over forty knots, but until it did she could use the cushion to move them straight and quickly. Before that she would reef the sails, and then she would continue to shorten sail as the wind strengthened. She should reef even sooner, but she wanted to move as quickly as she could and as far as possible. She would take the chance. By forty knots and before the storm completely enclosed them, she would have the last chance to determine the direction in which the storm was moving, and moving them.

"Now," she said, "I want you to take the helm. But we're before the wind, so you have to be careful of a jibe. You've got to be very careful not to get the wind behind the sails. I explained this a little before, but not in wind like this. I'll put the wind a little more over our starboard quarter." And she did so. "The boat is boring in a little deeper now; you can feel that, right? But that's OK for now. You keep us here. Don't bother with the compass. Don't even look at the compass. Look at your sails. If they start to slack, especially the foresail, then turn further into the wind. Turn this way, to port. Got it? This is very important. We're on the very edge now, over the edge, in fact." Already she had to shout to be heard. "Don't let the wind get on the other side of the sails. I've got to do some navigating below. And I want to check on your knots. And on the *Ark*." She pointed to the boat secured over the transom. "Keep Santucci out of the cabin. Make him stay on deck." She pointed to Santucci, who had sunk down with his back braced against the bulkhead of the forward cabin. Already he was beginning to sicken. "And concentrate. Before the wind like this, you really must keep the wind where it is. Don't let us jibe."

The *Ark* was the name she had given to the fourteen-foot boat she kept on davits, the deep, strong boat that Joe had built for her soon after she had acquired the *Marindor*. She had secured it as if the *Ark* were only one more piece of the *Marindor,* even though she could launch it in minutes. She went to it and saw that all was well.

Below decks she plotted their position as best she could and what they might expect, or at least hope for. She still could not read the absolute direction of the storm, what quadrant they would be in. She might never know that for certain. And of course Barstow would not know. But by now, she thought, it could not matter much. If there was intention in the universe ... Already the boat was moving more quickly, being pushed down. Soon she would have to take the helm back from Barstow. He would not know what to do.

And the people in the forecastle, they would have to wait a while longer.

Back on deck she patrolled the boat, looking at everything, every bolt and lanyard and shackle, every fitting. The smallest failure now could be amplified a hundred times. The smallest failure, the breaking of a quarter inch of a steel becket, could bring disaster. But she was as confident as she dared be. However much else in her life she had neglected, she had never neglected the *Marindor.*

She pulled and tugged and made adjustments as she moved easily enough around the canted boat. Before the wind, even with it on the quarter, the boat was sailing fairly flat. She went around it twice. She read strengths. Only strengths. Other than fittings and lines, which she had always promptly attended to, there were no weaknesses in the *Marindor.* Only in people.

She had tried to avoid thinking of Alan and Evelyn. But mostly now she avoided thinking about the day or two or three or even more of them all living down below, in the terrible motion, when even the wholesome *Marindor* would begin to stink. Now she wished that she could be like Barstow. She would have preferred solitary confinement.

But in the cockpit, he surprised her again. He *did* think about the days to come; the difference was that he did not care about what he was thinking in the way she did. First he had asked a substantive question. And now this.

"We'll have to leave them in the front. Locked in," he said.

"It's the worst place to be, the forecastle," she said. "In the old sailing ships, that's where the crew lived. The officers lived amidship. The captain lived in the stern. That's where the ship is most stable, the least motion. Before the mast is where it's least stable. If you leave them in there all the time, they'll suffer terribly." The wind was blowing more strongly; she could tell by how much more she had to shout to him. Later, far beyond a full gale, no one on deck would be able to hear another at all, but by then no one would be on deck. "Why not put Santucci in the forecastle? He will be useless." Through the past hour, Santucci had sat apart, wrapped in his clothing, already in descent.

"Santucci, he's going to suffer terribly too," Barstow said.

"Do you expect me to care about that?" she said.

But he did not care what she felt or thought about either the people he was going to lock up in the forecastle or Santucci, or about the suffering any of them were going to endure. They were all going to suffer, who or how much or more or less did not matter because it could not matter. There were no alternatives.

"Santucci is not good at suffering. Look at him," he said.

In front of them, supine on the deck behind the forward cabin, in Evelyn's expensive rain gear, he stretched out as white as the sails, whiter, for the sails had dampened down into gray.

"So?"

"So you can never know what someone like Santucci is likely to do."

"Like what?" she said.

"I have no idea. Santucci, he's good to have in a robbery. You take care of him, and he does what he's told. But alone, he gets confused. There is nothing in his head. Right now he has nothing in his head. He's not thinking about opening his restaurant, that's for sure."

"So what is your point?"

"I don't know yet. Except this. I can tell you this. It's just you and me left to do anything. You are right, Santucci is worthless, and Alan isn't coming out of the front room—the forecastle. You're going to have to sleep. Even me, eventually even me, I'll have to sleep. So figure out how that's going to work."

Then he left her, maybe because he recognized that unlike him, people like her did need to think about what was coming, and she could and he would not. He could not.

But there was nothing for her to think about. Only the next wave and the increasing weight of the wind. Only about when she would have to shorten sail again. Even now she was well beyond what sail she should have up.

She stayed at the helm until 1800 hours. The wind had turned into one solid thrust. It was mounting, but it was not gusting, which was good. The gusting was what could hurt you most. Now the wind was steady, and it was blowing away the crests of the waves and scattering the water like buckshot. At 1800 hours she brought in almost all the sail. To do that she had to get rid of the wind behind them. She brought the boat onto its beam and hauled the sails. It was a difficult maneuver. But there was nothing she could not do. And by now the wind was backing farther to the east, giving her a slight advantage. She signaled Barstow, who was at the helm, what to do as she managed the sheets herself. Then she set the self-steering, and she and Barstow went below. All this time Santucci lay on the deck, sheltered by the cabin. Now she jostled him and motioned him below too.

Below, she took off her outer gear and put it in a special hanging locker at the bottom of the companionway. "Keep the wet slickers in here. It will help to keep the rest of the cabin a little drier." But Santucci pushed by her and slumped down as soon as he could.

"We've got to think about eating," she said to Barstow.

"I'm not hungry," he said.

"It doesn't matter," she said. "You'll lose strength. And you'll lose heat without food. The heat is more important. You eat because you must. You eat because I say so; it's part of running a storm. Just help me open some cans. We can make a slop in one kettle and heat it while we can. Later we'll just eat it cold. Bread too. I've got bread in cans. And other tricks."

They set to work. She got the food warm enough on the gimbaled stove. She ladled it out into thick plastic bowls. Santucci refused, and neither she nor Barstow pressed him. Then she started toward the forecastle. Barstow stood up.

"They've got to eat," she said.

He did not agree. In the forecastle, locked in, they were not a problem. "They don't need heat," he said.

"I'm going to bring them food."

He did not want her to do that, but he could not stop her. Now he could not stop her from doing anything at all.

Now, and at last again, she was the master of the *Marindor* and in command.

In the forecastle she gave them the warm food and bread, oranges, and candy. Even a bottle of wine she had kept in her cabin. It was not yet as cold in the forecastle as it would become. They had enough light. They lay in each other's arms. She wanted to make promises to them, but she could not. Not now, not yet. Perhaps later, when they would all need promises. And at this moment, they did not need her. She said she would come back later and sit with them.

In the night, about 0200, the full storm caught them. She had slept a little. Now she was awake. She would not be able to sleep for a long time now.

From about 2100 the rain had come hard, and now the wind. Earlier she had taken in the yankee jib and the mizzensail and had put three deep reefs in the main, as much of the main as she could shorten. She would take the chance that she was sailing across the face of the storm and that therefore a quicker passage was to her advantage. If she was right, in two days she might get them to the coast, where there could be lessening wind and a chance to jog back offshore until she could move with some control to whatever harbor she might be able to find. If the storm was dead astern, then in an hour she would know that better, and then she would quickly drop the main completely. Then she would raise the small storm stays'l. Or else replace that sail with a tiny storm trys'l. Already the *Marindor* was beginning to hobbyhorse. She was pushing the boat too hard. But she understood what the *Marindor* could do, what her margins were, and she remembered how her father had told her that a boat would always tell you if it was unhappy. She would rather not work the sails in the darkness if she could avoid that. She could do it if she must. In an hour she would know if she could take one more hour of this wind until there was more light, or as much light as there was likely to be. The *Marindor* would abide for a time, for an hour or two more. Now she could only wait.

Santucci had already started to dissolve. He was shivering intensely. The warm air before the storm had nearly all been dissipated, and rain at sea was always cold.

"All I'm trying to say is that there is more to this. It wasn't nothing like rape. It wasn't like she wasn't looking for something. She was wet and scared, so I helped her. And this is what I get, you know what I mean? Jesus," he said to Katherine, "you got any heat in this place?" She did not know how long he had been talking. Barstow appeared not to hear him.

"In a few hours when the boat is on its main course, I'll make a fire in the stove." She pointed to the stove. "You can go up to the lazaret and bring down the coal."

"Not me. No fucking way. I'm not going up there." He pointed up.

"Then there won't be a fire, will there?" she said.

"This girl, see, I'm rubbing her dry. I'm taking care of her. She's in terrible shape. She's scared shitless. I put my arms around her, you know, to get her warm, to make her feel it's OK? You know? Like I'm saying you're safe now?" A spasm snapped through him. "Jesus, Barstow. You see what you got us into? I think I'm going to be very sick again."

She brought him a bucket.

"Keep this with you," she said. He bent over and retched out nothing. He began to shiver and spasm. It was as if he had shriveled as well, grown smaller. "How long is this going to go on?" he said. "When are we out of this?"

"I can't say. Two or three days, maybe more."

He did not answer that because he could not, she thought. Barstow was right about him; Santucci's mind was going everywhere at once. He was breaking down.

Barstow sat still. He would not respond to Santucci, who had begun to babble now, wildly justifying, blaming the girl, blaming Katherine for making her go up the mast. Images of the girl's flesh spurted out of him as he conflated his suffering with her, blaming her for what was happening to him now as if her accusation had somehow made the storm.

"That miserable cunt. The miserable fucking cunt. Nothing but trouble. I just knew it. You know how you know some things, so this is something I knew. And now we are on this fucking boat ... fucking boat ... fucking boat. Where's my money, Barstow? I want to see my money. Where is it?"

Barstow pointed to the forecastle. Santucci tried to struggle to his feet, but he could not.

"You gave them my money? You put the money in with them nutcakes? What the fuck is wrong with you, Barstow? I'm getting my money." He reached for the gun strapped into his ankle holster, but it was gone.

"Where's my gun?" He looked at Katherine. Then at Barstow.

"I've got it," Barstow said. "You don't need a gun. I've got your gun." He stood up. "I'm going to get you some coal, Louis."

12

At 0300 hours she knew that the time had come to make all her decisions. The storm was coming from behind them. They would be in the dangerous quadrant. All she could do now was stay in front of the wind as long as she could. She explained this to Barstow, and then at 0400 she went up on deck. He said he would help her, but she pointed to Santucci.

"What?" he said.

"I don't know what," she said. "You tell me."

"Louis is nothing right now. Later, maybe, when he feels so bad he'll really want to die. So what will he do; what can he do?"

"He could try to get his money."

"He won't. Not without his gun."

She had just enough sail with the storm stays'l to keep the stern of the *Marindor* into the wind and the following seas. She would lash the rudder tightly amidship. There was no longer enough purchase on the sea that the rudder could make; whatever steerage way they had was overcome by the seas that were driving by now faster than the *Marindor.* The small storm stays'l would be just enough to keep them from turning the beam across the waves. That time would come, she knew. But now she decided to use the storm trys'l instead.

On deck she snapped herself into the safety harness and hooked it up to the safety lines that ran fore and aft. She showed Barstow what she was doing, what to do. She showed him how to move down the deck or across it while staying hooked up. He was on deck with her, but she did all the work, although she showed him what she was doing and how to do it himself. It was what he would want to know. And she wanted him to know so he would understand that he could not do it himself, though she could, so he would know that he was helpless. That on this boat only she was not helpless. *That* he could trust.

Once again below, she started a fire in the coal-burning stove. It would not drive the increasing cold away but would slightly dull it, and it would make some warmth. Santucci had already crawled toward it.

"Nothing much more to do now," she said to Barstow. "Not for a while." And so they sat in the buck and heave of the boat as it rose up and surfed and then slid down into a following trough, but sometimes it would fall off a wave into a hole in the sea, and it would hit hard, shaking everything badly. It was like falling off a two-story building, she told him. She told him how off the west coast of Africa there were holes in the sea so great that sometimes supertankers would fall into one and break in half and sink in two minutes.

"They should go around," he said. "They should avoid that area."

"Many do. Most do," she told him. "But it's the shortest route. You can save thousands and thousands of dollars by going the shortest way in those supertankers. They cost a fortune to run. The fuel oil. A pretty irony. Twenty million gallons of crude in their tanks, and the price of the fuel oil is a problem. Not crew. They run those tankers more and more by electronics. Maybe only half a dozen men, a captain, and a cook. That's all it takes. Docking gets a little more complicated. But someday soon it's going to be all computers and satellite navigational systems."

"But not on your boat," he said.

"No," she said. "Me and the *Marindor,* we're too old to change too much. And look how well we've managed without."

And then they were silent for an hour.

As soon as it happened, she knew what had happened. The *Marindor* canted sharply and rolled down into the sea as if it would roll over. The small storm trys'l had blown away and the *Marindor* had given herself to the sea like a piece of flotsam. They were ahull now, and nothing would serve them except the durability of the boat.

Santucci began a low, moaning howl. He crawled back to them.

"We're sinking." He looked up from the cabin sole, a slithering creature.

"No," she said to him. "Not even close."

But it was no use to him. Her words were beyond him, all words, nearly all comprehension. He crawled back toward the stove.

Few motions are worse than a boat, bare poles, lying ahull in a storm. On its beam ends, it rises and falls and rolls with every wave even as it is twisted and pitched. It is moving in three axises at the same time.

There was a hammering from the forecastle. Barstow became alert. Katherine went to the bulkhead.

"What happened?" Alan shouted through. With her ear close, she thought she could hear Evelyn crying.

"Lying ahull," Katherine shouted through the door. "Nothing to worry about."

"We've got to pee," Alan shouted.

"They've got to pee," she relayed to Barstow. He stood and braced against the deep rolling cant of the boat. His gun was in his hand.

"Let them out, one at a time, to use the john. Head."

"You can't use the head in this sort of sea. The outlet is underwater. You need a bucket."

"Good," he said. "Give them a bucket and let them stay in there."

She would not confront him yet. Let him absorb the situation. Let him arrive at his conclusions.

She took the plastic bucket that Santucci had used earlier. There was little left in it, only a little mucus. Whatever he had retched had spilled out. At the forecastle she opened the door and explained. When they handed out the bucket, she took it to the galley sink, high now on the port side of the boat, and poured. She went back to them and entered.

The forecastle was warmer than the main cabin. Their bodies were heating the space. They had vomited.

"Listen to me. I know it's hard to believe, but we are going to get through this storm. You've got to believe me. Believe *in* me." But she thought they had passed beyond one level of fear into another, where the fear of death was replaced by the purity of suffering. She had seen it before in Vietnam. She had experienced it herself there in the bunkers, where the relentless thump of the artillery shells coming in became a rhythm to which you could actually sleep, and you pushed yourself down so deeply that you no longer existed here. So she would not disturb them where they were, where they were going. She would not tell them about Steven. Let them use their suffering to escape. They were better off in here than they would be in the main cabin, where Barstow and Santucci and their unbearable presence would bear constantly upon them.

She went up onto the deck to check on the sail that had blown away. It was gone except for a thin strip where it had been hanked onto the stay. The halyard had been keep taut by that. Good. It was not flinging about. Everywhere the sea was white and breaking. She thought now that the wind was above sixty knots, but because the *Marindor* was so far over on its beam, its masts and rigging were low and the wind could have less purchase on them. The wind was blowing on the hull. Some of the waves were forty feet high, but they would not roll the *Marindor*. She would not capsize. Mostly the hull rose and subsided with the waves, less punished than when it was going forward. Now the pressure was not directly on the keel except when a breaking wave caught her upright, and then the sea crashed against the entire side of the hull. If you stared at it, the sea annihilated everything in the fundamental catastrophe. This is what it must have been like at the beginning of time.

She went below and tightened the hatch completely. She would not go above decks now until the storm had passed over them or the force of the quadrant had flung them outward, out of it and toward a reckless shore.

In both cabins she settled down whatever had been displaced. Not much. She thought that in her passing years at sea she must have read every book on voyaging ever written, and it surprised her and even made her angry how so many accounts described the cabin coming apart in the worst storms. Pots and pans and cans and books and clothing and even electronic equipment—everything that wasn't nailed, screwed, strapped down—would fly about. The mess the narrator would bemoan. The loss of important things, the depression of cleaning up what had spilled or been broken, and the difficulty of doing it under raging conditions. But surely, Katherine had thought in her chagrin, these people going to sea were certain that they might eventually be in harm's way; they could have anticipated and prepared. Would prepare. It was not a difficult thing to do, and she had done it. All her cabinets were secured so that they could not spring open. And anything that could move about had a place that could lock it down. Even the coal scuttle had a lid that locked down. And now, even though lying on its beam and rolling, the *Marindor* was an orderly ship, just as Slocum's *Spray* had always been neat and tidy. Except for the inescapable dirt— the ashes from the stove, the general damp scum of confinement, the whiff of backdraft of diesel exhaust, the inevitable seepage on even the tightest boat from the decks when they were awash. But the Marindor was well contained.

Then through what was left of the day and through the night there was nothing but the long and endless motion before the wind and through the sea. Wallowed as deeply as the boat was, the motion, though constant, was not violent even in the midst of the violence of the storm. The motion described a kind of three-dimensional parabola. But some-times the boat would lurch and fall down and everything in it would be shocked and would quake, the boat falling into a hole, the crash. At that Santucci would moan loudly. Now all they could do was sit or lie down and wait. For Katherine the worst part of lying ahull was not a thrum-ming anxiety of destruction and death but having nothing to do.

From the beginning, long before the storm, in the sunny days and languorous nights of absurdity as she carried them swiftly down to the Carolina Canyon, she had periodically run the diesel in order to charge the batteries that would give them light, and this she continued to do. And now, as well, she was running pumps in the bilge off the batteries and a small generator especially for that purpose. Only the port side pump, where whatever water there was would gather with the boat in this attitude.

She had taken off all her clothes and dried herself and put on dry things. She wrung out what moisture there was and put the clothing near the stove, in a kind of open basket over it. What had salt in it would not dry completely until it was washed in fresh water.

She brought food to the people in the forecastle and took out their bucket and dumped it. Barstow had sat up when she unlocked the door.

"Do you think they will try to escape? Where would they go?" she said to him.

"I'm just ready for whatever can happen."

She pulled Santucci high up to the windward side of the boat. He seemed barely awake, as if he were fighting himself down into unconsciousness. She placed her hands on him, his head, under his sweater and Evelyn's slicker, which he still wore. He was very cold, colder than he needed to be even under these circumstances. The *Marindor* was cold but mostly from dampness. It was endurable, but it was threatening Santucci.

"He's not in good shape," she said to Barstow. "Maybe if you could rouse him, get him to eat something."

"Louis," he said to the slumped man, "can you hear me? You've got to eat something. I've got some bread here. I'll put some jam on it." Santucci turned toward the voice but shook his head, and then he fell back upon himself. He had ventured too far. There had not been much to him, and now he had gone too far beyond that. She had also seen this in Vietnam, a soul slipping away.

She ate some thick slices of bread on which she had spread deviled ham. She opened a can of lima beans and ate them cold. It was food much like what she had brought into the forecastle. The *Marindor* had a sizable electric refrigerator, but in the storm she had turned it off. Most of the food would keep. She also had a very large ice locker in which she kept less perishable things. The ice was all gone, but enough of the cold had stayed to do some good. From it she took out carrots and a handful of lettuce. She offered Barstow some of what she was eating, and he took it.

"I'm going to sleep," she said. She got into her berth and went to sleep. She had been in storms before with her father, some as severe as this one. And fifteen years ago, she and Tom and the children had been caught well off to the east of Nantucket in a fierce storm that she could not dodge or outrun. And they had lain ahull. They were all good sailors, good at being in boats. But bad storms need comfort even more than skill. Then she had had to keep herself moving, always doing something. Cooking real food even with the boat on its beam ends, working against

206

necessity. Assigning tasks. Taking them out of whatever terror might seed itself and germinate. And it had been a fast storm, over in less than twenty-four hours. When it had all passed and a good sun had come up and they were arranged and scudding before a good wind toward Owl's Head, she had assembled them on deck and turned up the music and ordered them into a prancing jig. She had explained that it was the way to thank Poseidon, who loved a good dance as much as the next god. It had been a fine hour for her, and some of that elation, or at least the memory of it, came back now to touch her a little. Storms pass.

But now there was nothing more to do. This was a longer storm, probably a tropical depression that had risen to the lower edge of hurricane. The barometer had gone well down into that range. Every two hours she would check the compass and extend a line on the chart from where she had last imagined them to be. She looked to see if she could find some pattern. They were being blown to the northwest, as she had expected. What she hoped for was at some point to find that they had been turned more toward the west-southwest, which would mean that the quadrant was swinging away from them and might sling them out of its grip the way a spaceship might be flung away from a planet by its gravity. But if the quadrant held them and took them with it, then there would be nothing more she could do than what she could do now. Nothing.

She gave herself up to the sea as the *Marindor* had given herself up. As she drifted down into sleep, she tried to think about what had befallen her, but she could not. Where would she start? Where had she begun? Surely long before she had been seduced by Agare. But when? There was no isolated event. Inside the box was always another box. She wanted to think about Joe Mackenzie and about the structures he had spoken about and written about that had always, all her life, been just out of her reach. But she could not think. More than fatigue prevented her; the time, she thought, even now, has not yet come to think about infinite schemes. Even now, she had not come far enough to know anything.

Earlier, in the afternoon, lying in the main cabin, she had looked up through the thick, steel-mesh-reinforced glass in the doghouse that sat atop the forward cabin. Once she had thought to replace it with Plexiglas, which might have been stronger, but the idea had violated her sense of the *Marindor.* Slocum had sailed around the Horn in worse than this with glass not even as strong. And Culler had lived with it for twenty years.

In the long afternoon, she had lain beneath the glass with the pitch and roll of the boat in her and watched water race over the glass and then fall off, rush and fall. Often the movement of the water across the skylight was the rhythm of the boat. It brought her into harmony. That is what she thought about now, and then she slept.

At 0600 hours she felt the pump stop, and it brought her awake. Sailing, especially under this stress, was like a context. Nothing made a specific difference unless it was suddenly not present. But there was no great urgency. She dressed in the increasing cold and darkness. From a below-decks station, she checked some gauges. The batteries were reading well. And the muffled clatter of the generator continued. There was no indication of an electrical failure or burnout in the pump. Even if there had been, if the pump was badly broken down, she could run a piece of flexible tubing to the starboard pump and use it. Or even repair the pump. She had replacement parts for everything on the boat. And the skill. She thought maybe something had clogged the pump and it had shut itself down, as it was supposed to do. It was something she would be able to fix. Something to do.

In the main cabin, Barstow was working at making coffee. He had gotten the galley stove lit, but he was having trouble keeping the kettle from sliding off. She showed him the special fittings on the side rail used for just that purpose. Santucci seemed not to have moved through the night. Occasionally she could hear him murmur, the sound rising and falling like a chant.

"What is he saying?" she said to Barstow. His face, his skin now, was more unusual than ever. He had stubble, but it did not grow where his skin had been fractured. Now the lines, the dendritic pattern, were even more pronounced, even as he had otherwise whitened. The salt in the air leached color out of everything, brined the skin as it had brined the beef in the barrels of the ships that sailed two hundred years before. The image of the sun-darkened sailor was not true of the older sailors and fishermen of the northwest Atlantic, the fishermen of the bleak fishing villages of Nova Scotia and Labrador. They were often as white as the flesh of the cod they hunted. When they were young, the cold would make them red as the blood rushed to warm them, but as they grew old, if they lived to grow old, the vessels would break and restrict and disappear, and then they would turn white.

"He's praying," Barstow said. "Sort of. Holy Mary, mother of God. Over and over. It's like in prison. You hear that sometimes."

"There are cans of fruit I'll open. Do you want some? And I'll open more bread. I think I can heat up some canned stew. We're holding steady enough. I've got to get some food to Alan and Evelyn." She went to work, gauging herself against the shift of the boat, riding it, her body flexing, but she was born to this.

"I was good in prison," he said. "You don't like it. But some guys do like it; it's the closest to a society that they've ever had. They even get to like the food. I didn't like prison, but I could do it." He stretched. "Louis, he wasn't in prison much, but it was all a very bad time for him. He told me about it."

"But this is worse for him?" she said. "Worse than prison?"

"Much worse," he said. He stretched again.

"You slept," she said.

"I slept good. I never said I didn't sleep. I said I didn't need to sleep. I didn't need much of it."

"And what do you need?" she said.

"Right now, what I need is to pee."

She took out a special bracket made to hold coffee cups in bad seas. She measured out the instant coffee.

"Two big spoons for me," he said as he came out of the head with the bucket. A larger wave shifted them so that they both sought handholds. Santucci's cry rose up into a small scream. There was banging on the forecastle door. Katherine went to it. "I'll open it soon. I'm making you some coffee. And some stew. Some fruit and bread." She returned to the galley. The water had started to boil. He poured.

It took her four trips to get the food into the forecastle. Each time Barstow turned to watch. Ready. Then she took her own fruit and coffee and bread and stew and ate it quickly.

She told him that she was going to go down into the bilge to inspect the pump. The boat was riding more deeply than she wanted. The increased mass had brought it up a little straighter, and the motion had lessened. That was because there was water in the bilge, she explained, like ballast.

"So why not leave it?" he said. "It makes us more comfortable, so why not leave it?"

"Because sooner or later the water becomes too much water, and if water in the bilge starts to move around, then it can pound you from the inside out. It can do more damage than from the waves. A boat is built to take pressure from the outside, but not from the inside. And you also want to know where the water is coming from. Or the water can get to the batteries."

"You know what you're doing," he said.

"I certainly do," she said.

"Me too," he said. "I know what I'm doing."

Santucci screamed louder: "Holy Mary, mother of God."

But if there is intention in the universe?

She put on bilge clothes, the worst of things. There was no dirtier work, and there was no use in using clothes against it. In the bilge, shining a powerful flashlight, she saw that there was more water than she had expected. She saw why. A seam high up above the garboard plank had started to weep. It was above the water, and that was good. But the pounding of the seas had opened it just enough so that waves, when they did break full that high on the hull, forced water in. It was not unusual. Wood hulls all made a certain amount of water. However tightly built, a wood hull was nonetheless a flexible structure. One reason it could take so much punishment was that it *did* move by infinitely small fractions, giving way a little, absorbing the blows of the waves. The water in the bilge had drowned the pump, but she could deal with that later. For now she would work in some caulking where the seam seemed to spring most. She rested her hand at that point and ran it down the plank for about eight feet. Yes. She could feel it. As if her hand were on the flesh of a great animal. The thick oak ribs like the ribs of a great whale, and though she kept her bilge exceedingly clean, still it was a bilge and had its stench, however slight in

210

the *Marindor.* While below, she made up the connection to the starboard pump and set it going. She saw that it could outrace the leak. She would go up and make a proposition to Barstow, though it would actually be a demand. She wanted Alan to come down into the bilge with her to hold the flashlight while she caulked the seam. Then, if possible, she would go above and raise a small foresail and try to flip the boat. Alan would be at the helm, and as she raised the foresail, he would turn into the wind and the *Marindor* would come about and fall down, get knocked down, onto its other side. Then she could get to the port side pump and get it fixed. And she could also inspect the seams on that side of the boat. That side had been hull down in the sea for nearly two days, actually more. Some water could be making through it. The maneuver might not work. There might still be too much wind, but if she picked her moment, she might be able to do it. She would herself drag Santucci into her cabin out of sight. Evelyn she would keep locked in the forecastle.

She felt the possibility of affect surge in her. Even as her hands worked surely on the thin line of thread that she hammered into the seam and spread some flexible sealant over, she pictured what she would do on deck. Which sail. How she would find her hole in the storm. The way she would signal Alan at the helm. She finished her work in the bilge.

As she pulled herself through the bilgewater toward the steps up and out into the main cabin, she heard the crash and then the bark of Barstow's gun. She scrambled up into the dull light.

Alan had smashed the door out of its frame. As it came down, it had caught itself on the cast-iron stove and twisted over so that it landed on edge on Santucci's ankles, maybe breaking one of them. Barstow had shot Alan, hitting him in the arm, spinning him back. The girl stood in the shattered doorway of the forecastle, stiff with shock.

"Go look at him," Barstow said. "See if you can fix him."

First she went into her own cabin and brought back the large medical chest. She examined Alan's arm. Santucci made small yelping sounds.

"It's a flesh wound. It didn't go through the arm." She tended it.

"I couldn't stand it," Alan said. "Evey, it was getting so bad for her. We had to get out. Take a chance."

"Shush," she said. "Just be quiet for now. Don't say anything."

"I'm not going back in there," he said.

"Shush. Don't say anything. Don't say anything at all. Nothing. Nothing. Do you hear me? Do you understand?" But in her hands she felt that he did not. All she could feel in him was that he was young.

She bound his arm after spreading an antibacterial ointment over the rip. There would be more danger from infection than from the wound itself, which was not serious. But the danger from Barstow now was greater than that of infection.

Barstow could not put them back into the forecastle; there would be no way to secure them. And not in Katherine's cabin either.

"What about Santucci?" he said to her.

She examined the ankle.

"It looks broken. It's swelling badly. There's nothing much I can do. I can chill it with a chemical icepack. I can splint it. I can give him some painkillers." She looked at Santucci. But the pain from his ankle had already entered into the totality of the pain he had become, and that she could not lessen. At some threshold, suffering is indecipherable, and Santucci had passed that threshold.

"Later," Barstow said. "Sit over there." With his gun he motioned Alan and the girl to a place at the far end of the cabin. Evelyn could hardly move by herself. She was matted into her filth and anguish.

The *Marindor* lurched up off its beam to about thirty degrees. The upward position was suddenly odd to them.

"It's a lull," she said. "It happens. The storm is deciding which way to go." She told him her plan for bringing the boat onto its other side. "Let me have Alan. Even with one arm, he can do this. Or he could even use the bad arm. Raise your arm over your head," she said to him. He did. "See? Let him come up on deck with me and down into the bilge. I need someone to hold the light so I can work on the pump. Give him to me."

"No," Barstow said. He was making himself clear to her, as he had all along. It was the same thing. If she understood him perfectly, then she could trust him, and that way he could trust her. And now he had new decisions to make. He would stay with what he had at the moment. He would have to consider what had changed, and he did not want to think

212

about more than one thing at a time. Alan moving about—on deck, into the bilge—he did not want to deal with that.

"Please," she said.

"No," he said.

"Then I'll have to try to do it myself."

"You'll do it," he said. "You'll do it. You don't need him."

Riding more or less upright for a minute at a time before getting knocked over, the *Marindor* bobbed about roughly now. The wind and the waves blown off were still blinding, but the angle of the boat gave her a place to stand. She could get the sail on the stay and up. She would leave the sheet free until the last moment, when she was back at the helm. She would bring in the sheet and stiffen the sail and bring the helm across the wind and hope that the sail would not be blown away and that the boat would come about and through the wind and then fall down again on its starboard side. She guessed that the wind was above eighty knots now.

She could not allow herself to think about what had happened. She needed every instant now for herself, the rote of the memories of all her old skills at sea, the inch by inch and second by second of procedure. And the pace. Her father had taught her. The worse the conditions, the slower the pace. Move with the pace of the boat. Storms are furious, and the wind, but the actual boat when it is entirely depowered is moving slowly, more slowly than it seems. It is a waterlogged bulk of wood, deeply submerged, hardly visible. A dead man, it is called, because a wooden hull jamming into a dead man while moving with some power through the sea could get a hole punched in its hull. A dead man. A hull in a storm like this.

Moving down the lee deck, shielded a little by the cant of the boat, she had tied the sail into a package, and this she had tied to herself. Her hands were free to help her into the bow. She had brought the standing end of the cutter halyard with her. She let it run through her hand as she pulled down the tattered luff of the sail that had earlier blown out. She snapped the halyard into the new sail and hanked it onto the stay. Then she worked back to the helm. She unlashed it and felt it spring to life, thrashing and flailing. She had to be certain that the wheel did not get free of her and spin. She put one leg over a spoke and leaned down across an opposing spoke. She lost much leverage this way, but that couldn't be helped. Now she had to raise the storm sail quickly and then bring in the sheet, cleat it, and turn the wheel.

Now was the moment to wait. Feel the boat find itself until what you want to do can best be done. Wait.

Then Katherine hauled in the sheet and the sail rose up the stay quickly even as it jerked and tried to pull out of her hands. But it went up, and she cleated the sheet and then turned the wheel. The *Marindor* swung smartly across the wind and immediately slammed down onto its starboard beam. She had done it. She lashed the helm again, hauled in the small storm sail, secured it, and went below.

The shift in the attitude of the boat had forced them to sit down to leeward. Otherwise nothing had changed. The children sat forward, Evelyn in Alan's arm. Barstow still held his gun. Santucci had slid down to leeward and lay there crumpled.

In her cabin she changed again out of her deck clothes into her bilge clothes. She smiled at her own odd decorum, her modesty. How would it have mattered if she had stripped in the main cabin? What was at stake? What was protected? Especially here, now. Maybe all that was left of order was this particle of decorum. Maybe when it was gone, when the last molecule was broken apart, then everything else would fail. Maybe there was a curve of binding energy and it all came down to her; maybe the universe depended upon her changing her clothes in private.

In the bilge she discovered that a seam on the new, exposed side had also sprung slightly. There was no great danger from this leak either. But it was the protocol of her existence. She managed to secure the flashlight and move it along as she worked down the length of the seam. It was good work. She liked the sound. She could not really hear much, but it was as if she could feel the sound through her hands as the caulking hammer hit on the broad head of the caulking iron. Someone else might have simply run a bead of sealant into the seam, but that would be inconsistent with her boat. Culler had built this boat so that it could be double caulked, outside and inside. He had written about it, and it was a controversial idea, but a good one. It put more of the fate of your boat in your own hands. And once sealant was in and hardened, when the *Marindor* was back in a dry dock to be reconditioned, the sealant would have had to be scraped out down to the original oakum and cotton. No. She would do this the boat's way. It is what Slocum had done and what Culler, the builder of this boat, had called for. The *Marindor* was her boat, but it belonged to those others as well.

After she had filled the seam to her satisfaction, she worked on the pump. It was an odd but simple problem. She smiled at it. Someday she would write a letter to *Cruising World* to describe it. The problem was that even in the few days that the pump had been submerged, enough barnacle sprat had settled out of the bilgewater onto the primary ignition switch to jam it. A little filing and a little sandpaper and it was fine. So much depending upon so little. Sermons on barnacle sprat.

She finished her work and sat in the bilge in the dark. It was the lowest and deepest place in the boat, where it was most rooted in the sea, the elemental bottom into which everything eventually drained. Maybe she would stay here until ... until what? Until the boat was in dry dock? Until she could write her letters? Why were they here? To get more money from Agare? That seemed preposterous even though it was true. And she understood that only the storm kept them, not together but locked into the coils like sons of Laocoön. That only the storm had meaning any longer.

At last she hauled herself up out of the bilge and into the main cabin.

She looked for the others. Where had he put them? He watched her look around, struggling to imagine how he had fixed his problem. Only Santucci lay inert. He watched her stagger against the cant of the boat to the forecastle and then back to her own cabin. Nothing.

"They're gone," he said at last.

"Gone?"

"Gone," he said. He pointed up and over his shoulder with his thumb.

"Topside?" she said. "In this weather? The wind is coming back."
The lazaret. "You put them in the lazaret? Both of them?" She started
toward the companionway.

"No," Barstow said. "Not the lazaret. Gone. Over the side."

"I don't understand," she said. "I can't understand."

"They're gone is all."

"I don't know what you mean. I must know what you mean. Stop
this. Stop this. What happened? What have you done?"

"I told Alan to take Evelyn up on deck. I told him it would be good
for her, the air, even the rain. I told him to do it or else I'd shoot him in
the head. He took the girl up, and then I backed him off with the gun,
and then I took her and threw her over the side, and then I shot Alan and
threw him over the side. And now I'm going to take Santucci up and
throw him over the side, which will be easy."

"What do you mean? What can you mean? How can you say this?
You threw them over the side into the ocean like pieces of electronic
equipment?" she said, and was surprised that she could speak at all.

"Exactly," he said.

"Monstrous," she said. "Monstrous. Monstrous." She sank down onto
her knees. "You killed them? You killed two people?"

"Think about it," he said. "You think we could have gone on like
this? Alan on the loose, the girl? Santucci about dead anyway? Do you
think we could have all sat around for another day and maybe another
day, for who knows how many days? And if we got to port, and if we got
to Agare, then what? Santucci is useless. Worse than that. And what
good would the kids be? You think they would work Agare? People in
situations like this just want out. They're not tough. They were already
in pieces. Everything was busted up into pieces. Nothing was going to put
that back together. That was the situation, and now this is the situation.
It's much better this way. For me."

"They're human," she said. "They were human."

"OK," he said. "Human. You think I don't understand what that
means, what you mean? You think I can't measure what I did? I can, but
that is not the point at all. Maybe being what you call human isn't enough
for doing some kinds of things. Like conducting a negotiation with a guy

who has raped your girlfriend or a guy who has shot you. With people
who are robbing you. With storms like this. Santucci fucked it up. After
that, there was no use. Nothing was going to work out after Louis raped
the girl."

"So now it's only you to negotiate with Agare. Did you think of that?"

"Forget Agare. Agare is later, or probably never. It's too screwed up
now. But it's not that important. I've got the two hundred thousand dollars. What's important is you get me ashore, and then I get to live, and
then you get to live. That is what is important. That is now the situation.
Them?" he said, his thumb up and over his shoulder again. "They can't
be important now, can they? Nothing is going to change anything that has
happened. Nothing that you think. Nothing that you care. In Vietnam,
did I think? Did I care? About government policy? About making the
world safe from communism? About any of that bullshit? You were there;
do you think any of us gave a shit about any of that? So what were we
thinking? What we cared about was not getting killed. Killing someone
else first was easy. There was nothing personal about it. Nothing complicated. So you think that was OK, what I did then, but what I did now
wasn't OK? Is that what you think? Is that *how* you think?"

"That was a war. This isn't a war," was all she could think to say. She
waded through shock; she felt the waves of it sweeping through her, con-
vulsions without rhythm, like seizures.

"But you'll have to kill me too, won't you?" she said. "Finally, you'll
have to kill me too."

"Why? What's the point to that?"

"I'm a witness," she said.

"To what?" he said. "Who is Louis Santucci? Who is Alan or Evelyn?
You don't have bodies. You never will. You don't even have a weapon, see."
He showed her the empty ankle holster. "What do I need a gun for now?
I pump up the inflatable, and I go ashore with my money, and that's the
end of it. What, do you think you can get Agare in on this? What kind of
witness could he be? And to what? And he wouldn't care. Do you think he
would care? You get him his disk if you can, and what, he's going to get involved with what? You want the disk, you've got it. Do what you want
with it. No, Katherine Dennison. That's all over. You get us to shore, that's

all I want now. The problem with you, with people like you, is that when you think about alternatives, you never think about *all* the alternatives, only the nice alternatives, the clean alternatives. You would have made a lousy general, and you sure as hell would have made a lousy grunt."

He picked up the unconscious Santucci like he was a sack of air and started up the companionway. Katherine sprang at him, tried to stop him, to pull him down. But she could not. He did not even resist her. He waited until her grip loosed, and then he continued up.

She felt the boat spin lazily. At first she thought it was herself, the blood rushing out of her head or maybe into it. The moral vertigo spinning her down. But it was the boat.

Barstow returned. "Go where you want," he said. "Do what you want. You're free now. And I'm free now. Now it's simple. Get us to shore. Get *yourself* to shore."

"I am not your friend. Don't think that I am relaxed," she said.

"No, no. Of course not. I'm not talking about friends. We were never friends. We had some good talk. *I* had some good talk up in the cockpit at night. That's all. Now, hate me if you want. But it's all simple now. Now the boat sinks or it doesn't, but if it doesn't, then I'm free for my life, and you're free to go back to whatever your life was."

But that would not be possible, she knew.

"I hate what you are," she said.

"So what were *you* going to do? You were going to talk sense to him, to the kid? You were going to keep him off of Santucci or me? You were going to talk the girl out of what had happened to her, what was happening to her? You were going to rescue Santucci? You think you could have done that? You think that could have been done?"

"I could have tried," she screamed.

"Why?" he said.

"Because unless I did, nothing would make sense in my life ever again."

"Sure it would," he said. "If you live through this, everything will make sense again, or as much sense as it ever did."

"That's not enough."

"Sure it is. That's all there is. Just enough sense to get you through. The rest is bullshit."

"You're wrong," she said. "You are profoundly wrong."

In her cabin she watched the compass swing. She waited for the motion of the boat. She stayed in the cabin for an hour and then an hour more. Then she felt sure that the quadrant had released them. Already the *Marindor* had a less sharp list. Soon she might chance putting up a handkerchief of sail. And then what was she to do?

When she went back into the main cabin, he was fully stretched out and asleep. He did not trust her more than he could trust, but he trusted that she would not kill him. She could have taken a large knife from the galley and plunged it into his heart.

She made herself some food, and still he slept. Maybe he had not slept, not deeply, for days. Maybe that was the price of his weariness, three lives. But she did not want to wander into that.

13

In her berth through the night as she rose and fell in and out of sleep, she felt the storm coming apart. She dreamed, but not defined dreams; rather, she floated in a netherworld of tangled dreamscape, sinking through it down into sleep or rising up and out of it into horror.

When she awoke certainly, she felt the storm begin to stutter and trip the way anger subsides and then suddenly remembers itself. The first sure sign of the storm leaving was the gustiness. Instead of the constant unbroken onslaught of wind and wave, the metronomic pounding, now there would be bursts like a rearguard action. In some ways it was a more punishing situation: instead of the constant heavy push of the wind and waves, now it would be more like a hooking punch, and harder to prepare for. Now the holes in the sea grew larger and more frequent. And now was the time when rogue waves formed. Freed from the order of the organized force of the storm, now only the energy spun about in primal dislocation, taking any shape it might fall into. Waves that were once contained within the storm now could join other waves and rise up into truly crushing forces. Caught in such a wave, a boat, however strongly built, could be crushed or pitchpoled or capsized. And in the aftermath of big storms, the shoreline could suffer more in the storm surge than in the storm itself. Ahull, deep in the water and low, the boat was gripped in a sickening, unrelenting motion. Now, more upright, with no sail set or sea anchor to face it into the wind, all of the boat was in random motion. The shrouds sang as if they were the untuned strings of a harp, and the thick pine mainmast was strummed, a deep counterpoint bass to the strident rigging. The tightly set stays sagged and sprang taut again as the masts worked in their deeply socketed partners and steps. Everything was in vibration. Now, in the ending of a storm, the sea and the wind took the boat and shook it like a dog plucked up out of the water. Not the calm before the storm but the chaos at the end of it that mariners knew to fear.

She worked herself carefully into the cockpit and considered. She did not think that he would let her live. If she got him to shore, to some place where he could make a landing with his aluminum cases of money, though he would have no reason to kill her, he would equally have no reason to let her live, surely even less reason. Why should he take any chances at all? She did not think that he had decided to kill her, or that he had even thought about it yet. What Calvin Barstow would think about was her getting the boat to shore. He would think about this day. This morning.

These thoughts she managed in the cockpit as she watched the storm build again, and fade, and build. Falter and bluster, hesitate and then stagger back, swinging wildly. The air had grown lighter, though it still rained heavily. The smell of the storm-borne dirt in the air was less. By the end of the day, she would try to find where she was. Her father had taught her a simple trick. Take your wind-speed estimate and the direction you have been moving in. Divide the speed by one hundred, and then, to the scale of your chart, draw a line perpendicular to the main line of drift, a right angle to the west if you are moving north, to the east if you have been driven south, just as long as it is ninety degrees from that axis. It was, of course, very crude. And no one knew why it worked. But for those who went to sea, like much else, none of the magics were to be scorned. And all along she had had her father's fine chronometer. Once she could establish her local time, she would be able to find her longitude. The skies would have to clear much more for that. She would again need the sextant. But the drift was westward. Even with nothing more than a compass reading, eventually they would come to the land, but where could make all the difference to life.

Below, she told him that the storm was lessening.

"It doesn't feel like it," he said. "We're getting bounced around worse."

She explained how storms felt, how they worked when they wore themselves out or passed by. She managed to prepare food for them. She opened Agare's cans of pâté and sealed quail eggs and delicate prawns and smoked morsels of fish and other exotica, the food a fragile absurdity now. She always, even now, had to remind herself that he could not reach into imagination, go forward into anticipation or linger in an aftertaste.

She worked the formula and told him where she thought they were. She placed them maybe forty miles off the North Carolina coast, maybe fifty miles south of the Outer Banks. She told him that it was very approximate, more a guess than otherwise. But that did not matter to him. If that was all they had, then that is what they would use. He wanted her to know that; he wanted to assure her. About Santucci and Alan and Evelyn there was no mention, no indication that they had ever existed. What was past was past; for Barstow what was past might never even have occurred.

"If we're where I guess we are, or near it, we can make some sail; we could get to somewhere along the coast in a day. With luck."

"A day is good," he said. "Even two."

"With luck," she said.

Through the day the breaking of the storm did not abate. That night she did dream, a solid and precise and familiar dream. She dreamed *The Marindor,* the children's book she had made those years ago that had brought her so much of the rest of her life and that had brought her to here.

The book she had written and illustrated was largely a recasting of the tale of Noah, the building of his ark with the help of his sons, the stocking of it with the creatures of the earth. She had written it with a softly comic overlay by making Noah and the problems he faced ordinary and realistic. Unlike the Bible story, her story was replete with details—the trenels with which he hammered the planks of the ark together, the tar with which he sealed the ship, the coarse ropes the wives spun out of fibers, the provisioning with bales of hay and feed for the animals, the jars of honey, the bags of wheat. And Noah's fretfulness as he hurried about, fussing and encouraging and urgent. The realistic and somewhat bumbling but nicely concerned Noah would be attractive to any child, and it gave her a lot to draw as the ark took shape and then as the animals began to appear. And as the storm began to occur in earnest. They had to work more and more quickly as the skies darkened and as the last animals were hurried aboard. And where to put them: Could the cats and the pigeons be close to each other; would the lambs lie down with the tigers? And then the rains began. And at the last, just before Noah and his family went aboard and sealed themselves in to await God's awful will, there came a great shaking of the earth and a great light shining over the hill of the valley in which the ark had been built. The light grew brighter, but it was unlike any light anyone had ever seen before. It was like a light that shone with all its components—white light broken up into its prismatic range, like a rainbow, but amorphous. A rainbow everywhere. The light emanated from three magnificent animals, animals never seen before, never even known of. They were like horses, and yet not horses. Much larger, great creatures, with a beauty and a stateliness so intense it made the senses ache.

They wanted to come aboard the ark. Noah told them that he could take only two of them. But they were three, their leader said. Noah explained. God's will. God's command. Two, not three. But we are three, the creature said. We are the Marindor. "I just can't do it," Noah said. "I wish I could, but I can't. Two, not three." But no, the Marindor said. No. And then the great animals wheeled away. Never mind, they said. We are the Marindor. And Noah ran after them even as the rain became torrential. He pleaded with them. Such glory should not perish, as perish it surely would. Two, he begged. But the great beasts did not relent, and the last he saw of them was the emanation, their light pushing away the rain. And then they were gone.

Of the majestic Marindor, besides their ineffable beauty, she remembered best their dignity and their courage. She did not know how much children would capture that—or be captured by that—but it had mattered to her that children should have that chance.

The defined part of the dream was the book itself. The undefined part of the dream was without images; it was only the feeling that the Marindor, book and boat, that had brought her here, would take her farther, would take her home, but at the thought of home everything grew even more diffuse. Where was home? What was it?

When she awoke and dressed and went out into the main cabin, Barstow was still asleep. Without waking him or eating anything, she went up on deck.

The wind was still very strong, but not impossible. She could get some sail up. But she waited. She waited and summoned herself, letting her temperature adjust, letting her sense of herself and the sea come together again. After all the time below, she needed to meld again with the sea and her history. And then she thought, we are the Marindor, and with a smile moved forward firmly into the bow.

She measured out about thirty-five feet of anchor chain and stopped it off around the old-fashioned capstan. Carefully she opened the plate to the switch of the donkey engine and disconnected a wire and replaced the plate. Then with an ax she chopped through the thick line which held the starboard anchor tightly cradled to the boat, and with a shove she pushed the anchor out. It fell quickly and jerked short at the end of the thirty-five feet of chain, and immediately the boat skewed off and put its bow into the waves. Quickly she returned to the cockpit and hurried down into the main cabin. Barstow was awake. The sharpened angle of the boat and the grating rattle of the anchor chain against the hull had pulled him out of sleep.

"The starboard anchor has broken free. It's dangling about thirty-five feet down. We've got to raise it," she said. If everything she told him was the truth, then she would not make a mistake that would alarm him, break his odd faith in her. There would be nothing for him to know. He would believe her—believe *in* her—as he had up to now.

"I heard something up from the front," he said.

"If you listen you can hear the boat drive into the anchor chain. Enough of that and it can pull a chunk out of us. We either raise the anchor and secure it or let the anchor and the chain go altogether, but that wouldn't be as easy as it sounds, and it would pull us deeper down until we could get it free. Not a good idea. Besides, it's a problem we can solve. We can get the anchor back."

"But you, you would have a good idea," he said. "What to do." It was a statement, not a question.

"Yes. First we stop the anchor from swinging and pounding against us. Then we can work to haul it in. What we have to do is raise the mainsail enough to bring the boat up into the wind on a port tack." She showed him with her hands what that meant.

"What about the wind?" he said.

"What about it?" she said.

"Right," he said.

On deck she took him forward to show him the anchor on its chain and how the chain was already grinding into the boat.

"We've got to get the boat over so that the chain is lying still. If we try to bring the anchor up now, swinging as it is, we could catch a wave and punch the anchor into the boat. It probably wouldn't put a hole in us, but it could stick in us and maybe even start to pry. Not good. It would take too long to raise the anchor by the capstan, and the donkey engine won't start." She flicked the switch three times to show him. "But if we can turn the boat, that will stabilize the anchor and its chain, and we can take our time to bring it in. And maybe we can even get us moving. West." She pointed. "Come," she said.

At the mast partner, where the mast entered down into the boat and where the greatest pressure under sail was exerted, just at this point, the support was massive. The mast was ringed with belaying pins around which were cleated various lines. She handed him one of the lines.

"This is the peak halyard. It raises that yard." She pointed back to where the gaff yardarm lay across the mainsail, furled and stopped across the heavy boom where it rested in its gallows. "I'll show you where to stand. At the right moment, I'll give you the command, and you haul up on it. Brace yourself well, because you'll be raising the top of the sail right up into the wind where it's strongest. When it's up as far as I want it, I'll give a shout and you go forward to this pin and cleat it down. Like this." She showed him how to turn the line around the pin and how to lock it down on itself. "But even if you don't get it right, just get it tight. Once the sail is peaked up, we don't want the gaff coming down on us. Do you understand?" She shouted as the wind howled but dropped almost into silence so that her voice was suddenly loud and hung there.

"Yes," he said.

She stood on top of the doghouse so she could unstrap the mainsail and the gaff from the boom. Then she went back to the mast where Barstow stood. She took a block and attached it to the ring around the mast and ran the peak halyard through it.

She had worked out over the years all the arrangement of tackle that she needed to control the sails from the safety of the cockpit, but now she bypassed that. Now she had gone back to the old way, into danger, and she took Barstow with her.

"This will give you more purchase," she said. She took the throat halyard and started it. The boom rose slowly out of the gallows that supported it. The sail started off the boom and up the mast, and immediately the wind whipped it. Quickly the boom snapped to starboard. She took a turn around a pin and held the sail until the wind released it, and then she hauled it up another foot. And took another turn and waited. With each few seconds that the wind was out of the sail, she gained another foot until the sail was up as far as she needed it to be, and then she belayed it. "Do you see where I was standing before, just now when I unstrapped the sail and the boom? Up on top of the doghouse?"

"Yes."

"When I tell you, go there and haul up the peak halyard, and then when I tell you, come back to here and cleat it down to this pin. Can you remember this pin? That's important. Keep focused. Listen for my commands, and remember which pin. Have you got that? Listen for my commands and remember this pin."

"Yes."

She checked once more to see that the mainsail was where she wanted it, the wind slapping and slatting the sail violently. The sail popped and exploded like gunfire. Or cannons. She would have only one chance to do this.

"OK," she said. "Now I'm going back to the helm. Listen to my command. And remember which pin. And one last thing. Keep your safety line secured." She plucked at the safety line, tugged at the safety harness he was wearing. "OK. It looks good. Don't go up on top of the doghouse without your safety line hooked on. Is that clear? Take your time. Not too much time, but enough time." Her voice came in and out of the wind. The slatting of the sails was sometimes deafening but sometimes nearly silent. The boat careened or stood still. It was difficult for him to keep his footing, but not for her. "As soon as you get your sail up and I sheet it in, everything will stabilize. Are you ready, Mr. Barstow? Ready to come about? Hard alee, remember?"

"Ready," he said.

Back in the cockpit, she waited. She scored the wind against the wave action. She scanned for something large enough and full. She read the sea and the wind and the *Marindor,* and she filled with certainty, a lifetime coming together at least in this.

"Now," she shouted to him through the wind. "Now."

Carefully he mounted the doghouse. He snapped into the safety line and brought the peak halyard with him.

"Now," she shouted again. "Up." She pointed up in the air. He hauled on the peak halyard. It was hard work. The peak of the gaff should ordinarily be raised along with the throat. But now the gaff was pointed down and swung and jolted him through the halyard, but with the wind pressing on the hull she could maneuver just enough to ease the strain, though she wanted him to work hard at what he was doing, to keep him thinking about that and nothing else. The peak came level to the throat and then slowly rose up above it, pivoting from it, until it was well above the perpendicular. The sail filled strongly now.

She felt him waiting for the command. She felt the strain of the line in his hand and his determination to hold on and to raise the peak higher, to do as she had told him. And she waited for the wind and the position that she needed, against everything she waited until the time and the condition came, and then she spun the helm as swiftly as she could so that the sail jibed. It came across the top of the doghouse with a force even greater than the wind behind it because it was also driven by the mass of itself. It came across with a snap so quick the eye could not follow it. It scythed across the doghouse and swept Barstow into the sea. The safety line was worthless against such a force. In the last instant, she believed they saw each other and that he was not surprised but had only confirmed that he had trusted her and that is what had killed him. And then he was gone.

But the boom continued, roared into the starboard shrouds and parted them and continued into the cutter forestay and the main head stay and brought them down, and with nothing supporting it, the great mast shattered ten feet above the partner and crashed down across the boat, all its top rigging dragging in the sea, its chords of wire and rope, with the fittings still attached to the ends of them, suspended and swinging. The broken mast crushed into part of the doghouse, opening the cabin to the sea and the rain. The chain-plates to which the shrouds had been attached bent and skittered everywhere, large pieces of wood still bolted on. And the massively built partner had been pulled partially free. The *Marindor* was listed over by the weight of the broken mast and rigging. Wave-driven rain and waves entered the boat. She had known that this would happen.

The thing to do now was to free the wreckage from the hull and to raise a jury rig that might get her to the coast, but she would not be able to work on the jury rig in the storm's remnant. The wreckage, especially with the mainsail in and under the water, pulled the boat down and forced it to turn in a slow circle, giving the weather and the waves every advantage over it. That she would have to cut free.

The boat was slowly taking on too much water. She started both pumps, but unless she could get the boat up and on some protected course, eventually the rising water would overwhelm the generator and the batteries. With the ax she began to chop through every binding. First she let the anchor fall off, and where the chain was shackled to the rope, she cut through it. She had hoped to save the gaff yard to use in the jury rig, but it was too deep in the sea, and the heavy boom as well. With a saw she cut through the splintered mast. The shattered partner was all that held the mast to the boat now, and when the mast went, it would pull the rest of the partner with it, opening the cabin further. At last she was finished. In the next revolution of the boat, it would all slide free. She moved far back and checked that no stray line would snag her. And then the slide began, slowly and then quickly, and then all at once everything went over the side and the *Marindor* bobbed up, shorn.

She hauled all the spare sails she had and hammered them down over the large hole in the deck and the doghouse. There was no more she could do now. She could not move the mizzenmast; it was too heavy. In the morning, if the storm had died down enough, she would saw off a piece of it in making up the jury rig forward. But other than a little steerage way, it would not be enough to move a boat as large as the *Marindor.* She started the diesel engine, but that would not do much in seas like this either, as they subsided. Still, what could be done should be done.

Below deck, as she had planned, not much was thrown about. But water was spurting up through the floorboards. The bilge was filling. She went down into it. The stump of the mainmast, no longer stayed, rose and fell with every surging wave. Relentlessly, it was battering an opening along the garboard planks. She hammered wooden wedges in around the mast and down into the step. It stopped the mast from working, but it would not be permanent. Every hour she would have to come down here and hammer in the wedges.

In the cabin, she waited. She prepared food. The water rose. Even the sails could not keep all the water out, and more water was coming in from the bottom. At 2300 hours, the generator failed as the rising water shorted it out. The pumps stopped. She went to sleep. And did not dream.

She awoke at 0600 hours and understood the wallowing of the boat. Even though the wind had dropped considerably, there was a lot of it, but it would drop further now and stiffen; the tear in the ocean and the air would begin to heal. But within that wind, she felt the *Marindor* falling slowly into the sea, turning into a dead man. There would even be sun today. September would come back.

In the cabin, water had seeped up above the floorboards.

She patched together a breakfast and perched up where it was drier, although the interior of the cabin was everywhere sodden, clammy, damp. Where was she? Somewhere off the coast of the Carolinas. Adrift. The work of making the jury rig would not matter. Nor would the diesel engine. It could only give her some steerage, and there was not much fuel. She might be spotted by an airplane flying over, but that was unlikely. No searchers would be looking for her. And no other boats would be out here now. She was too close to the hazard of the shoals off the Carolina banks. Nothing large would be this close under any circumstances, least of all in the aftermath of such a storm as this had been. And small boats would have run far in for cover and would stay there. They would not be out here, not for days at best. So here she was. She did not even bother to establish a position. She was here off the coast at some distance and might drift ashore or else circle in the eddies of the sea until the *Marindor* dissolved or she did. But she would not die this way. You don't have chances, she remembered. But in some other sense, maybe there was a second chance.

Above deck now, she was bundled warmly, but the day was becoming pleasant even with the wind, which had dropped down to thirty knots but steady. With more coffee, she sat in the cockpit. The wind was blowing everything free. Now she was here again alone, she and what was left of the *Marindor* and what was left of herself.

She thought of watercolors, the work that she had done that created the illusion of accident even as she denied it. That had been the limit and the essence of her art and craft. And of her life. Not the inspired accident that could result in discovery from having worked to an edge of mystery, but the controlled accident of watercolor, which had been no accident at all, only a pleasant fuming. Books for little children.

She was a palimpsest upon whom error, like the pentimento of mistake, still could be seen beneath her life, a dull glow up through the soaking and scraping away, a permanent stain forever stealing away the intensity of the subsequent layering of new and vibrant glazes, the brilliant translucency gone.

She drank her coffee as the day brightened, the air of the wind becoming a long sigh as if it were itself relieved from the pressure of the energy that had possessed it. Like herself. She thought about Joe Mackenzie. She thought how she had understood everything and nothing of what he had told her all her life. She remembered reading and rereading his letters over the years and how she agreed with everything and how it had not mattered. She compared it to the way the young understand that they will die but do not believe it in the way in which they will some-day come to believe it. Only with her it had been different; with her it had been her life that she had understood but not believed in. Until now, off the coast of the Carolinas in the *Marindor,* which was dying. She drank her coffee. There was time enough for her to do what she would do.

Without his letters, but in his voice, how would he now commend her to herself, as he always had?

She had never been able to imagine more than she could bear. In Vietnam the photographs she had made were finally easy to make because there was nothing to imagine. It was enough to be there to get the photographs. Even the poems she had written and sent to Joe Mackenzie had collapsed the experience. She had not found her war but had found instead only a dangerous and exotic adventure, just as Joe Mackenzie had warned her. She had not found an answer because she had not even found a question. Even under the excellent tutelage of Joe Mackenzie and the urging of her heart, she had resisted—even as she did not know that she resisted—the lesson of Macken Island.

It was as if the life she did have was only the metaphorical substitu-tion, the illusion of the grail she always believed she believed in, as if one fine day she would turn in a pathway or sail into a small harbor, and there it would be, a life at last commensurate with her capacity to imagine it. But now, aloft in the *Marindor,* she knew as simply as she could ever have hoped to know that she had come at last out of metaphor and illusion and into the unadorned starkness of narrative itself.

She saw with clarity—accepted with clarity—that the *Marindor* had always been a retreat; it had never been simply an entertainment or a recreation or a creative pleasure. It was her center; it was where, even when away from it for a long time, she always wanted to be, on the *Marindor,* back at the beginning of time, in the Garden, alone. But she had miscalculated, and instead of being the master of the *Marindor,* she had become only its cargo, a dull ballast to its great beauty. And with the betrayal of Tom and the death of Steven, the boat had become not even a retreat but a prison ship. If she could not go forward, had *never* gone for-ward, now she could not, could never go back. She *was* like the Dutchman. She *was* like the Ancient Mariner.

Even without intention, she had cursed the life of life.

Now she saw in the raw wind that finally, at last, only the clarity itself was the intensity she had pursued through her life. The clarity itself, the certainty that life itself was what she had not been satisfied with, the clarity that reveals that life *is* its limitations, and all we can do is live in such a way that we make more rather than less of its diminishment. Through the wind and in the sea, she watched the waves breaking less, ebbing down into the long swells, the water turning blue again.

She had not trusted the surfaces. She had always wanted something behind them. She had never accepted that behind life there was nothing but life. Joe Mackenzie had told her long ago that she wanted to go behind the surfaces into the center—the center of the universe, but that universe was spurious. She had never accepted, as Joe Mackenzie had urged, that she was as we all were already in the center of the universe: the trick was to realize that and to realize that in the center it is as dark as it is light.

She had believed without even thinking of it carefully enough as a belief that at some point she would be touched by an intensity so great that the heat of it, the illumination from that heat, would light everything else, a belief that something like that condition actually existed, a kind of singularity where all the forces of the universe came together in an ur-atom out of which singularity came the big bang in whose radiation one could live forever after. Just as in the fairy-tale-like world of children. Maybe that is why children's books had become the measure of her soul.

Why this silent and unstated and untended assumption that had been the dynamic of her life? Why a life that had been so vulnerable to a delusive passion? Why a heart so impervious that it could not be broken by dancing? She could not say. There was no saying it. We are what we are.

In the marrow of her bones she felt the *Marindor* begin to split, to soften, the sprung seams in the hull widening. The boat would not sink quickly. It might not even go all the way down. But it would sink deeper, wallow, suffer. And if she were to be spotted, if the Coast Guard flew over and found her on a routine patrol, all they would do was take her off and note the position of the boat to give a warning to other ships at sea. More than likely, they would at last send out a cutter to sink the boat.

Even if she stayed, there would be nothing much to tow. And what would be left? What would she be trying to hang on to, even now, the boat or the metaphor?

Below, the water was rising. She gathered up food and water and what was dry for clothing. She bound everything together carefully. She took her father's magnificent chronometer in its brass-bound cocobola wooden box and sealed it carefully in plastic bags within plastic bags. The aluminum cases of money she left, and the case with Agare's disk in it. The medals and citations above her bunk she left as well.

Above deck she loaded everything into the *Ark* and lowered it into the sea and set it off from the *Marindor.* She raised the mast in its tabernacle and freed the tiller and rudder. She hoisted sails and set them after first putting a single reef in both. She settled in the stern sheets and took command, the quickness of the small boat an exhilaration. There was still gustiness in the wind, but she could spill what she didn't need or come up into it if necessary. The wind would push her westward. The surge of the seas was westward. Sometimes at the very top of a high swell she thought she could judge the slightest smudge of the purple in the air above land. Somewhere to the west. Thirty miles, maybe forty. This weather would not go bad again quickly. In her good clothing, she would be warm enough. She listened to the boat in the sea. When she looked back to the *Marindor,* she had already left it a quarter of a mile away. And when she was low in a trough, the rail of the *Ark* no more than inches from the water, she could not see the *Marindor* at all.

The *Ark* was sturdy. And so was she. She had never had fear of the sea because there at least she had stayed within the limits. She had never made of the sea more than it was. There was no need or maybe even no possibility of that. She would get to the coast easily. The *Ark* was making a good four knots and could go faster, but that would mean a harder sail. Go slowly if you had the sense and the nerve for it, and she did. At four knots she would make landfall in ten hours, and maybe even find herself enough of a harbor to come to land. If not, she would sail the coast until she found what she needed. In the *Ark* she could do that. Now there was nothing to doubt, nothing to linger in. All she had to fear was gone now. Barstow and Santucci. Already it was hard to remember the past days, so unlikely, so improbable. And yet so ordinary too. She had survived that, but more to the point now was that she had survived herself. Now she had destinations. It was all very simple. She had a wedding to attend. And an island in Penobscot Bay to go to. And, having found her clarity at last, so she would.